Deceptive Lies

JANE BLYTHE

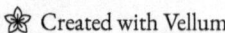

Acknowledgments

I'd like to thank everyone who played a part in bringing this story to life. Particularly my mom who is always there to share her thoughts and opinions with me. My wonderful cover designer Letitia who did an amazing job with this stunning cover. My fabulous editor Lisa for all the hard work she puts into polishing my work. My awesome team, Sophie, Robyn, and Clayr, without your help I'd never be able to run my street team. And my fantastic street team members who help share my books with every share, comment, and like!

And of course a big thank you to all of you, my readers! Without you I wouldn't be living my dreams of sharing the stories in my head with the world!

CHAPTER

One

July 9th
    10:57 P.M.

The loudest sound he'd ever heard ripped him from a deep sleep.

It sounded like an explosion only ...

Why would someone be blowing up his house?

Thirteen-year-old Cooper Charleston jerked upright, his heart hammering so hard in his chest it physically hurt, blood pumping so furiously through his body he felt strung out, like he'd just run a marathon even though he'd just been sleeping.

"Coop?"

The trembling voice came from the other side of the room, and he looked over to see his twin brother's shadowy form also sitting up in bed.

"What was that?" Connor asked, voice scared.

He was scared, too. Frozen in fear.

Some unknown instinct inside him screamed that he needed to move, to do something, but he had no idea what. Something was wrong, that much he knew, he just had no idea what it could possibly be.

"I don't know." He managed to force the words out through a throat that felt like it was closing up.

Before either of them could say more, the door to their room was flung open.

Connor screamed.

Maybe he did too.

He wasn't quite sure.

The fear inside was too much. There was no fight or flight for him, just fear, just freeze, just sit there in the bed as four huge figures dressed in black stormed into the room he shared with his twin brother.

Another scream fell from his brother's lips, and from the corner of his eye, he saw his brother scramble out of his bed.

That's what he should be doing.

Trying to escape before the men got them.

They lived in a big house with five bedrooms—one he shared with his twin, one was shared by their older and younger brothers, one was used by their baby sister, one was used by their two stepbrothers, and the master was now for his mom and stepdad. Only six months ago his dad had been killed when his Delta Team had been attacked. The only survivor of the attack was now married to his mom. Nine people lived in this house, and if four men had gone running into all those bedrooms, there were at least twenty men who had broken into their home.

Why?

Who were they?

What did they want?

The questions ran through Cooper's mind as his body shook, stuck in place as two men approached his bed. The other two had gone to Connor's bed and yelled at him as his twin tried to fight them off.

A high-pitched scream echoed through the house.

Cassandra's scream.

His little sister was only five years old and wouldn't start kindergarten until the fall, she was just a baby.

Yet there must be men like this bursting into her pretty, pink princess bedroom in the middle of the night, scaring her.

Anger ignited inside him, shoving away some of the fear.

No one got to hurt his little sister and get away with it.

Just as the men tried to reach for him and pull him from his bed, Cooper launched to his feet. The window was right between his and his brother's beds and right outside was a huge oak tree. How many times had they gotten in trouble for jumping out the window and into the tree?

Hundreds of times.

Last winter when little Cassandra decided to follow her big brothers and do what they did, she'd attempted the jump only to fall and break her arm. All four boys had been in huge trouble for not stopping her.

Now nothing was going to stop him.

He was going to get out that window, into the tree, then he was going to scream as loud as he could and get to the closest neighbor's house and get them to call the cops.

"Don't do it, kid," a voice warned as he jumped toward the open window.

For a second, he hesitated at the authority in the man's tone, but Cassandra's screams still filled the house, and they spurred him on.

At the window, he went for it.

He jumped.

Only to be caught before he could reach the tree.

A hand snapped around the T-shirt he was wearing and yanked him roughly back into the house.

"Damn kids," a voice muttered.

"No wonder given who the mother is," another grumbled.

Helplessness filled him as he was set on his feet, a hard grip on his shoulder preventing him from going anywhere other than where he was marched. Helplessness had been the catch cry of his life these last six months. From learning that the dad he idolized was dead, to his mom marrying someone just a couple of months later, to having to learn to live with a new man and two new kids in the home he had shared with his family.

But this was worse.

Lights began to flicker on throughout the house as Cooper was marched out of his bedroom, his brother behind him. His fifteen-year-old brother Cade was fighting against the two men manhandling him, and eleven-year-old Cole was crying. Stepbrothers Jake, who was fourteen, and Jax, who was twelve, were both trying to break free of the men holding onto them, as all six of them were dragged down the stairs and into the living room.

"Get your hands off my sister," Cade growled in a deep fury-filled voice Cooper had never heard his big brother use before.

When he saw one of the men in black carrying a shrieking Cassandra down the stairs, the anger inside him surged.

Nobody touched his sister.

With four older brothers and six years between her and the next youngest, Cole, there was no denying that Cassandra was spoiled. No one in the family was any good at saying no to the little girl, but despite being pampered as she was, there wasn't a sweeter child in the whole world than Cassandra.

"No one is hurting the girl," the man carrying her snapped like they were the problem and not him.

When Cassandra continued to wail, she was thrust toward Cade who immediately took the little girl into his arms. "Shh, boo," he whispered, calling her by the nickname she'd gotten as a toddler because of her complete love and obsession with hiding and then jumping out when you walked past her hiding spot and screaming boo at you.

"Why won't she shut up?" one of the men grumbled.

"She doesn't have her bunny, that's why she's crying," Connor informed the men hovering around them, his blue eyes shooting daggers at each and every one of the men who had broken into their home tonight.

"Go get the kid the bunny," the man holding Cole ordered. After casting a glance at his oldest brother, the eleven-year-old ran back upstairs after Cade nodded his ascent, returning a minute later with Cassandra's treasured bunny.

Once the little girl had it in her arms, she began to quieten, her sobs becoming sniffles as they all stood around and ... waited?

Cooper had no idea what was going on.

No idea who these men were or what they wanted, and they didn't seem inclined to offer any answers. From his spot in the living room,

Cooper could see that the front door had been rammed off its hinges, that must have been the boom that woke him. These men in his home all had weapons and given that he didn't hear the sound of sirens and knew that the attack on his house must have been loud enough for some of the neighbors to hear, he had to wonder if maybe the men in black *were* the cops.

But why would the cops break into his house?

And where was his mom?

It was Jax's gasp that had his head snapping up. His stepbrother was looking toward the top of the stairs, and the look on his face told Cooper that whatever Jax was looking at, he wasn't going to like.

He didn't want to look.

Yet he had no choice.

His head turned of its own accord.

There, at the top of the staircase were his mom and stepdad.

Both were in handcuffs, both had blood on their faces and fresh bruises already forming.

Just like that his world changed forever.

Cassandra, Cole, and Jax all began to cry. Cade and Jake began to shout angrily at the men who had turned their world upside down while he and Connor stood there in shock.

"Mommy," Cassandra wailed. "I want my mommy! Mommy! Mommy!"

Cooper woke with a start, his baby sister's screams from that night eighteen years ago still echoing in his ears with as much clarity as they had when he and his siblings had been forced to watch as their parents were dragged down the stairs and thrown into the back of a van.

They hadn't been allowed to say goodbye.

There had been no last kiss, no last hug, and no last exchange of I love yous.

That was the last time he'd ever laid eyes on his mother. A couple of days later, his family was informed that his mom and Jake and Jax's dad had both committed suicide in their cells.

The charges that put them there—treason.

A crime neither he, his siblings, nor his step-siblings believed.

He was now sitting on a plane on his way to Egypt to hopefully finally prove his mother and her husband were innocent of that crime.

∽

July 9th
    11:32 P.M.

How was she supposed to sleep when her entire body ached and throbbed?

Willow Purcell groaned as she shifted slightly on the thin mattress she'd been given to sleep on. A mattress that did one step away from nothing to protect her from the hard stone floor of her underground cell.

It was so dark in there that it was impossible to see her hand even when she held it directly in front of her face. And that was after being locked in there for hours.

Every day for almost two weeks it had been the same thing.

Beatings.

Torture.

Starvation.

She did her best to keep a record of the passing of the days the only way she could, by gouging another mark into the floor of her cell with the end of the chain keeping her bound to the floor.

Twelve marks.

Twelve days.

Twelve horrific days filled with pain, terror, and the dwindling hope that she was going to be rescued.

No one was coming for her.

That was finally beginning to sink in.

Instead of coming to Egypt to find the proof she'd been looking for to bring a dangerous man to justice, she was going to wind up becoming a casualty of that same man. She'd thought she had what it took to make it in this industry, she wanted to be a good journalist, one who cared more about finding the truth than fame and fortune.

Not like them.

Not like the people who had gotten her father killed.

Shifting her battered body again, Willow did her best to ignore the way the hard ground dug into her. After being given nothing but a little stew to eat once a day since she'd been caught, not only was she weak, but she was beginning to lose weight, her bones protruding where they never did before, making sleeping on the floor that much worse.

Over these last two weeks, she'd moved through a gamut of emotions.

Fear, of course, she'd come here to try to do something good and it had spectacularly backfired. Anger had followed, there was no way she deserved to be subjected to this when she'd come here with the best of intentions to find proof a university professor was, in fact, recruiting young men to join Allah's Warriors, a small but steadily growing sect and terrorist cell. Acceptance was the next step, she was going to die in this house that looked nice enough on the outside but on the inside was run by a vicious man who enjoyed inflicting pain just because he could.

Now she was mostly numb.

She wanted this to be over.

Not that she had any intention of rolling over and giving up. That wasn't in her nature. She was a fighter, she had to be after living through what she had as a child.

Eight had been much too young to learn that every person in her life had an ulterior motive and most didn't care who they hurt as long as they got what they wanted for themselves.

Valuable lessons, hard as they'd been.

Accepting her fate didn't have to mean giving up. It just meant that she was ready for death when it came for her, but she'd still try to hold it off for as long as possible. Just in case fate decided to throw her a helping hand.

Not giving up meant taking care of herself the best way she could.

Which meant trying to sleep.

Doing her best to ignore everything else, the suffocating heat, the hard ground, the pain coursing through her body, Willow concentrated on evening out her breathing, relaxing each muscle, and calming her brain until finally, she drifted off.

Only sleep wasn't restful here.

It was just another way to suffer.

Just like that, she was eight years old again, climbing out of her bed when the sounds of someone hammering on the front door dragged her from sleep.

Like the curious child she'd been, Willow climbed out of bed and went to her window, looking down to the front door below to see who was there.

There were men.

Lots of them.

At least twelve that she could see.

She didn't recognize them, but they were yelling her dad's name, so maybe they were his friends?

A scream stuck in her throat when her dad opened the door and the closest man grabbed him, pulling him out into the front yard.

"No!" Willow screamed as the men began to hit her dad.

Over and over again.

There were too many of them.

Twelve against one wasn't fair.

Her mom always said picking on one kid was never fair. If all your friends were being mean to someone, you were supposed to stick up for that person and help them.

But no one was helping her dad.

They were all hitting him.

Red.

Blood.

It was all over her dad.

She had to help him.

Had to make the men stop.

Why were they hurting her daddy?

He was a good daddy, she thought as she ran down the stairs. He read her bedtime stories every night, and he went to every one of her ballet recitals. He had tea parties with her and let her put makeup on him. He was a teacher at her school, teaching the fourth grade, and she wanted to be in his class next year. He coached her cousin's soccer team, and he helped out at the Kids Club at their church.

When she got downstairs, she saw her mom standing in the doorway watching.

Watching as those men hurt her daddy.

Why wasn't Mommy helping?

If Mom wasn't going to help then she would.

She'd help her daddy. She loved him so much.

"Daddy!" she screamed as she ran toward the front door.

As she tried to get through it, her mom grabbed her, held her back, and stopped her from getting to where the men were still hitting and kicking her dad, who now lay on the grass in their front yard, right under the tree where they had their tea parties in the summer.

He wasn't moving.

"Daddy," she sobbed again. A couple of the men looked over at her, but they didn't stop.

They didn't care.

They wanted to hurt her daddy.

"Why?" Willow begged the men she was old enough to understand were killing her father right before her very eyes. "Why are you hurting my daddy?"

"Because he's nothing but a disgusting child killer," one of the men sneered, delivering another hard kick to her father's head which no longer looked the way a head was supposed to.

"No," she whispered as she collapsed into her mom's arms.

They were wrong.

Her daddy would never hurt anyone, especially a kid, and he'd never ever kill anyone. Killing was bad, and her daddy knew that.

He wouldn't.

"He wouldn't," Willow said, waking on a sob.

After twenty-one years, that night was still as vivid in her mind as it had been when it played out in front of her.

It didn't hurt any less either.

That was something no child should ever have to witness even if it was true that her father was a child killer.

And it wasn't.

Her dad was no killer.

An overly eager journalist wanting to build a name for themselves by breaking the story first had named him as the cop's number one suspect and the parents of the murdered children had acted on what they believed to be correct intel.

Only it wasn't.

And her dad had paid the price.

"I'm not like them," Willow said aloud as she shoved to her feet, ignoring the pain from the litany of bruises covering her body.

Even though she had watched what happened to her father as he was beaten to death, it was only in these last two weeks that she'd had first-hand experience of what it was like for him that night. The pain he'd suffered, the fear as blows came from all directions and he was powerless to do anything about it.

"I came here to do good. I wasn't lying or making anything up, I just wanted facts." Tears tumbled down her cheeks as she hobbled around the small underground cell. "I want to go home. I don't deserve to be here."

There had been no real justice for her wrongly accused father. The men who had beaten him to death that night had all got slaps on the wrists, as had the journalist who started it all and the paper who had published unsubstantiated claims.

Nobody cared that an innocent man had died for crimes he had not committed. Crimes that only a month later the real culprit had been identified, only after he'd taken another young life.

Would anyone care if she never came home?

Would anyone try to find out what happened to her?

Would there be any justice for what was happening to her?

Or would she simply become another statistic, another death in a country that could be unsafe for a woman to travel to alone?

CHAPTER

Two

July 10th
   8:49 A.M.

He was a little early for his nine o'clock meeting, but Cooper was happy to have this time to survey the house in question, and the area of the city in which it sat.

The house was on the outskirts of the nicer side of Cairo. By most American standards, the house was nothing fancy, a simple two-story brick house set on about an acre of land. There was a vegetable garden, a few crops planted, and a couple of farm animals. At this hour of the morning, the building appeared quiet, there was no movement he could detect, and he had no idea how many people were inside.

Knowing he could be walking into a trap had him on high alert, but trap or not, there was no way he wasn't coming here to gather whatever intel he could to prove his mother and stepfather's innocence.

Eighteen years he and his siblings had known something wasn't right, and they had yet to find a single shred of evidence to prove it.

It didn't matter that the night his mom and stepdad had been taken into custody, all of the kids had made a discovery that shook up the core of their world.

While Jake and Jax had lost their mom when they were small, so the idea of their dad moving on with someone else hadn't been a big deal to him and his siblings, their mom remarrying just a couple of months after their dad's death had led to a whole lot of anger.

It was only after he realized there was more going on than he had known at the time that he regretted those last few months of his mom's life. The anger he'd taken out on her, the belligerence that came from confusion, and the way he'd spoken to her when he was talking to her at all. At thirteen, he'd known his parents loved each other, and it made no sense to him or his brothers that their mom would remarry so quickly.

No sense at all.

But after his mom had been hauled away in handcuffs and someone from child protective services had shown up and ordered them all to pack bags, they'd found something that changed what they thought they knew. A sofa bed was in his mom's bedroom, one that someone had been sleeping in before their house was stormed by cops.

His mom and stepfather weren't sharing a bed.

Even as a young teen, he knew that meant more was going on than he'd been aware of.

The problem was that other than his brothers and stepbrothers, nobody else seemed to care.

Branded traitors who conspired to have his stepdad's Delta Team ambushed and killed so they could continue their illicit affair, they would have spent the rest of their lives behind bars if they hadn't committed suicide.

Which never sat right with any of them either.

No way would his mom give up like that. She was a fighter, and she'd instilled that same fight into every one of her five children.

They would never give up. None of them. Not until they proved that their mom was no traitor, no killer, and that she had been murdered not taken her own life.

That was what he was hopefully going to do while he was there in Egypt. A couple of months ago, their inquiries had led them to a university professor who claimed to know something about their mom and her CIA career. A career neither he nor his siblings had even known that she had until she'd been ripped away from them.

It wasn't fair and he intended to right those wrongs.

So he climbed out of his vehicle and headed toward the quiet brick house.

There was no movement as he approached, and when he pressed the buzzer at the front gate, he almost wondered if he was in the right place. Even though two months had passed since their search for answers had led them to the professor, it had taken this long just to pin him down for a face-to-face meeting.

Paranoid didn't begin to describe the man. He took the meaning of the word to a whole new level. He would communicate only in brief, heavily coded messages sent from throwaway email addresses, unable to be traced. When they'd insisted that they needed more, he would only agree to meet with them in Egypt. It was obvious the man must know something about some pretty powerful people if the only way he felt safe to speak to them was in a whole other country.

About a minute after pressing the buzzer, the front door to the house opened, and a man came strolling out. He wasn't dressed in traditional Arab clothing, just jeans and a black T-shirt, with sneakers on his feet. His hair was mussed like he'd just climbed out of bed, but his eyes were clear, although distrustful, when he pulled out a key and unlocked the padlock, swinging open the gate.

"Cooper Charleston?" the man asked.

"Professor Mahmoud?" he asked back.

Giving a brisk nod to confirm his identity, Cooper also acknowledged his with a nod. The professor said no more as he followed the older man down the short path and inside the house. Despite the heat of the day, it was cool inside and quite dull. They bypassed a small living room to the left, and what looked like an office to the right before coming into the large room at the back of the house. It was mostly a fairly basic kitchen compared to what he was used to back home, with a huge wooden table taking up most of the remainder of the space.

Other than himself and the professor, two other occupants were in the room. One was an older woman who he assumed was the wife of Tarek Mahmoud, and the other was a person dressed all in black sitting in the corner of the room. From the baggy clothes the person wore, it was hard to tell their gender, age, or anything else about them.

Whoever they were, unless they had information on his mother and why she'd been betrayed and labeled a traitor, Cooper didn't really care who they were or why they were there.

His purpose for coming to Egypt was singular.

Get answers.

Prove his mother's innocence.

Nothing was going to get in the way of that.

Taking a seat at the table when the professor indicated that he should, Cooper waited expectantly. It had been a long night. After his nightmare, he hadn't attempted to go back to sleep, he was tired, hot, and dirty, and he didn't want another year to pass without being able to clear his mom's name.

The professor, on the other hand, didn't seem to be in any rush.

He took his time, collecting a cup of tea and a plate with some Egyptian bread from his wife. Once he had everything set up at the table, he nodded at his wife who quickly hurried from the room but didn't bother casting so much as a glance at the figure in black.

Shoving aside his natural curiosity, Cooper focused on his goals. "What do you know about my mother?" he asked, tired of waiting.

"I recognized her picture when you were asking questions about her," the professor replied, which wasn't really an answer, he knew that already.

Ever since he and his siblings had grown up, they had been asking around about their mom and stepdad. All six of the boys had joined various military branches, and now they worked together as the world-renowned Prey Security's Charlie Team. With the support of their boss, billionaire and former SEAL Eagle Oswald, they used most of their time when they weren't running an op for Prey to look into what had happened to their parents.

Of course, they had pursued all the obvious steps, trying to get answers, evidence, and proof of guilt from the military and the government, for which none was ever produced other than a form letter stating their mother's guilt without providing anything to back it up. They'd then started doing their own investigations, eventually leading them to the world's most renowned Egyptology professor.

Tarek Mahmoud.

Who had somewhat reluctantly reached out to them when they were asking around.

Who now sat before him with an inscrutable expression Cooper couldn't decipher and a relaxed demeanor that belied their paranoid interactions before he arrived here.

Frustrated and close to the end of his rope, his patience snapped.

Before Professor Mahmoud knew what was happening, Cooper was out of his chair, had a hand around the man's throat, and his back shoved up against the wall. "For almost two decades, I have thought of little else but clearing my mother's name and proving she didn't do what she was accused of. I'm not playing games. You are going to tell me everything you know about her and what happened to her or I am going to cut you apart piece by piece until there's nothing left of you."

∾

July 10th
   9:12 A.M.

Yes, please do that.

The thought ran unapologetically through Willow's mind as she watched the big American man threaten Professor Mahmoud from her spot chained and gagged in the corner.

Not so tough now, are you?

Satisfaction soothed away some of the pain from this morning's beating. Despite her promise to herself that she would fight until the end, Willow was starting to realize that the end might be coming sooner than she would like.

Already, her body was becoming too weak.

So far, Professor Mahmoud had been careful not to hit too hard, break bones, or cause internal damage. He wanted her alive and suffering for as long as he could draw it out. But a blow to her arm this morning when she'd instinctively thrown it up to protect her face, had sent nauseating pain spiraling through the limb and out into the rest of her body.

Broken?

Maybe.

There were no outward signs of a break, but that didn't mean the bone hadn't splintered. Without the benefit of an x-ray, there was, of course, no way to confirm, but she was sure that at least a couple of ribs were cracked, and the throbbing pain in her face from yesterday's beating told her that her cheekbone might be fractured as well.

Besides that, she was positive she was a tapestry of black and blue from her head to her feet.

The end *was* coming.

Definitely sooner than she wanted.

But what if this man, towering over Professor Mahmoud, who was trembling like the coward he was, was in fact, the answer to her prayers?

Was it possible he was here for her?

It wasn't like she had come traipsing to Egypt without telling anyone where she was going. Willow had to tread carefully with what information she shared with her friends and colleagues. Professor Mahmoud was well-connected. A celebrated Egyptologist, he traveled the world lecturing as well as working for one of the top schools in the country.

Messing with him was dangerous, but it was more dangerous to allow him to keep doing what he'd been doing. It wasn't even a question of whether or not he was doing it, Willow knew that he was, she just needed proof if she was going to stop him.

Which was why she was there.

Only she hadn't expected to get caught and wind up a prisoner of the man who knew exactly what she was doing there.

When she hadn't returned home or checked in, she was sure that at least one of her friends or colleagues would have reported her disappearance to the cops. They knew enough to know that she was investigating the professor for ties to a terrorist organization. Surely, when the cops learned that they'd pass along the intel to the appropriate agencies. Then someone would come for her.

It was a hope she'd been clinging to valiantly these last two weeks, and now she hardly dared to believe that this man could be here to rescue her.

From his height and the muscles bulging beneath his black T-shirt, stretching it to the limit, and the confidence he exuded with every movement, every word, there was no doubt that he was military. If he was here for her then likely special forces. It wasn't like the government could start a war over one missing journalist, but surely, they'd do something to try to rescue her.

"Tell me what you know about my mother," the man growled again, this time his words registered.

His mom.

Whoever the American man was, he thought the professor knew something about his mother.

If she could, she'd tell him that Tarek Mahmoud didn't recruit women, he recruited men to join Allah's Warriors. Young men. This man looked like he was probably a couple of years older than her own twenty-nine years, which would mean his mom was most likely around fifty, much older than the professor's target demographic.

"Y-yes, of c-course," Professor Mahmoud stammered, no longer the tough guy he was when he was beating on her. It was one thing to pretend you were strong and powerful when your victim was so much physically smaller than yourself. It was quite another when the man staring you down with hatred in his eyes was bigger than you.

Releasing his hold slowly, the American nodded at the table, and Professor Mahmoud scurried over to it. Instead of taking a seat alongside him, the man stood beside the professor's chair, his arms crossed over his broad chest, a glare on his face.

"Start talking," he ordered.

Mahmoud nodded like his head was one of those bobble-headed statues people put on the dashboards of their cars. "I d-don't know much," he prefaced. When the American did nothing but stare him out, he continued, "I recognized the picture. Such pretty green eyes. The kind you don't forget. I saw her here in Egypt a long time ago. Eighteen years."

That sparked something in the American's eyes. "How do you

remember it was eighteen years? That's quite specific considering it's almost two decades ago."

Another manic nod from the professor, his eyes darting about as though seeking help from somewhere. However, she was the room's only other occupant, and she sure as heck wasn't going to help him. Not for any reason, but certainly not when she wasn't sure if the American was here solely about his mother or if this was some sort of ruse to get intel on whether or not she was alive and being held there.

Wishful thinking, Willow.

Of course it was, she just wasn't ready to accept that yet. If the man was there because of her, he would have done more than give a single disinterested glance in her direction. As badly as she wanted to rid herself of the gag and call out to him, beg him for help, tell him that she was being held against her will, she held back because she couldn't know for sure he was a good guy.

American, yes. Military, she'd bet everything she owned on it. But that didn't mean he was one of the good guys. What if he was one of those guys who had become a mercenary or something? What if he was a bad guy now?

Or what if he *was* one of the good guys and had a whole team waiting outside to swoop in and save her? If she did anything now, not only would she incur the professor's wrath in the form of another beating—he'd informed her before the American arrived that he had a visitor coming, and if she spoke or drew attention to herself in any way she'd be punished—but she might ruin whatever plan her potential savior might have.

"Y-yes, yes. Eighteen years. The year I married my wife," Professor Mahmoud explained. "That's where I saw her. We threw a large party, and she was one of the attendees."

From the expression on the American's face, he was trying to take that information and figure out how it fit into what he already knew or suspected.

"That's all I know," Professor Mahmoud said, a hint of defiance in his tone now.

Given what she knew of the man, she was positive that was a lie. He knew more. If he didn't, he wouldn't have told this man that he had recognized his mom's picture. Whatever game the professor was playing, it didn't seem like it had anything to do with her.

Which meant this man likely didn't have anything to do with her either.

That meant she had nothing to lose.

Even if the American was a threat, she'd only be exchanging the frying pan for the fire, it wasn't like her position could get any worse than it already was. If she stayed, then all she had to look forward to in her future was pain and then, eventually, death.

If she risked it, then maybe the American would save her even if that wasn't why he was there.

As though he could read her mind, Professor Mahmoud immediately got up. "I'm sorry, I must ask you to leave. I have a speaking engagement this morning that I must get ready for. I'm sorry I don't have more information for you, but at least now you know that your mother had some sort of business here in Egypt not long before she died."

Clearly, the American was debating his options, and Willow was about to risk screaming through the gag and begging for help, but Professor Mahmoud shot her a murderous glare. Even if the American was inclined to help her, it didn't mean he'd be able to get her out of this house alive. The Warriors owned this whole street. All the professor had to do was alert them, and neither she nor the American would be leaving this house alive.

Defeat had her snapping her mouth shut before she made a sound.

Why risk the American's life when there was the tiniest thread of hope that he was there for her, that he did have a plan in place, that maybe she would be going home?

Finally, the American nodded. "If you think of anything else, please contact us."

"Of course," Professor Mahmoud said like he actually cared about anything other than himself and his own beliefs and goals.

Watching the American walk out of the kitchen, Willow couldn't help but feel that her only chance at survival had just walked out with him.

Had she made the right choice?

Or had she just sealed her own fate?

CHAPTER

Three

July 10th
    12:13 P.M.

The only way Cooper could describe how he felt as he lounged on the bed in his hotel room a couple of hours later was unsettled.

Nothing about this morning's meeting felt right.

From the fear in Professor Mahmoud's face when he had his hand around the man's throat, to the information the man gave him, to the figure in black huddled in the corner.

None of it.

That the professor knew more than he was letting on was as clear to him as the sun shining brightly in the clear blue sky.

Of course, he'd expected to instill fear when he wrapped his fingers around the professor's neck, that had been the entire point, he'd wanted the older man to know that he wasn't someone to be messed with. But there was more to it than that. Nothing specific that he could put his finger on, just a gut instinct.

There was something the professor didn't want to share, and Cooper would bet that whatever it was, it was the key to unraveling this

entire mess and proving that his mother was no traitor and that whatever happened to cause his father's team to be ambushed had nothing to
do with her and her second husband.

At the back of his mind, there was always that tiny niggling bit of
doubt.

A voice whispering *what-if*.

What if he and his siblings were wrong? What if they were grasping
at straws because they couldn't accept that the mother they adored
would ever betray them all by conspiring to have their father killed?
What if she really was a traitor and had gotten exactly what she
deserved? What if she'd committed suicide because she was guilty and
didn't want to live with the consequences of her actions?

Those questions had been a constant for almost twenty years. But
every time they spread their insidious doubts through his mind, he
focused on the facts. His parents loved each other. Sure, he might have
only been thirteen at the time, but he knew what he'd seen, and he knew
that their marriage was rock solid despite his dad's unpredictable sched-
ule. He also knew that his mom and stepdad had not shared a bed.
They'd married for a reason other than love, and he believed it was
because they knew they were being set up and were trying to stop it
from happening.

Innocent.

Despite the whispers of doubts, he knew his mom was not guilty,
and that determination to prove it only grew with each passing year.

When his phone began to ring, he saw his twin's name on the screen
and quickly accepted the call. After returning to his hotel room after his
meeting with Tarek Mahmoud, he texted to tell them the meeting was
over, and he'd been sitting there expecting their call.

As soon as Connor appeared on the screen, Cooper felt himself
settle. He and his twin had always been close. Cade was only two years
older than them, and Cole was two years younger, but he and Connor
shared a bond. One that had only grown after their parents' deaths.
Thankfully, their grandparents had stepped up, moving into their house
so they could remain in their home and not endure another trauma.
They'd even fostered Jake and Jax who had no other family to take them
in. So even though he was close with all three of his brothers, both step-

brothers, and his baby sister, nothing could come close to that twin bond.

"How'd it go?" Connor asked, shifting the phone slightly, and Cooper could see Cade, Cole, Jake, Jax, and Cassandra all come into view. They were all looking at him with expectant faces, and he hated that he had nothing concrete to give them. They'd all wanted to join him in Egypt, but they couldn't all come over because together, they were an intimidating group, and there was no way they'd get anything out of the professor if they showed up together.

"I don't know," he said slowly.

"What does that mean?" Cade demanded. From the look of the man, you'd never guess that he could be an absolute marshmallow when it came to his four-year-old daughter. While he was big, almost six foot seven, with a muscled form and a dark expression that intimidated almost everyone he met, Cade never hesitated to get down on the floor and have makeup parties, teddy bear tea parties, or dress up as a fairy princess with the little girl he adored.

Cooper took a moment to consider his answer.

There was nothing concrete he could put his finger on. There was no one thing he could say about why he was feeling so unsettled, yet he wasn't going to discount his feelings. All they needed to do was a little more digging around, and once he had a better read on Professor Tarek Mahmoud, he'd take another crack at the man.

"Something wrong, Coop?" Cole asked. Of the four Charleston brothers, the youngest, Cole, was the most laidback. He was charming, calm, and relaxed, usually smiling, which didn't mean he wasn't just as deadly, but he was the one you wouldn't immediately pick as a former special forces operator.

"No, nothing wrong," he confirmed. "I just ... Professor Mahmoud explained why he recognized the photo of Mom, but ..."

"But you think he's lying?" Jake asked. Like Cade, he was an intimidating man, not quite as tall but every bit as broad. He had a temper that seemed to be always balancing on a knife's edge, and the smallest of things could send him tumbling over it. But he was a good man, one Cooper respected and cared about, and considered a brother just as much as the ones he was related to.

"Yeah, he was lying, no doubt about it," he confirmed.

"What did he tell you?" Jax asked. The younger Holloway brother was definitely similar to Cole, much more charming and outwardly likable than Jake, yet every bit as deadly.

"Said he recognized Mom from his wedding," Cooper informed them.

"From his wedding?" Cassandra asked. Despite losing both her parents when she was young enough that she barely remembered them, despite the accusations thrown at their mother, and despite the fact that she had six overprotective big brothers, she was like a breath of fresh air. She was sunshine and roses in a world that was, more often than not, far too dark and depressing.

"Doesn't sound likely," Cade said. Of all of them, he was the only one who'd ever been in love and gotten married. Unfortunately, his wife had passed away almost two years ago, leaving him a single father to little Esther, who was utterly spoiled by all of them, much to her daddy's annoyance. Given their unpredictable job hours with Prey, Cade had a nanny, Gabriella, who lived with them and was always there if he had to be called away.

"Exactly. He's getting married and yet happens to remember the face of a woman he doesn't know eighteen years later. Doesn't sound believable," he agreed. "The fact it was two decades ago, and he should have had other priorities that day tells me it's a lie. Even if he wasn't invested in the marriage and wedding, I don't think he'd notice Mom enough to remember her this many years later."

"Mom has those green eyes that are hard to forget," Cole suggested.

"He mentioned the eyes, and they were amazing, but I still find it hard to believe that they would stick in his mind that long that he could pick her out in a picture," he said. "It was more than that, though, I can't put my finger on it, but there's something else going on there. I rattled his cage, but he looked more fearful than he should have, considering he knew I believed him to have information I needed. I don't know what, but he knows something, I'm sure of it.

"We'll figure out what he knows," Connor said confidently like it was already a foregone conclusion.

Right now, he needed his twin's optimism because he was feeling pretty tapped out.

"Was there something else?" Jax asked.

"Nothing to do with Mahmoud. There was just this figure dressed all in black in the corner of his kitchen. I just ... got a weird vibe about it." When he'd been getting ready to leave, he'd sensed that whoever was in the corner had been going to say something, but they hadn't.

"Probably nothing," Cade said, brushing it off. "They do things differently over there. I wouldn't worry about it, remember what you're there for."

His big brother was right. Whoever the person was, whatever they were doing there, whatever was going on, it wasn't any of his business. If the person wasn't safe, he hated leaving them to their fate, but he had to focus on what was most important. Clearing his mother and stepfather's names so they could all finally move on with their lives.

If he messed up this chance at getting intel, they might not get another.

~

July 10th
   6:24 P.M.

The sounds of the trapdoor being opened to her overheated prison told Willow that her time was up.

When the American had left Professor Mahmoud's house this morning, she'd been prepared to take the beating she knew was coming. But she'd been given a reprieve. No sooner was the stranger out of the kitchen, the front door closing behind him, than the backdoor was opening, and a half dozen men she'd seen before had come barreling in, demanding to know what the American had wanted.

She knew what the professor had been afraid of.

Like her, he'd wondered if the American had come for her.

Just because he had connections in both the US and Egypt didn't mean that Tarek Mahmoud was completely above the law. He did his business quietly, hiding who he really was behind his enigmatic personality and love of his parents' country.

But if you looked closely enough you saw the truth.

Like she had.

While it seemed on the surface like the American was here solely to learn answers about his mother and presumably what had happened to her, that didn't mean there weren't other reasons.

Please be other reasons.

Because if there weren't, if he really wasn't in Egypt to rescue her, or because he too knew what Professor Mahmoud was really doing, then it was as good as over for her.

Feet appeared in the hole and even though she knew it was pointless, instinct had Willow pressing her back against the concrete wall of her cell. There was no escape. From the coming beating, from her inevitable death at the hand of the man she had been attempting to bring down, from the likelihood that no one would ever recover her body.

That she'd just disappear, and in the end, nobody would truly grieve her.

Even though her father was proven innocent and the real killer brought to justice, it didn't undo the damage that had been done. Her ability to trust grown-ups had been shattered. Not only had those men been content to kill her father right in front of her, but her mother hadn't done anything to try to stop it from happening. She'd believed in her husband's guilt.

Which had left lasting damage to her mother's psyche when the truth came out.

Ostracized by the other children, no longer trusting anyone, and taking on the role of caretaker when her mother became too depressed to function, Willow had changed, too. No longer was she carefree and outgoing, now she held her cards close to her chest and struggled to make friends. At the back of her mind there was always a question of whether or not the person could be trusted regardless of their words or actions.

Luckily, she supposed, she didn't have that problem with Professor Mahmoud.

She already knew he couldn't be trusted.

At least he wore his intentions on his sleeve. He was angry that she'd managed to see through his façade and had the audacity to actually take him on. He wanted to punish her, enjoyed her pain, and got off on her fear. It made him a sadistic psychopath, but at least she could read him easily. There was no guessing, which took away a little of the fear.

"You were going to disobey my orders this morning," Professor Mahmoud said as his shoes became his whole body and he landed on the floor of her tiny cell just a couple of steps away from her.

Even though the air outside wasn't much cooler than the stifling air trapped in her musty little oven of a cell, it was still cooler, and for a moment Willow ignored the maniac standing before her and took a few gulps of it. Since the heat was pretty close to unbearable, there was a constant sheen of sweat on her skin, it made her skin slippery, and every movement had the cuff around her wrist slide around. At first, she'd thought that it could be a way to slip her hand right out of the cuff, get the drop on Mahmoud when he came for her, and find a way to escape.

Now she knew it was just another thing to cause her pain.

Now as she stood slowly, shakily, it banged against her already bruised and torn skin.

Every ounce of pain as she drew herself up straight, refusing to cower before this coward of a man, served as a reminder of how quickly her life was rushing to an end. It was like her body had been turned into an hourglass, each beating caused a little more sand to fall from one side to the other. When all the sand was gone ...

Then she would be too.

But that didn't mean she would cower.

No way.

She knew she was doing something dangerous when she decided to follow Professor Mahmoud to Egypt. She'd weighed the risks against the gains and concluded that it was worth it.

If this was how she was going to die, she could at least hold her head up high and know that she'd done her best to take her father's tragedy and turn it around, make it something good.

"I didn't speak a word, I followed your rules," she told the professor, gaining a small rush of satisfaction at the annoyance that flared in his eyes.

This was the only bit of power she possessed in this situation. Her ability to stand her ground and not fold before the man who thought he had a right to do as he pleased and hurt whomever he chose.

All Willow could pray for was that she could hold onto that strength right until the end. That even as she took her final breath, she didn't give this psychopath the satisfaction of begging, pleading, or cowering.

"You were going to," Professor Mahmoud snapped.

"But I didn't. And you have no way of proving otherwise." That was kind of a silly comment to throw at him since proof meant nothing there. She wasn't being charged with a crime and wasn't standing before a judge in a court of law. There were no rules, there were just men who would do whatever it took to force their beliefs on the rest of the world.

"You are not very smart are you, Ms. Purcell?" Professor Mahmoud snarled as he stepped closer, snapping out a hand to wrap around her neck and shoving her back up against the wall just like the American had done to him several hours ago. "You do not seem to learn your lesson no matter how many times I teach you."

That's because the lesson he wanted to teach her wasn't one she was willing to learn.

She didn't believe, as he did, that women were nothing more than vessels to be used to provide the next generation of boys they could train to become just like them. Slaves to cook, clean, and cater to their every whim.

Nothing he could do would ever make her believe that.

It killed the professor that it was a woman who had been trying to bring him down, and while he was enjoying inflicting his punishments, it was infuriating to him that he couldn't bend her to his will. Which was why it was so important that she stood firm.

Stay strong.

You can do this.

If you don't believe in yourself nobody else will.

The pep talk was enough that she only grunted when his fist connected with her stomach, shoving the air from her lungs.

Another followed quickly after, and then a third.

Predictable as he was, Professor Mahmoud stepped back after that.

When his hand left her throat, Willow sagged forward, dragging in breaths and doing her best to compartmentalize the throbbing pain in her stomach.

"I will break you," he snapped as he pulled out a key and unlocked the cuff from around her wrist then threw her over his shoulder. Like always, he passed her up to one of his men standing above the trapdoor, then climbed up to join them.

Snatching her from his friend's arms, the professor literally threw her onto the ground, her body bouncing from the force, then stood above her sneering down at her. With the bright blue sky surrounding them and the sun highlighting him from behind, making him appear more shadowlike than human, Willow felt she was looking directly at the devil.

This man was pure evil, there was no other way to describe him.

The only comfort she could take in her death was knowing that upon it, every scrap of evidence she'd managed to uncover would be sent directly to her boss, the cops, the university the professor worked for, and a government contact she had. Before getting on the plane, she'd left instructions with her lawyer that if no one heard from her in a month, he was to access her files and pass them along to the designated people.

If Professor Mahmoud thought killing her was going to solve all his problems, he was wrong. While she didn't have enough evidence yet to bring him down, she had enough for people to start asking questions, and add in her disappearance and likely death, and she was sure that in the end, she would be the one who came out victorious even if she was no longer alive to celebrate her victory.

"You are nothing," Professor Mahmoud snarled as he slammed his foot into her body.

Instinctively, she curled in on herself, protecting her head and vital organs as best as she could as his foot continued to make contact with her body.

Like she always did, Willow mentally reached out to her father, who had suffered the same fate she currently was.

Help me, Daddy. Help me be strong like you were. Help me to hold on. Help me stand up for what's right and not cave no matter what.

Give me a miracle and send someone to save me.

CHAPTER

Four

July 11th
10:32 A.M.

He was walking around the pyramids—*the* Pyramids of Giza—a place on many people's bucket list, and yet Cooper could barely give it any of his attention.

It wasn't that the pyramids weren't spectacular, they were, and you could spend an entire day walking around, taking pictures from different angles, capturing their size and magnificence. The problem was him.

It didn't matter how amazing the pyramids were, he felt like he should be doing something productive. This was no vacation, he wasn't there to marvel at the wonders of ancient Egypt, he was there to get answers on who set his mom up to look like a traitor and why.

That wasn't all that was on his mind.

The person in black in the corner of Mahmoud's kitchen was as well.

Cooper couldn't seem to get them out of his head. The body was too small to be an adult male and too big to be a young child, so it was either a woman or a teen boy. Given where they were and the big, baggy clothes the person had been dressed in, he was leaning toward a woman.

Who was she, and how had she gotten mixed up with a man like Tarek Mahmoud?

Was it possible that the professor was wrapped up in more than just whatever happened to his mom? Could he be into human trafficking? Prostitution? Was the boy or woman a slave? A prisoner?

His brother's words kept echoing in his mind. He shouldn't worry about it, he was there for a reason and one he had to focus on. He had to keep his mind on the ball and not allow himself to become distracted.

But ...

What if the person needed help?

If they were in trouble, could he really just ignore it because he had his own issues to deal with?

That wasn't who he was. Wasn't who he had been raised to be. While he and his siblings had believed that their mom worked for an aid agency and that's why she had to travel sometimes, they'd always known that she was strong and tough. To travel to dangerous countries and build a successful marriage with a special forces operator who was away sometimes for months at a time, you had to be. Learning she was actually in the CIA was a huge shock but had also filled them all with pride.

Their mom had been an amazing woman which was why he and his siblings were determined to clear her name.

It was the least she deserved.

So stop thinking about the person in black.

Whatever was going on there wasn't his business. There was every chance that the person wasn't in any trouble, and even if they were, it wasn't like he had many options to do anything about it. Sure, he worked for Prey, and he had his boss' okay to be there, but this was no official mission and he couldn't just barge into a respected professor's home and demand that he hand over the person in black. What if they were there of their own free will? They might not even want to be rescued.

Best to just let it go.

There was enough to focus on without adding to the mix.

To that end, he did his best to shove all thoughts of the huddled black figure in the kitchen corner from his mind.

This might not be a vacation, but he *was* in Egypt, and he *was* walking around the pyramids, he really should take in their grandeur and make the most of it. As he wandered around, heading toward where the Sphynx was situated, he even pulled out his cell phone and took a few photos. No selfies, they weren't really his thing, but he did snap some great pictures of the Sphynx with the pyramids in the background.

It was only when he was turning around to walk over to the other side of the pyramids, that he noticed it.

A man who seemed to be paying a little too much attention to him.

There was nothing outwardly suspicious about him. He looked like all the other tourists wandering around, only at the same time, he didn't. Dressed in jeans and a long-sleeved T-shirt, he had a pair of sunglasses on so there was no way Cooper could confirm that he was looking at him, but he *felt* eyes on him. The man was angled so he could watch Cooper, and he didn't have a cell phone in his hand.

Almost all the tourists had phones in their hands, laughing and smiling as they took photo after photo.

Only this man just stood there, staring.

At him.

Cooper would bet everything he owned on it.

To test his theory, Cooper started walking. Keeping his pace slow and even. He headed back toward the pyramids. Walking around them, he headed across the large sandy area to another good photo opportunity spot. It was where he was heading anyway, but it would give him proof that he was being followed. There was a road that most of the buses were taking to drive to the second spot, and only a handful of people were walking it.

As he walked, he stopped regularly, snapping more pictures, he may as well take as many as he could and make his little sister jealous since the pyramids were indeed on her bucket list.

Every time he stopped, he spotted the man.

Following.

If he was doing his best to look unobtrusive, he was doing a terrible job. He still hadn't pulled out a cell phone and at least attempted to look like just another tourist.

Why, if you were going to follow someone, would you make it so obvious?

Did they *want* him to know he was being followed?

Was it one of Professor Mahmoud's contacts?

That would be the only thing that made sense. He wasn't there for Prey, so there was no reason for anyone to follow him around because of his job. And he didn't look like he was wealthy, and given his size he clearly wasn't an easy target. He was definitely not who you would pick out if you were there to rob someone, even if he was alone.

When he reached the other spot, he stopped for a moment, took more pictures, then angled his phone and zoomed in, snapping as many pictures as he could of the man following him. From this distance, he couldn't get a clear picture of his face, and the sunglasses definitely made it even more difficult, but he'd take what he could get. Once he had a whole range, he tapped out a quick email to his brother, attached all the pictures, and asked Cade to pass them along to Prey's computer people. Maybe there was something they could pull from them to help identify him, and even if they couldn't, at least they'd have them for reference if the man tried anything.

Which so far he hadn't.

Other than following Cooper wherever he went, the man didn't try to get too close, and from what he could see it didn't look like he was armed. It was like he had just been hired to tail him and see where he was going and what he was doing.

If it was Mahmoud, could it be because the man wanted to see if he was going to meet up with anyone?

After their meeting yesterday, Cooper had the feeling there was more to Tarek Mahmoud than the man was letting on. He just had no idea what it could be.

Again, the image of the figure in black huddled in the corner filled his mind.

Could that be related to him being followed?

If the figure was a victim, perhaps the professor was worried that he'd been caught red-handed, and Cooper was there for more than just to ask questions about his long-dead mother.

It wasn't true. He was there for no other reason than to find out what Professor Mahmoud might know about what was more than likely his mother's last job with the CIA. Verifying the date Tarek Mahmoud had gotten married, it was just a month before his dad was killed, and then just six months after that his mother was arrested and died.

Whatever had happened in Egypt had to be related to what happened to his mom, all seven of them agreed on that, but that didn't actually bring them any closer to finding out what exactly it was that had happened.

If the man following him really was here at Tarek Mahmoud's orders, then it confirmed that the professor was more deeply embroiled in the plot to set up his mother to look like a traitor. Whatever the man was hiding, whatever he didn't want Cooper to discover, whatever reasons he had for having him watched, there was no way he wasn't going to uncover those secrets.

~

July 11th
    5:02 P.M

It sounded silly, but the worst part of being held prisoner on Professor Mahmoud's property in this tiny little underground cell was the heat.

The pain from constant beatings was awful, and the unexpected claustrophobia those first couple of days had been as terrible as it had been confusing, given that Willow had never worried about small spaces in her life.

But the heat ...

It was inescapable.

It clung to her body in a horrible sheen of sweat.

It was stifling and made it feel like every ounce of air had been drained out of this dark space.

It made her feel like she was being slowly cooked alive.

Of course, the temperatures in here weren't actually hot enough to kill her. If they were she'd be dead already. But they were hot enough that they kept her in a constant state of dehydration. What little water she was given, she always drank too quickly because she was so thirsty her mouth felt as dry as the desert outside. No matter how many times she coached herself to go slow, take sips, and make it last, as soon as that water touched her tongue, she lost her mind and guzzled it down as quickly as she could.

Which only served to start the process all over again, and by the time the next bottle of water was delivered she was so thirsty she couldn't think straight.

This was a horrible way to live.

In fact, a lot of the time, Willow just wished the professor would hurry up and do it already, end her suffering, and put her out of her misery.

The rest of the time she remembered why she had to fight.

The promise she'd made to her dad on the day of his funeral hadn't been fulfilled yet. Even at eight years old, she'd felt the injustice of what had happened to her father so deeply that it was forever ingrained in her soul. That day, as she'd stood beside his coffin in the church empty but for herself, her mom, and the pastor, she had promised her dad that she would do something with her life to make him proud.

At eight, she hadn't known what that thing was. All she'd known then was that the people who should have trusted and believed in her dad had failed him, and somehow, she had to make it right. The church they'd attended every Sunday had been empty only because she'd refused to go to the funeral if the people who had let her dad down were there. They knew him, and yet they had refused to allow his funeral to take place there until he was cleared.

Then they cried crocodile tears.

But it was already too late. The damage had been done and she never stepped foot inside that building after the funeral.

As she grew older and thought more about the journalist who had written the lies that led to her dad's death, she realized that was the way to honor the father she adored. To take what had killed him and make it mean something important.

So, she'd begun on this journey.

One that had already given her a well-respected name and sustainable career. One that had shown her that not all journalists cared solely about being first to break a story, about ratings and views, about fame and fortune. Some cared about gathering evidence and sharing with the world stories that needed to be told.

Those people were her tribe, and she was clinging to hope that they would alert the authorities about her disappearance.

Not that she was pinning all her hopes on anyone else to come swooping in on a white horse to save her.

If she wanted to live, she had to find a way to save herself.

Which was exactly what she planned to do.

The American would be back, she was sure of it. She'd studied human behavior, and even from the little she knew about the man, she was confident she could predict at least that aspect of his behavior. His mom had been gone for eighteen years, he had to be around her age, probably a couple of years older, which meant he'd lost his mom as a kid.

There was no way that hadn't shaped the person he had become.

She knew, she'd lived it, too.

Her dad's death had shaped her entire future, and she believed it was no different for the American man. For whatever reason, he believed that Professor Mahmoud knew something about what happened to his mother, so he'd come back to try to get more answers from him.

When he did, she'd be ready.

This time she wasn't keeping quiet.

It was obvious the American wasn't there for her, and despite the professor's guilty conscience, she doubted he was there for him either. This was all about his mother, which meant there was no team waiting in the wings to rescue her. There were no plans to risk messing up, so when the man returned, she was going for it. She'd find a way to alert him to the fact that she was in trouble and needed help and pray he would be willing to give it to her.

Don't let me be wrong about this.

Please.

The familiar clank of the padlock being unlocked had her closing her eyes. It was the best way to deal with the onslaught of light when the trapdoor was flung open.

Even with her eyes closed, she felt that light cut straight through her skull.

"Get up," Professor Mahmoud ordered, and she sensed him standing before her even though her eyes were still closed.

Normally, she'd shoot back some sort of retort, but today, she just didn't have the energy. It was becoming increasingly evident that her body had already given pretty much all it had to give. Her tank was almost dry, and once it was, it was only a matter of time.

A foot connected with her hip, and she had to bite on her lip to prevent a moan from falling out. Almost empty or not, she was not going to give Professor Mahmoud the satisfaction of breaking her.

"I said, get up," he ordered again, delivering another blow to her hip and making the entire left side of her body feel like it had caught fire.

Gathering what scraps of strength she could find, Willow managed to drag herself to her feet. As soon as she was standing, the metal cuff on her wrist was unlocked and she was picked up and thrust up into the arms of one of the men who worked with the professor.

From the voices chattering around her, she knew this was going to be bad. Most of the time it was just the professor who doled out his torturous beatings alone. But sometimes, he invited his friends along. Those days were always the worst, and not just because more people meant more pain.

It was how much it reminded her of the worst night of her life.

Somehow, the universe seemed to get off on continuing to torture her with her father's death, even twenty years later making her life turn into an echo of his murder.

Before anyone could get to her, Willow managed to scramble to her feet. She swayed precariously, almost going back down again, and with nothing to reach out to and use to steady herself, she had to cartwheel her arms a couple of times to remain upright, but she managed it.

The men surrounded her, looking at her with curiosity. She wasn't like the women they were used to, she didn't cower, didn't blindly obey, and had a role beyond what they believed women should have, and she loved that all of that angered them.

"I know who you really are, professor," she said, her voice weak from pain but still confident. "I know what you do. I know what all of you do," Willow added, letting her gaze roam the gathering of men in this dusty yard. "I know that you're recruiting as many young men as you can so that you can groom them, convert them, then instill them in positions of power in the countries of your enemies. I know you're planning a Trojan Horse kind of thing and that you want to destroy everything that doesn't align with you and your beliefs. If I survive, I'm going to shout it all from the rooftops and bring you down."

The men laughed like that declaration was the funniest thing they'd ever heard, but they knew she had enough intel to destroy them if she really should manage to escape or be rescued.

It was why she had to keep fighting, even when they converged on her and blows began to rain down on her already broken body.

Why giving up wasn't an option no matter how much her injured body pleaded with her to do so.

When the American came, she was going to do whatever it took to make contact with him.

Because it was her last hope.

If the American didn't save her, nothing else would.

CHAPTER
Five

July 11th
6:47 P.M.

This time he wasn't walking away until he was sure he'd gathered every piece of intel to glean from Tarek Mahmoud.

"Hey, Coop, you gone inside yet?" the voice echoed inside his ear from the comms unit he was wearing. Tonight, he was going into the professor's home wired. Anything the man said would be heard by all three of his brothers and both his stepbrothers. Cassandra had opted out, although they never hid anything from her, she had decided to take a different path in life than the rest of them, and they all respected her boundaries and her desire to keep out of danger and away from the filth that littered the earth.

"No, just pulled up outside," he answered Connor's question.

"Good, we got an ID on the guy following you today at the pyramids," his twin informed him.

"Cass is still jealous that you got to see them, and she hasn't," Cole added with an amused chuckle. "You're going to hear all about it when you get home."

"Don't doubt it," Cooper replied, a small smile curling his lips up.

If there was one thing you could say about his sister, it was that she wasn't shy about making her needs and wants known. Growing up with six big brothers, she'd had no choice but to learn how to stand up for herself if she didn't want to get lost in the crowd. That confidence was going to help her get whatever she wanted out of life, and already she was on her way to making her dreams come true.

"So, who is the guy?" he asked. After walking around for a solid hour at the pyramids, making sure the man was still following him, he'd risked an encounter with him. Doubling back abruptly, he'd left the man with no choice but to either make a run for it and make it obvious what he'd been doing or stand his ground.

The young man—who looked like little more than a college kid—had chosen to stand his ground, and Cooper had managed to get a close-up picture of him. Wanting to see how he would react, he'd then asked the kid if he would mind snapping a few pictures of him with the pyramids in the background because he didn't want to pay one of the men who worked there to do it for him.

Although looking extremely uneasy, the kid had complied, which gave him a fingerprint that he'd been able to send to Prey for them to run through databases. While he was no forensic analyst, Cooper was grateful for the few things he did know because now he had an ID that could be the key to getting the professor to talk.

"He's a twenty-year-old by the name of Aston Duncan. Just finished his sophomore year at the same college Professor Mahmoud works at," Connor informed him.

Coincidence?

Nope.

Not a chance.

"What's he in the system for?" Cooper asked. If they could ID the kid through his fingerprints, then at some time in the last couple of years he'd committed a crime.

"A couple of possession arrests during his freshman year," Cade replied. "No charges were ever pressed. Dad's got some money and made a deal for his son to do rehab instead. Seemed to have worked. No arrests at all this year, and he's passed all his drug tests with flying colors."

"He in any of the professor's classes?" he asked.

"Nope. Not a one," Connor answered.

So, what was the kid doing here in Egypt following him around tourist sites?

The college was a connection between the young man and the professor, but how would they have met? And did the fact that the kid had been on drugs at some point play into it in any way?

"All right, I'll see if I can use that to get Mahmoud talking," he said as he unsnapped his seatbelt and climbed out of the car. One thing for sure he wouldn't be missing when he got back home was driving. These Egyptian drivers didn't bother following any of the alleged road rules, and they'd never met a horn they didn't enjoy using. If you weren't able to drive assertively, you'd never make it over there.

"Remember we're listening in on everything," Cole reminded him as he strode purposefully across the street.

"I'm going to put you guys on silent now," he told his brothers. Just because they'd be listening to everything he said didn't mean he wanted anyone to hear what they were saying. There was no way that Mahmoud didn't know who he was or who he worked for, but he also had to make sure the professor believed that his reasons for being there were personal only.

The last thing he wanted when he was alone over there was for things to spiral out of control.

Depending on what he learned, he may take it home to his team and Prey, and see if they needed to plan some sort of op. But for now, he was there merely on an intel-gathering mission and didn't want things going sideways.

After pressing the buzzer, he waited. How the professor approached this unexpected visit would hopefully tell him just how deeply involved the man was in whatever had led to his mother's death.

Nervous.

That's how Cooper would describe the older man when he came hurrying down the front path.

"Ah, Mr. Charleston, I was not expecting another visit from you," Mahmoud said but still unlocked the gate and allowed him to enter.

"I think we have a couple of things we need to discuss," he said, voice low, a hint of menace in his tone.

The man's eyes flared but he gave a nod and ushered him toward the front door. "Yes, yes, of course, I actually would have reached out to you again anyway."

"You would?" Cooper asked, not believing it in the least. There was no way the professor had any intention of ever contacting him or his siblings again. Whether it had to do with his mother, the figure in black, or something else entirely, he was pretty sure that Tarek Mahmoud was rethinking his decision to reach out in the first place because he had secrets he wanted to keep hidden.

As he walked through the house, he couldn't not wonder about the figure in black. No matter how many times he tried to convince himself it wasn't his problem, that he was there to clear his mom's name, he couldn't get the person out of his mind.

They were in trouble, he was sure of it, and it killed him not to be able to do anything about it. But again, he was there on his own, his siblings were counting on him to get this intel, and he couldn't let them down. Not for anything.

"Yes, yes, of course," Mahmoud babbled as they entered the kitchen.

Immediately, Cooper's gaze moved to where he'd last seen the figure in black, and just like before, it was there again.

This time it was huddled right in on itself, looking more like a pile of black material than a human being. But it was a human. A person who he was positive was not sitting in the corner of the room, swathed in material, of their own free will.

"I was looking for photos," Mahmoud continued.

"Photos?" he asked, tearing his gaze away from the figure in black. "What photos?"

"From my wedding," the professor told him. "After you left, I felt bad that I hadn't had much to give you so I thought I'd go through photos and see if I could find some of your mother."

"And did you?"

"I did." Nodding at the table, Mahmoud took a seat and pushed what looked like a photo album forward.

Intrigued, Cooper took a seat and opened the album. Flipping through the first few pages, which were all photos of the bride and groom and their families, he then found some of the guests. Scouring the groups of people sitting around tables eating and drinking, he finally spotted her.

His mother.

Just as he remembered her.

She was wearing a bright green dress, in line with what all the other women were wearing, and even though she was at the back of a table, barely noticeable, he could see how it brought out her eyes. No wonder she'd stood out that night, she looked gorgeous, those stunning eyes were enough to stick in anyone's mind because they were such an unusual and almost unnatural shade for a human's eyes.

But was it really the reason Professor Mahmoud had remembered her almost two decades later? And why had she attended his wedding in the first place? It wasn't like the two were friends, and this had to be the final mission she ever worked for the CIA before she was arrested and died.

Feeling like he had opened Pandora's box and had no idea what the consequences would be, Cooper fixed a hard stare on the professor and asked the most pressing question. "Why were you having me followed?"

∼

July 11th
   7:08 P.M

"Uh ..." Professor Mahmoud stammered, his gaze darting all around the room but not settling on anything.

Willow was listening to the conversation only because she was waiting for the perfect opportunity to make her move.

Determination was flowing through her system. It was giving her strength her body so badly needed and was dulling the pain throbbing inside her, almost stealing her ability to function.

There was no time to waste on resting.

As nice as it would be to just curl up in a little ball and close her eyes, drift away into sleep, and forget for a little while that she was in danger and had to constantly watch her back and be prepared for the next assault, that wasn't possible. If she wanted to live, she had to fight for her life.

Maybe she wouldn't win that fight, but she was going to give it everything she had.

So, she clung to that determination and forced her mind to focus.

She didn't really care what the two men were talking about. Not that she wished the American any ill will. She hoped he would find the answers he needed to be able to get closure on whatever had happened to his mom almost two decades ago, but she couldn't let that be her focus right now. At the moment, she had to use every drop of strength she had left to get herself out of hell.

If he helped her, she'd certainly do anything she could to help him find the answers he sought. But right now, she had to just focus on surviving. So, whatever the two men were talking about was only relevant to her in that she had to time this perfectly if she wanted it to work.

One chance.

That's all she had.

If she blew it, it would be gone along with her hopes of rescue.

Willow still wasn't even sure if this man would help her, like her, it seemed he only had one purpose, and he might be prepared to sacrifice her—a complete stranger whose story he didn't know—to achieve his goals.

Even if he did decide to help, what could he actually do? Besides the professor, there were a couple of the men who had been beating her earlier still there. Some had scattered when the American showed up, but others were in the house, waiting in case Professor Mahmoud needed help.

Though she was positive he was military, he could only do so much if he was outnumbered. And maybe he wasn't even armed. The professor and his friends most certainly were, although they preferred using their fists on her, she had seen the guns lying around.

Reaching out to the American would be putting his life at risk, but it was the only chance she had. She just hated that it made her feel selfish because she really might get him killed.

Hope wavered inside her.

No, don't give up.

She couldn't.

Giving up meant certain death.

Blinking away the tears threatening to blur her vision and give her yet another disadvantage, Willow hardened her heart. She didn't want to put the American in danger, but she also had to do what she had to do to survive.

"I ... don't know what you're talking about," Professor Mahmoud said with a nervous laugh.

"So, the name Aston Duncan doesn't mean anything to you?" the American asked.

Even from there, with her head down, mostly covered by the niqab she had been forced to wear, Willow could see the professor's pupils dilate in fear. He knew the name all right.

Clearing his throat, Professor Mahmoud tried to make his voice strong but failed miserably. "No. It doesn't."

"Twenty-year-old kid, just finished his sophomore year, goes to the same school you work at. Does that sound familiar at all?" the American pushed. His voice did, in fact, come out strong, full of confidence, and completely calm. It was like he knew he was in the presence of a potentially dangerous man, he just didn't care.

That was exactly the kind of energy she needed right now.

Chancing a glance at him, this time around Willow took the time to really *look* at him. Even though he was sitting down, she could tell he was tall, and this time, like last time, he wore a T-shirt that showed off his muscled chest and arms. There was no doubt he was fit and strong, and she could tell from the way he carried himself that he had the training to back it up.

If anyone had a shot at saving her, it was him.

If he wanted to.

She even believed he had the skills and abilities to get her out of there even if they would be outnumbered.

Again, if he wanted to.

Lifting her gaze to his face, she searched for signs that he was the kind of man who had a heart, who would care that she was in trouble and take her out of there. He had scruff and brown hair that was longer on top, but it was his eyes that captivated her.

A pretty shade of gray that reminded her of the sky right before a thunderstorm. There was anger in them, and she shrunk in on herself at the sight of it even though she knew it wasn't directed at her. But there was more there, too. Honor, integrity, and loyalty, everything she needed to see to know that this was a man that could be trusted.

Unless she was seeing only what she wanted to see.

Only right now she didn't have time to worry about it.

She had to take this chance.

Had to.

It was the only one she was going to get.

The American might not return, and if he didn't, and her one shot at escape disappeared along with him, then she'd never be able to forgive herself. Whether she continued to stand up to Professor Mahmoud and his friends or not, her self-respect would be left in tatters, and right now, that was all she had left.

"Doesn't sound familiar," Professor Mahmoud said, leaning back in his chair and waving a dismissive hand. If he was aiming for nonchalance, he was failing miserably.

"I don't believe you," the American said.

"You can believe whatever you want but I—"

Slamming his fist into the table loud enough to make both the professor and her flinch from the sound and the violence behind it, the American leaned closer to Professor Mahmoud. "I said I don't believe you. I think you know exactly who the kid is, although how he's connected to you, I have no idea. You told him to follow me, I want to know why. What are you hiding, Professor Mahmoud?"

She could answer that question.

Would if her mouth wasn't currently covered with tape in an attempt to keep her silent.

Given that he knew she'd been thinking about trying to contact the American to beg him for help on his last visit, Willow knew the professor would be a lot more confident if she wasn't there. Unfortunately for him, the American had shown up without warning, and he hadn't had time to return her to her cell. His own need to have her close so he could lord it over her, how she was his prisoner, was coming back to bite him.

Now, she lifted her head and shifted her body as best she could while chained to the wall.

The American noticed her movements and turned to look at her, something flared in his eyes as their gazes met. If nothing else, then the fact that her eyes were blue when the vast majority of the population of Egypt had brown eyes had to give him at least an inkling that something wasn't right.

Quickly realizing things could fall apart in an instant, the professor stood, moving between them and breaking the connection their gazes had made.

"Darius," the professor called out.

Almost immediately, another man appeared in the doorway.

"Take her," Professor Mahmoud ordered, inclining his head in her direction.

"You have a woman chained up in your kitchen?" the American demanded, shoving his chair back and pushing to his feet. "What the hell is going on here, Mahmoud?"

Whatever excuse the professor gave, Willow wound up not being privy to it. Jerked to her feet fast enough her head spun, she was dragged out of the room before she even properly got her feet beneath her.

Instead of taking her back outside, Darius pulled her into the office at the front of the house. She'd been in this room only once before. The night she was captured while following the professor, tied up, thrown in the back of a van, and brought there.

Tonight, she was bent over the desk as Darius planted a foot between hers, preventing her from closing her legs. One of his hands moved to circle her neck while the other shoved at the long black dress she was wearing, pulling it up to bare her backside.

Hot breath touched the side of her face while a hand connected with her backside. "I've been waiting to have you all to myself," Darius whispered in her ear.

Was this it?

Was she going to be killed now, while her chance at surviving was only yards away in another room?

CHAPTER

Six

Ignore it.

It has nothing to do with us.

Nothing to do with why we're in Egypt.

Cooper could practically hear his brother's voice in his head even though he still had the home end of the comms on silent so neither he nor anyone else could hear what his siblings were no doubt currently discussing.

"Explain," he barked at Mahmoud, loud enough and harsh enough that the man began to tremble.

"It is complicated," Professor Mahmoud hedged.

"Uncomplicate it for me," Cooper ordered. The woman had blue eyes, so it was highly unlikely she was of Egyptian descent, although, of course, not impossible. If she was in Egypt as a tourist, there would be no reason for her to be sitting on the floor in a professor's kitchen, chained to the wall as she'd been.

All along he'd had a bad feeling about the figure in black, who he now knew was a woman. Something had been off about it, and he always trusted his gut. He'd just allowed himself to put his own needs first and not done anything about it.

Because of that, a woman had been hurt.

There were bruises on the small part of her face that had been visible between the black material covering her head and most of her face. One of her eyes had been partially swollen, and the remains of black and blue marks were clearly evident.

"Now," he growled when Professor Mahmoud offered no more information.

"She's my wife's sister's daughter," the other man blurted out.

"And? Why is she chained up in your kitchen?" Cooper didn't believe that. Mahmoud's wife was also Egyptian, and while yes, her sister could have a Caucasian husband and they could have produced a child with blue eyes, he didn't think that was the case. Hopefully, his brothers were looking into it right now, checking to see if that was true, and if it wasn't then they'd have proof that Mahmoud had a woman held against her will on his premises.

Something they could definitely use as blackmail to make him talk.

Which made Cooper feel uneasy, dirty almost. From what little he'd seen, the woman had been abused, and instead of thinking about how he was going to get her out of there, he was thinking about how he could use her trauma for his own gain.

Not that he'd leave her there.

Yes, he was cold enough to use the intel to make Tarek Mahmoud give up whatever intel he was hiding about what his mother had been doing in Egypt and how it played into everything that had gone down. But he wasn't so cold that he wouldn't do everything in his power to get that woman to safety.

"She ... the girl ... it's complicated." As though realizing his mistake in saying that again, Mahmoud quickly hurried on. "She is unwell. Sick. Mentally. She has Schizophrenia and sometimes she has violent delusions. She is a danger to herself and others, and sometimes we don't have any choice but to contain her to keep her safe."

Nope.

He didn't believe that.

Not for a second.

The woman's gaze had been clear, there was no confusion in her eyes, nothing to indicate that she wasn't in her right mind. There had been pain and fear, but also a determination he couldn't help but admire. She'd wanted his attention and she'd got it.

"So, you keep her chained up in your kitchen?" he asked, arching a brow to show he didn't believe that at all.

"It's the safest place for her. She doesn't like to be alone, so we don't leave her upstairs in her bedroom. This way she's close by, we can keep an eye on her, and she has company, but we also know that everyone is safe. Her and us."

"Why isn't she with her parents?"

Professor Mahmoud's gaze did a quick round of the room before settling on him. "They were overwhelmed after caring for her for many years, and we offered to take her for a while to give them a break."

"Will she be returning with you to the States when you go back for the fall semester?"

"She ... she does not like to fly. She could not cope with so many hours sitting in such a small and confined space."

Lies.

All lies.

There was not a chance in hell that the woman he'd seen dragged out of there was a relative of Professor Mahmoud or was mentally ill. She was there for some other reason. Whatever it was, he needed to get her alone long enough to ask. Then he'd take the steps needed to alert the authorities that a kidnap victim was being held in the home of the world-renowned Egyptologist.

Or do whatever it took to take the woman with him when he left.

As much as it might frustrate his siblings, he couldn't in good conscience walk away, knowing an innocent woman was in imminent danger, knowing that she likely wouldn't still be alive when authorities investigated. Leaving her there would be as good as signing her death warrant himself.

Not who he was.

Not who his mother would want him to be.

And not what a single one of his brothers—blood or step—would do if they'd been the ones to come to Egypt and discover her.

It absolutely messed with his plans to gather intel, but he didn't see any other choice. Besides, it wasn't like he was going to have to be personally responsible for the woman. He'd take her with him, drop her off at the embassy, and then go back to doing what he'd come there to do.

Just as Cooper was about to demand to speak with the woman, Mahmoud sagged against the wall. "You were right."

"About what?"

"The kid. Aston Duncan. I *did* ask him to follow you."

Stepping closer, he crowded the older man. "Why would you do that?"

"Because I know who you work for and what happened to your mother. I've heard the stories and the rumors. I had to be sure you were just here to do what you said you were and not for any other reason."

"What other reason would there be?"

"I don't know, but I always know it's better to be safe than sorry. I should have trusted that you just wanted to learn about your mother, but I got a little paranoid. Maybe because I'm aware of the rumors about her. I don't know what she was doing the night of my wedding. She came as the guest of an invited guest. She looked stunning, and even though I love my wife, those eyes weren't ones you could forget easily. It was the first time I'd ever seen her, I exchanged a few words with her, and that was it. By the time I returned from my honeymoon, I heard the rumor that she was involved in the death of her husband and his team. I'll admit I gossiped about it a little, and I was aware that she had been arrested and committed suicide. Maybe because she was somehow connected, no matter in how small a way, with the happiest day of my life that I couldn't not reach out when I saw her photo floating around. But I don't know anything more, I'm sorry."

The speech was delivered emotionally, with all the right intonations and facial expressions, yet it didn't feel real.

Maybe because the professor kept darting nervous little glances toward the door.

The same door the mysterious woman in black had been dragged through.

It was obvious Mahmoud didn't want him getting too close to the woman. As soon as she'd made any attempt to connect with him, the older man had made sure she was taken away. The woman knew something, meant something, was somehow an integral part of this whole thing, and Cooper knew he needed to somehow get to her.

With a sigh, he dropped his head and stepped back, spearing his fingers through his dark locks. "That's it? That's all you know?"

"All I know."

"And you aren't lying?" he asked, shooting the man a look that clearly conveyed that if he was, there would be consequences.

"Swear, no lies."

"All right. May I use the bathroom before I go? After running from your little friend for half the day, I had to drink about a gallon of water once I got back to my rental car."

"Of course. There is one through there, take the door under the stairs."

As soon as Cooper was out of the kitchen, he heard it.

Muffled cries of pain.

Instinct had him heading toward the sound, and when he approached the half-open door to the office at the front of the house, fury ignited in his chest at the sight of the woman in black bent over a desk while the man who had pulled her from the room had his hand around her neck while he rained down blows on her bare backside.

For once in his life, calm, composed, and logical flew out the window and he just acted.

～

July 11th
   7:24 P.M

Slowly, the pain began to fade.

What had once been blinding terror at the thought of death shifted until it became acceptance, and something more.

Peace.

That kind of tranquility you found when you sat on the sand on the beach, listened to the sound of the waves, and watched the sunset on the horizon. Or when you were out in the middle of the woods, the tall trees stretching their limbs far above your head and up into the blue sky while scattered sunlight made dappled patterns on the ground and the twittering of birds mixed with a babbling brook.

As the hand around her neck squeezed a little tighter, Willow floated a little further away from the land of the living.

I'm ready, Dad.

Please be there waiting for me.

Maybe stepping over into whatever came next wouldn't be so scary if her dad was standing there with open arms ready to catch her.

Just as the world went black around the edges, all of a sudden, she could breathe again. The weight that had been crushing her body was gone. The hand that had been striking her bare backside was no longer there.

Weak as she was, her brain struggled to comprehend what had just happened. Why she wasn't dead. And why a strong set of arms gently gathered her up into an embrace.

"Hey, honey, it's okay, you're okay now," a voice crooned in her ear.

There was a hint of familiarity about it, but all she could focus on was dragging air into her starving lungs.

"That's right, honey, keep breathing. Nice deep, long breaths. There you go," the voice encouraged. Hands tugged at the material over her face, and she heard a muttered curse when he obviously discovered the tape over her mouth. "Sorry, honey, this is going to hurt," he murmured before the tape was ripped off, taking layers of skin with it.

If it wasn't for the fact that she could now drag in proper deep breaths, she might have cared about the sting, but honestly, Willow had gotten so used to pain over the last couple of weeks that it barely even registered.

While she sucked in mouthful after mouthful of air, the man just held her, smoothed a hand down her hair, and whispered words she couldn't even understand but that soothed her nonetheless. It was the American, part of her knew that even as part of her was struggling to just comprehend the fact that she wasn't dead.

Alive.

She was alive.

And safe now.

The strong arms wrapped around her kept her in a cocooned little bubble of security that she never wanted to pop.

"You saved me," she whispered through her burning throat once her breathing was finally under control. "Thank you."

A nod was all she got as an acceptance of her gratitude, and a niggle of unease settled inside her. The American had saved her from Darius, but was he going to take her away from Professor Mahmoud or was he going to leave her to her fate?

"What's your name?" he asked.

"Willow Purcell."

"Do you know how long you've been here, Willow?"

"Two weeks."

Those storm-gray eyes of his were a turbulent mess of emotions, and she still wasn't sure if he was going to help her escape even if he'd just saved her life.

The storminess grew when he lifted a hand and very gently traced a fingertip across the bruises she knew must be covering most of her face. At least she knew that anger wasn't directed at her.

"He did this to you?" the American demanded, his voice a low growl.

"Professor Mahmoud?" When he nodded, she did, too. "Most of them. His friends, too. Darius as well. Did you ...?" Willow trailed off, not wanting to ask aloud if the American had killed Darius or just incapacitated him.

"Dead. He had his hands on you and ... I snapped."

"Thank you," she whispered again. There was not a doubt in her mind that if the American hadn't intervened when he had, Darius would have killed her and suffered whatever consequences there might have been when the professor found out.

"Didn't do anything any decent person wouldn't have done," he told her gruffly.

"Hate to break it to you, but there *are* no decent people around here." Willow didn't mean in Egypt, in the entire country, she was sure there were lots, but in this neighborhood, there wasn't a single one to be found. "What's your name?"

There was a slight hesitation before he answered. "Cooper."

"You aren't ... here for me ... are you?"

"No."

Panic coursed through her at his simple one-word answer. "But you won't leave me here, will you?" Even though just moments ago death had seemed like an almost pleasant alternative, now that she'd been dragged back from the brink, she found she didn't want to die. She wanted to live. Wanted to fulfill her promises to her dad. Wanted to destroy Tarek Mahmoud.

Again, there was a pause, and his gaze shifted from her to what she assumed was Darius' body, then to the office door. "No, honey, I wouldn't leave you behind."

Relief swept through her, quickly followed by logic.

They needed a plan, and they needed one quickly.

"Thank you. I heard the questions you asked the professor. Once we're free, I'll tell you everything I know about him. I don't know if it will help you get the answers you need about your mom, but if nothing else, you can use it as leverage."

A smile curled up one side of his mouth, transforming him from handsome to downright gorgeous. "I like the way you think." When he sobered, a sense of dread curled in her stomach. "But I'm going to have to get back in there or he's going to come looking for me."

There was no way Willow wanted to say the words that had to pass her lips.

They made her feel ill.

They also left her in exactly the same position she'd been in before Cooper arrived if he decided to betray her.

But what choice did she have?

If she didn't, then the professor would come looking for Cooper, find the dead body, him holding her in his arms, and kill them both.

This was the only way they stood a chance.

With a sigh, Willow dropped her head to rest on Cooper's broad shoulder, relieved that at least for now, she wasn't in this on her own. "He's been keeping me in an underground cell. That's where Darius was supposed to put me. If you take me out there, lock me in, hide the body, then it will give you time to get away. Then, in a few hours, you can come back and break me out. If you try to get me out now, he'll notice, he'll go look for me the second you leave, and I'm pretty sure he owns everyone on this street. We won't get away."

Because he was holding her in his arms, she felt his body tense when she mentioned the underground cell, and she hoped it was because he just didn't like the idea of anyone being locked up like that. Not because he intended to leave her there and wash his hands of her altogether.

Trust had always been hard for her after her father's murder, but now, in these circumstances, it was the hardest thing she'd ever had to do.

She was quite literally leaving her life in his hands.

If he came back for her, she would be rescued and could go home, write her piece, and bring down Professor Mahmoud and Allah's Warriors.

If he didn't, then whatever punishment the professor doled out for her disobeying orders and trying to make contact with Cooper she would not survive.

There were no other options.

"Can you walk?" he asked as he lowered her feet to the ground but kept a steadying arm around her waist.

If he thought this last assault had wiped her out, he was mistaken. Willow would do whatever it took to survive, and she absolutely could summon the strength to walk herself back outside to her prison.

Cooper slung Darius' body over his shoulders and followed her as she slipped out the front door and guided him around to the back. Her cell was unlocked, but he'd have to lock it to make this look believable. She had no idea how he was going to unlock it when he came back for her, but she was going to have to trust that he could find a way.

It took all her willpower to make herself jump back down into her cell instead of just making a run for it and hoping for the best.

There was every chance she was making the biggest mistake of her life.

"I'll be back for you, I promise," Cooper said, looking down at her from the edge of the hole.

Unable to form words, Willow merely nodded, then sucked in a breath as the trapdoor clunked closed.

This was it. She'd either found an ally who would help her escape, or she'd sealed her fate, she just wished she knew which it was so she could prepare herself.

Please come back, Cooper. Please don't have lied to me.

CHAPTER
Seven

July 11th
7:52 P.M.

"I'm not leaving her behind," Cooper growled the words into his comms as he stalked across the street toward his rental.

If Mahmoud was onto him, the man hadn't let on. When he'd strolled back into the kitchen like he owned the place after dumping the body of the man he'd killed at the back of the yard where he wouldn't be discovered until morning, he'd merely implied he'd taken longer than anticipated. The professor hadn't questioned it and after a brief talk where Cooper threatened to tear the older man apart with his bare hands if he found out he was lying, he'd walked out the front door.

Leaving the property felt like he was walking over broken glass.

He was leaving Willow behind, and he was all too aware of the fact that she wasn't safe. There was not a single doubt in his mind that she was going to be tortured as soon as he drove off.

Maybe Mahmoud was already in his yard, unlocking the trapdoor to her prison cell and laying his filthy hands on her.

His own hands clenched into fists as he got into his car, then because knowing what he was leaving Willow to endure made him physically ill, he slammed a fist into the steering wheel.

Two weeks.

That's how long she said she'd been there, and from the bruises he could see on her face—and he was sure there were more beneath the clothes—he was positive that she'd suffered every second of those fourteen long days. He had no idea how she'd wound up in the hands of a world-famous Egyptologist, but it was going to be one of the first questions he asked when he got her the hell out of there.

Switching out the comms unit to a two-way one, he expected to hear demands from his brothers that he had to leave Willow where she was, call in the cops, and let them handle it. Already he had a whole defense planned out, what he was going to say, hell, that he was going rogue if he had to. Since they were on the other side of the world, they couldn't do anything about it.

They hadn't seen her.

Hadn't seen the bruises mottling pale, creamy skin.

Hadn't seen the fear, pain, and pure determination swirling in her turquoise eyes.

"I'm going back for her," he said again as he turned on the engine and drove away, fighting against the pull of the brave woman huddled in a dirty underground hole.

"She's a friend of Julia's," Connor blurted out.

His foot almost slammed onto the brake. Julia Garamond was married to a member of Prey's Alpha Team. She was an investigative journalist who had come into contact with Alpha Team while investigating the Bratva who were involved in a plot to overthrow the government. Along the way, she'd fallen in love with Dominick "Domino" Tanner, and despite a very rocky start, the two were now happily married and expecting their first child.

If Willow was a friend of Julia's, she was likely a journalist, too.

I heard the questions you asked the professor. Once we're free, I'll tell you everything I know about him. I don't know if it will help you get the answers you need about your mom, but if nothing else, you can use it as leverage.

Willow's words rang through his mind, and now he knew what she meant. She had something on Tarek Mahmoud, and whatever it was had gotten her abducted and tortured.

"Julia reported her missing when she didn't check in as she was supposed to. She doesn't know what Willow is investigating, just that the target was Tarek Mahmoud. Domino apologized and said Julia wasn't aware we were going to meet with the professor, or she would have given us a heads-up. Said Julia feels bad about it," Cole explained.

"Not either of their fault. Even more reason to go back for her," he said firmly.

"No one was going to argue otherwise," Cade said with a hint of irritation in his tone. "I don't know why you seem to think we would leave an innocent woman behind. It was one thing when it was just a figure in black with no way to know who they were or if anything was wrong. Completely another to leave behind someone who has been tortured. It's like you don't even know us."

Hanging his head, Cooper rounded the corner and pulled over to the side of the road. "I'm sorry. It's myself I'm angry with. I knew something was off and I ignored my gut. Because of that, Willow suffered two more days of hell."

"Not your fault," Connor reminded him.

Maybe, but he still felt guilty.

And anxious to get her the hell out of there.

"I'll have to keep her with me," he said, thinking aloud, using his brothers as a sounding board. "Mahmoud has connections everywhere, and I don't want to chance one of them getting to her before she gets home."

"Get her out, get her to your hotel, and we'll go from there," Cade told him.

"Be careful, Coop," Cole warned. "You're right, the guy does have connections, and I doubt he's afraid to use them once he realizes Willow is gone. He's going to connect it to you, you're the only one who's been there, and he had you followed."

"I'm betting because he was worried you were there for more than just answers about Mom," Connor said. "He probably thinks you're onto him, that you know whatever it is Willow knows. If you want, we'll hop right on a plane and come over, I don't like that you're there without backup, and soon you're going to have an injured civilian on your hands."

"I can handle it," he assured his brothers. "And if anything changes and I need the backup I'll let you know."

After saying his goodbyes there was nothing to do but wait.

And wait.

And wait.

He couldn't go in for Willow until he was sure Mahmoud and anyone else in his home were already asleep. Even then it was risky. He'd have to climb the fence, which wasn't an issue going in, but was going to be one coming out. Even if she hadn't been further injured, Willow was already in a bad enough state that he doubted climbing a fence was something she was capable of.

If she was even still alive when he got there.

Fear he would arrive too late curled and spread inside him, making his body physically tremble.

All the time he'd spent in this woman's company amounted to mere minutes, yet her bravery and determination had struck him deep. Not a lot of people could survive two weeks straight of torture and still be standing, still thinking clearly enough to come up with a plan.

And not a lot of people would willingly put themselves in danger to protect another.

Which was straight up what Willow had done.

She could have begged and pleaded with him to get her out right that second, and he would have found a way to do it despite the risks.

But she hadn't done that.

Instead, she'd allowed him to put her back in that hole in the ground, knowing she was likely going to be punished for trying to reach out to him because she was trying to ensure he made it out of there alive.

Respect didn't even seem like a big enough word for what he felt for Willow Purcell.

Four hours later, when Cooper finally slunk through the dark night toward Tarek Mahmoud's house, he was still in awe over Willow, still filled with desperation to get her out. There had been a lot of people he had saved in his career in Delta Force, a lot he'd saved in the years he'd been with Prey.

There had also been a lot of people he'd failed.

Cooper just prayed Willow wasn't going to be one of them.

Entering the professor's property from the back was easier, less conspicuous, and closer to where Willow was being kept. The need to get to her was growing. It wasn't just about rescuing her, Cooper found himself equally invested in tending to her, caring for her, and making sure she was okay mentally and emotionally as well as physically.

He'd never had feelings like that for a woman before. Sure, he'd dated from time to time, it just wasn't easy when you were away as much as you were home, and you saw in the closest of details the atrocities human beings inflicted on one another.

But something about Willow called out to some primal part of him.

An almost compulsive need to protect her consumed him.

By the time he'd reached the trapdoor, cut the padlock, and was reaching out to lift the door, his hands were sweaty, and his heart raced.

Was he going to find Willow dead or alive?

~

July 12th
    12:08 A.M

Her aching body trembled as moonlight tumbled down into her underground prison.

New bruises layered old, and the accumulated pain was almost more than she could bear.

Especially with her rescue so close.

Was it about to come or had Professor Mahmoud decided he couldn't wait until morning when his friends gathered to end her life?

The exhilaration that her and Cooper's plan had worked, that the professor had no idea Darius wasn't the one who had put her back in there, that Darius was dead now, had sustained her through the beating Professor Mahmoud had delivered after Cooper left.

But now ...

Now she was just too tired.

Exhaustion wasn't just washing over her, it was barreling into her over and over again with harsh waves that knocked her down and kept her down until even just lifting her head took more out of her than she had to give.

Death or freedom?

What was her fate?

"Willow?"

The whispered voice had tears welling in her eyes.

For once, fate was on her side.

"C-Cooper," she stammered.

"Can you stand, honey?" His figure knelt at the edge of the trapdoor, and even in the moonlight she could see his worried eyes looking down at her.

Or maybe it was just that she felt them roaming over her huddled body.

"Yes," she answered, not sure it was true, but no matter what, she'd find a way to make it happen. "But he has me cuffed to the wall."

"No worries, honey, we'll get you out." Cooper's voice was calm and confident, soothing her in a way nothing had in a long time.

With an almost elegant jump, he landed on the floor in front of her. Dressed in the same clothes he'd been wearing earlier, Willow realized that he hadn't gone back to his hotel to change, he must have stayed in his car, waiting until the neighborhood was quiet before making his move.

Knowing he'd been close by all this time, that he hadn't left her, moved her and those tears very nearly came tumbling out.

Somehow, she managed to hold them in. Watching, he moved toward her, knelt, and reached out with those large hands of his to very gently circle her wrist. For a moment he stilled, staring at it, his fingertips almost absently skimming across her bruised and torn skin.

Then he pulled out a tool, bolt cutters she realized as he snapped the handcuff binding her in place.

When her hand dropped to her side, the relief she felt was overwhelming.

Not just psychologically.

Physically too.

The thought that freedom was within her reach sent her entire system haywire, and she began to shake. Not just tiny little trembles but huge wracking shakes that made her already aching muscles spasm, and she had to clamp her lips together so she didn't cry out.

The last thing she wanted to do was embarrass herself in front of Cooper.

A hand cupped her cheek, and it was pure instinct to lean into it. A single tear escaped, and Cooper caught it with the pad of his thumb.

"Hey, honey, listen to me." He waited until she lifted her gaze to meet his before continuing. "You've done amazing. I'm in awe of what you've survived, of how brave you've been. It's okay to need a little help now."

Giving him a shaky nod, Willow dragged in a deep breath. She had to do this.

Had to.

This was her only chance of escaping.

At living.

There was no way she was going to shoot herself in the foot.

"You got this, Willow."

His words of encouragement gave her enough of an infusion of strength to allow his hand to shift to her elbow and help her keep her balance as she pushed to her feet.

Without his help, she likely would have fallen right back down again. But with his steadying arm, she made it the few steps across her cell to the bottom of the trapdoor. This was the last time she'd ever have to set foot in this hellhole again, and she couldn't wait to get as far away from this place as she could.

"I'm going to need your help to get you out of here," Cooper told him.

It might be dark, but she fixed him with a fierce glare. "I survived two weeks of daily beatings. I'm not about to fall apart now. You tell me what you need me to do, and I'll do it."

A chuckle rumbled through the cell. "Don't doubt it for a moment. I'm going to boost you up, but I'll need you to help pull yourself up onto the ground."

"I can do that," she assured him.

Shifting so he was behind her, Cooper's large hands circled her waist, and he lifted her with ease. As soon as she could reach the top, Willow dug her fingers into the dirt, and even though her arms shook with the effort, she somehow managed to drag herself onto the ground.

It took almost everything out of her that she had left, and all she could do was lie there, panting and staring up at the stars shimmering in the sky.

Without a word, Cooper climbed up beside her, then without hesitating, he scooped her into his arms and took off running. This time there was no pretending that nothing had happened, that she was still in her cell, or that nothing was wrong. As soon as the professor looked out into the yard in the morning, he'd know she was gone.

A part of her wished she could see the look on his face when he realized she was free. She'd told him exactly what she was going to do if she got away from him, and that was destroy him.

She couldn't wait.

When Cooper reached the fence, he stopped, and she could feel the tension emanating from him. He was worrying about her ability to assist in her own rescue, and she had no intention of being deadweight. She might be dangerously close to empty, but she had a determination that could last for days. Never give up, that was her motto, and it held as strong today as it did the day she was taken.

"Can you make it over the fence?"

"Yes."

"Need to know the truth, Willow. No shame if you can't, we'll find another way."

"But this is the fastest. I can do it. Maybe with a little help," she conceded.

"I'll boost you, then all you have to do is swing your leg over. If you can't do the drop, wait for me to get over and catch you, I don't know how badly you're injured, and I don't want you to aggravate anything."

"No way to avoid it," she mumbled as Cooper shifted his hold on her to better be able to boost her up. Since she was in his arms, she felt his brief pause and realized she shouldn't have mentioned that right now. There would be time to worry about her injuries later, but not now.

Shaking from exhaustion, spurred on only by sheer force of will, somehow Willow managed to grab the top of the fence when Cooper boosted her up to it. It wasn't an easy fence to climb, well, not covered from head to toe with bruises, but somehow, she managed to swing a leg up and over.

Her plan had been to wait there on the top for Cooper to get over so he could help her down the other side, but her trembling arms gave out and she lost her grip. Hitting the ground hard, her body sort of bounced off the concrete and then just lay there.

She was done.

Even though she wanted to, she just had nothing left to give.

Feet hit the ground beside her, and when Cooper once again bent and gathered her into his arms, she couldn't help but wince. All she wanted was to be free from pain, even just for a minute or two. Her body had been pushed beyond what it could endure, and while she was proud she'd made it this far, she just wanted it to all be over.

"Not long now, honey, hold on for me just a little longer," Cooper urged as he took off running full speed.

They were almost to the road when the first shot came out of nowhere.

Hopelessness hit hard and fast.

How could she have thought she was going to be able to escape?

Of course, fate wouldn't be on her side. It never was.

Cooper muttered a curse, and Willow shoved aside all negative thoughts. This wasn't just about her. Cooper was here, too. Risking his life for her.

"Do you have a weapon?" she asked when he slowed. "I know how to shoot."

A second later, it was thrust into her hand, and even though she couldn't see what she was shooting at it didn't matter. She would lay down as much cover fire as she could to give them a chance.

If she failed, they'd both be dead.

CHAPTER
Eight

July 12th
12:16 A.M.

With the number of bullets being fired, there was not a chance in hell that they weren't going to wake the entire neighborhood.

While Cooper had no idea if the people in the area were friends of Mahmoud, if they were aware of or involved in the imprisonment of Willow, or if they would just call the cops, he did know there was every chance the professor would have at least one cop on his side.

Which meant the last thing he wanted was to get caught.

As he reached his car, he threw open the passenger side door, thrust Willow into the seat, snapped her seatbelt on, and then eased the weapon from her hands.

Silence.

Blessed silence.

"I think I got him," Willow wheezed like she was the one who'd just run flat out down the street.

Maybe she hadn't exerted herself in that way, but with her injuries and obvious weakness likely from dehydration and starvation, just pulling herself out of her prison, over the fence, and then laying down cover fire so they could get away had obviously tapped her out.

"You did amazing," he told her, scanning the dark night. Getting rid of whoever had been shooting at them gave them a fighting chance at escaping, but it didn't guarantee it.

"Didn't want you to get hurt because of me," she mumbled, words starting to slur as her eyelashes fluttered on her cheeks. Then she was out.

As badly as he wanted to check her out now and determine how badly she was hurt, if he had to chance a hospital, if he could handle them himself, if she was stable enough to fly. The best option was to call Prey for an evac, Cooper knew they couldn't risk staying there a second longer.

Keeping his weapon in his hand, he closed Willow's door, hurried around, and jumped into the driver's seat. Seconds later, he took off as fast as he dared down the street. Lights were beginning to flicker on in the houses around Mahmoud's and he wished he knew what Willow did about the man so he had some idea of what he was up against.

Thankfully, Willow's ability to shoot meant he had a clear ride out and he took it.

This late at night, there were still quite a few cars on the street as soon as he left the residential area and got back into the main part of Cairo. His hotel was nice, and while he was going to draw attention to himself carrying Willow inside, with the long black clothes she still wore, it wasn't likely that anyone would suspect he'd just rescued her from a hell one of their own people had put her through.

Even with her sitting passed out in his car he couldn't quite believe it.

This was not at all how he had envisioned his trip to Egypt going. A few days there to gather all the intel he could from Tarek Mahmoud, then head home to dissect it with his brothers. That was all that was supposed to happen. Instead, he had a kidnap victim who was now his responsibility to take care of and protect.

Although Willow could certainly hold her own.

The drive to his hotel was eventless, and by the time he was parked and rounding his car, Cooper could feel exhaustion tugging at his mind.

Just because this trip had taken a wildly different turn didn't mean it wasn't mentally exhausting. For almost two decades, he and his siblings had carried around the weight of what happened to their parents and the deep injustice of it.

Now that he was possibly teetering on the precipice of blowing this whole thing wide open, it was like all those years, all that weight, had caught up to him all at once.

Unbuckling Willow's seatbelt, he paused to look down at her. Even with the bruises marring her soft skin, she was beautiful, and in sleep she looked so peaceful and angelic. How could anybody hurt something this gorgeous? What did she know that had gotten her abducted and tortured? And was it possible it was in any way connected to what happened to his mother?

Answers would have to wait until Willow was strong enough to give them. Right now, she needed rest, time to recover, and let her body bounce back a bit.

When he gathered her into his arms, she stirred, a small moan falling from her lips. Since he wasn't sure if it was from pain or fear, he touched his lips to her temple in a kiss that felt far too natural given he'd met this woman only hours ago.

"Shh, honey, I've got you," he murmured.

At the sound of his voice, she immediately settled back down, and Cooper bumped the door closed with his hip, then carried her inside.

Thankfully, the hotel lobby was mostly quiet, although several workers and a couple of guests gave him odd looks when they saw him carrying a figure bundled in black in his arms.

"My wife didn't sleep the whole flight here and then crashed in the car," he explained to no one in particular as he strode toward the lifts.

It wasn't until he was safely in his room, with the door locked behind him, that he actually felt his body relax. They were safe there. There was a chance—probably a good one—that Mahmoud would associate Willow's abrupt rescue with him. The shooting had likely woken him, and even now, he might be aware of the fact that she was gone. Even with his contacts, it would take the professor a while to locate the hotel where he was staying, so they should be safe for the night.

Tomorrow, he'd check out and check them in at another hotel under an alias. He'd brought a couple of different IDs with him, not that he'd thought he would use them, but it was better to be over-prepared than under-prepared.

Laying Willow down on the bed, he hurried into the bathroom, grabbed a washcloth, ran it under the faucet, and then returned to the bed. Willow was still unconscious, and he hoped if she woke in the middle of this she would understand he was only trying to take care of her and not take advantage of her in any way.

Peeling back the layers of black material, Cooper's heart stilled in his chest until it felt like it had stopped beating altogether.

Beneath her clothes Willow was naked.

Barely a single inch of skin remained untouched.

Bruises in every shade of black, blue, purple, yellow, and green marred her skin.

Literally from her feet all the way up her body to her head.

"Damn," he muttered, uncharacteristic helplessness hitting him hard.

This woman had been through hell.

Yet despite that, she'd been clear-headed enough to help him come up with a plan, to assist in her own rescue, and to save both their butts when they were escaping.

Who was this woman and how was she so amazing?

Honestly, he'd known special forces operators who couldn't pull through what she had with as much determination and strength.

Doing his best to avoid her most intimate areas, Cooper got to work cleaning the dust and sweat from her body, focusing on her legs, arms, stomach, and face. Several times he had to return to the bathroom to wash all the dirt out of the cloth. But by the time he was done, she looked mostly clean, at least well enough until she was strong enough to shower.

Next, he eased onto the bed beside her and very carefully lifted Willow's upper body until it rested against his bent legs and went to work on untangling the knots in her mane of blonde hair. It had been a long time since he'd brushed someone's hair, not since Cassandra got old enough to do it herself, but it brought back a lot of memories.

It probably took him close to half an hour to get them all out and make her hair soft and smooth again. It definitely needed a good wash like the rest of her, but for now, he was confident that Willow would be able to rest comfortably.

Easing out from beneath her again, Cooper went to his bag and rifled through it. They'd have to do something about clothes for her later, but for now, he didn't want her to feel exposed and vulnerable before him. So, he grabbed a pair of his sweatpants and a T-shirt and took them to the bed.

It was a testament to her exhaustion because Willow didn't stir as he worked the sweatpants up her legs and over her hips, or while he slipped the T-shirt over her head. The clothes made her look even smaller and more fragile, and he had to remind himself that this woman was tougher than most. She was strong, resilient, and whatever she'd been through she'd find a way to survive and come out the other side, probably stronger than she'd been before.

There was a small couch in the room by the balcony, it was definitely the option he should take.

Yet Cooper found himself shifting Willow so he could pull back the covers, then stretching out beside her. When he had them both tucked in, he let his eyes fall closed. Even if this did wind up ruining his chances of getting intel that could help prove his mother's innocence, rescuing Willow was worth it.

With a small sigh, she turned and snuggled her body into his.

Back away.

Although the voice in his head screamed at him to put distance between them, Cooper found he couldn't.

Instead, he snaked out an arm and tugged the woman closer. He had no idea what he was getting himself into when it came to her, but he couldn't fight against whatever was pulling him toward her.

Didn't even know if he wanted to fight it.

Consequences be damned.

~

July 12th

6:31 A.M

Blows rained down on her.

One after the other.

They struck her everywhere.

Willow clamped her mouth shut.

She wasn't going to scream.

Couldn't give Professor Mahmoud the satisfaction.

But the blows wouldn't stop.

They just kept coming.

Her whole body throbbed with pain.

There was darkness all around her.

Seeping inside her.

Consuming her.

It was eating away at her resolve.

The pain was too much.

She'd done the best she could, held out for as long as she could.

But it wasn't going to be enough.

The scream was already building inside her.

Willow could feel it.

Expanding, curling out from her stomach, invading her limbs, working its way toward her mouth.

She fought against it.

Didn't want to scream.

Didn't want to show an ounce of weakness before this evil, soulless man.

It was the only leverage she had, and once she lost it, it would be all over.

There would be nothing left.

She'd lose herself.

Once that happened, she would be as good as dead.

There was no way to stop it though.

It slithered up her throat.

Then her lips parted.

Her lungs sucked in air.

Then she screamed.

"Willow. Wake up, honey. Now."

Wake up?

She wasn't asleep.

Trapped in a nightmare but one that had nothing to do with sleeping.

Her nightmare was all too real.

"Come on, honey, snap out of it."

If only she could.

If only escaping from her tormentor was as easy as opening her eyes.

"Wake up for me, Willow. Now."

A sharp sting on her cheek ripped her from sleep.

Panting, shaking, confused, Willow's gaze roamed the area trying to figure out what the heck was going on.

"It's okay, honey, you're all right. You're safe. You're in my hotel room."

The voice was soothing, washing over her overheated skin like a cooling balm. It calmed her racing heart even before she could properly process and figure out who it came from.

"There you go, that's good, honey, calm your breathing for me."

A face leaned in close, and slowly her vision cleared enough for the features to come into focus.

Storm-gray eyes.

Framed by long, dark lashes.

Thick dark hair framing a strong face.

He was shirtless and in the bed beside her.

Heat emanated off him, but not the kind of stifling heat that had surrounded her in the underground cell. This was pleasant and cozy and made her want to snuggle into it, bury her head in the sand, and pretend this whole mess was over and she'd never have to worry about the evil professor again.

But she couldn't do that.

Even hurting as she was, even exhausted as she was, even with the lingering fear of the nightmare fresh in her veins, Willow knew she had a long road ahead of her. A long fight to make sure Professor Mahmoud was brought to justice.

"Your skin feels like ice," Cooper murmured, running a hand up and down her arm, leaving a trail of fire in its wake.

It was only then that she realized she was no longer wearing the black dress the professor had put her in the day he abducted her. Now she was wearing a black T-shirt that was more like a dress on her, and a pair of sweatpants covered her legs, which were twisted in the covers. Her feet were bare, the sweatpants rolled up several times around her ankles. The clothes had to be Cooper's. He must have undressed her while she was unconscious.

"I just cleaned you up and put my clothes on you," Cooper told her, reading her mind. As though expecting his proximity might push her over the edge, he shifted away from her, moving to get off the bed.

The second she lost the contact of his hand on her forearm, Willow reacted purely on instinct. Reaching out to curl her fingers around his, clinging to him in a way that certainly didn't prove she was the strong woman she believed herself to be.

Right now she needed Cooper.

Not just to rescue her, he'd already done that, it wasn't even need in a way she could explain, even to herself. All she knew was that she wanted him close. His touch didn't scare her, and while she might have preferred him not to see her naked while she was vulnerable, she already knew he wasn't the kind of man to take advantage. He'd been taking care of her, and after spending two weeks in hell, she was so very grateful for his tenderness.

"Thank you," she whispered, meeting his gaze so he would know she was telling the truth.

For a moment, Cooper studied her gaze. She could feel the tension emanating from him in the tense way he held himself, then it faded, and he relaxed. "You're welcome. Although I think given half a chance you would have found a way to escape on your own." He winked, and the smile he gave her transformed his entire face into something that was beyond words, sexy and gorgeous.

His words pulled a small giggle out of her, but then she winced as the pain throbbing through her body came roaring back with a vengeance. For the last two weeks, she'd had to ignore how bad her injuries were because she didn't have the luxury of spending time catering to them.

But now she was safe, at least for the moment, although given Professor Mahmoud's reach, she couldn't guarantee she'd stay safe, and she could no longer ignore the pain.

Again, Cooper seemed to know exactly what she was thinking. Giving her fingers a squeeze, he released them and then climbed from the bed. "You need some painkillers. Water and food, too. I'm going to order some room service. Do you need help going to the bathroom? I thought once you were up to it you could shower. We're going to have to check out soon, though. I'm here under my real name and don't want Mahmoud to track us down. You need some time to rest and recuperate."

That was too many things for her to process all at once.

Overwhelmed, Willow sunk back against the pillows. The sweat that had dotted her skin as her body panicked in her nightmares now made her cold, and she tugged up the covers, wincing as her body protested even that small movement.

For now, she didn't want to have to think about showering and traveling to another hotel, she just wanted to curl up and sleep for about a week.

"Here, take these." Cooper's arm curled around her shoulders, and it took all her strength not to just turn into him, burrow into his warmth, press her face against his neck, and refuse to ever let go.

When he tipped the pills into her hand, she dutifully put them in her mouth, then swallowed them down with the water when he held a bottle to her lips. The water felt like a little slice of heaven as it slid down her throat. Cool and refreshing. She'd never ever take for granted again the simple blessing of being able to take a drink of water any time she wanted.

"I'm not really hungry," she said, allowing her eyes to slide closed.

"You have to eat, keep your strength up. I need to know how badly you're hurt," Cooper told her, and she could feel his presence right beside the bed. "Do you think anything is broken?"

"My face probably, maybe my arm, possibly some cracked ribs," she rattled off. The truth was, her entire body felt like it was broken.

"Okay, not a lot we can do for the ribs or your face right now, other than keep up the painkillers. I'll bandage your arm though."

Too tired to open her eyes, Willow listened to Cooper bustle about the room. When he settled beside her, she felt a warm kind of peace settle around her. Maybe the painkillers were starting to do their job because she didn't even care when he picked up her arm, gently probed it, and then began to wrap a bandage around it to keep it stable.

When he gently set her arm down on the mattress, he tucked the blankets tighter around her and then just hovered there.

Blinking open her eyes, she looked up to see him looking right back down at her.

"I'm sorry," he whispered.

Her brow crinkled. "For what?"

"I could have gotten you out a couple of days sooner. But I didn't. Because I could only see what was important to me."

Reaching out with her good hand, she grabbed his fingers. "You didn't know I needed help."

"I knew something wasn't right."

"And when you knew what, you got me out. I hate to break it to you, Cooper, but even if you'd got me out two days earlier, I still would be covered from head to toe with bruises. I've been with him for two weeks, and his favorite game was beating on me. In the scheme of things, those two days didn't mean anything."

A huge yawn tugged at her lips, and the room began to fade around her.

Willow knew she needed to tell Cooper what she knew about the professor. She also knew he was right, they weren't safe there. With his reach, it wasn't a matter of if but when Professor Mahmoud found them.

But right now, she was powerless to fight against the exhaustion weighing down on her.

She'd just have to trust Cooper to look out for both of them.

That wasn't easy for her.

She didn't trust people.

Ever.

Yet for some reason, Cooper seemed to make it easier than she'd expected.

CHAPTER

Nine

July 12th
11:00 A.M.

Grateful for the late check out, Cooper glanced at his watch and then the bed where Willow was still curled up fast asleep. As much as he'd love to let her sleep as long as she needed to, he was wary of the fact that they could be tracked, and his need to protect her was currently outweighing his need to take care of her.

Never in his life had he met a woman like Willow Purcell.

While she was sleeping, he'd checked in with his family and made sure they knew that he had successfully extracted her and they were both okay. He'd also asked them to quietly let Julia know her friend was safe but not to publicize it in any way yet. For now, it was safer for Willow if Tarek Mahmoud only knew she'd been taken but not that any cops or agencies alerted to her disappearance knew she had been rescued.

After that, he'd spent the rest of his time reading through all the articles she'd ever written. She was good. No doubt about that. There was a way she told her stories that felt so raw and authentic. She was one of those people who were able to really and truly step into someone else's shoes and actually empathize with them. Clearly, she wasn't writing to sensationalize anything, she wasn't in it for fame, fortune, or views.

Willow truly cared.

Curious as to what had led her to become a journalist and how she'd come to be such a brave, strong, and compassionate person, Cooper had dug a little deeper.

What he'd found had broken his heart.

Poor Willow had witnessed her father's murder when she was only eight years old. Having witnessed something similar but not as traumatizing when their house had been stormed and his mom arrested, he couldn't imagine how hard it had been for her. To then learn that it was all because of one journalist jumping the gun and naming a suspect too early in what had been a volatile and emotionally charged case had obviously influenced her own career choices.

Career choices that had put her in danger.

Before they'd had a chance to talk, Willow had fallen asleep again, so he didn't yet know what she knew about Professor Mahmoud, but he had zero doubts it was about a case she was working on.

Fighting the urge to let Willow keep sleeping, Cooper kept his priorities on safety and reached out a hand to gently brush his knuckles across Willow's cheek.

"Wake up, honey," he crooned softly. The last thing he wanted to do was scare her, but he also needed to get some food and some more water into her, then she needed a shower or bath. They had an hour to get all of that done and then be checked out and on the road. He had a plan for the remainder of the day, and a hotel planned for them to check into tonight. Then depending on what he learned from Willow, he'd decide what happened next.

Getting Willow on a plane back home was top of that list.

"Come on, Willow, time to wake up," he said again, thankful that at least this time he wasn't trying to wake her from a nightmare. Cassandra had had lots after their mom was arrested, and he and his brothers had become accustomed to her screams waking them at all hours. But that was a long time ago, and when Willow's petrified shriek had filled the room this morning, he'd almost had a heart attack. Being unable to wake her immediately had only made things worse. She was suffering, and he hadn't been able to fix it, for some reason that had hit him hard.

"Cooper?" she mumbled sleepily, lashes fluttering on her cheeks before lifting, leaving him staring into turquoise depths. "What time is it?"

"An hour before check out."

"Could have slept another week at least," she grumbled even as she went to push herself into a sitting position.

Still wary of touching her given what she'd been through, he couldn't assume just because she'd reached out to him last night meant she was okay with all physical contact, he held back until she groaned and froze.

Then his arm was behind her shoulders, supporting some of her weight. She felt so small leaning against him, so fragile, yet he already knew she was the opposite. What she'd survived in her life, what she did for a living, how she'd handled her ordeal, it all made Willow Purcell the very definition of strength and bravery.

"Thanks," she murmured, resting against him for a moment before shifting so she could swing her legs over the side of the bed.

Worried she would fall back down again, Cooper quickly realized he shouldn't. There didn't seem to be a limit to what this woman could endure. No matter what, she just kept going, and he respected the hell out of her.

"A shower does sound nice," she said.

"I ordered some clothes for you while you were sleeping. Got some makeup, too, since we're going to have to do something about those bruises, or we'll attract everyone's attention no matter how careful we are."

"Yeah, I'm sure I look a mess."

Her words showed a thread of self-doubt that he didn't like one little bit. Even though this woman had shown him she was strong and brave, he had to remind himself that she was still human. No one, no matter how determined, could walk away unscathed after living through what she had.

"Hey." Placing both hands on her shoulders, lightly as he was mindful of all her bruises, Cooper bent his knees so they were eye to eye. "Without sounding wildly inappropriate given I saw you naked while you were unconscious, you are gorgeous. Easily the most beautiful woman I've ever seen." The blush that tinted her bruise-free skin pink was the prettiest thing ever. "More than that, Willow, you're beautiful in here." Pressing a hand to her chest, above her heart, he maintained eye contact so she could see how serious he was.

"Thank you." Willow drew in a shuddering breath, then lifted her hands to rest against his pecs. "I needed to hear that this morning. It's been a long two weeks." Unshed tears shimmered in her eyes, and he ached to take away her pain.

"It's okay to be struggling," he reminded her.

Willow gave a shaky nod. "I'm not used to having a partner."

"Well, this time you have one. I'm not going anywhere. You're going to shower, get dressed, eat something, and in the car you're going to tell me everything you know about Tarek Mahmoud. Then together we're going to bring him down."

"But you're here for information on something about your mom." Her nose did the most adorable, confused scrunch and he couldn't help but smile.

"Yeah, I am. But that doesn't mean I'm going to walk away and leave you to handle this alone." Cooper meant every word of that, too. Just because he'd come to Egypt with one purpose only, didn't mean he wasn't one hundred percent committed to helping Willow. And not just because he hoped he could use what she knew to his own advantage. Even if there was no way to use Willow's intel to force Tarek Mahmoud to give up more information on what he knew about his mother's final CIA mission, he wanted to help Willow.

The woman got to him.

In a way he'd never experienced before.

Whenever he'd dated before it had been for fun and companionship. He loved planning dates, taking his girl out, and enjoyed having someone to come home to after a mission, but he'd never once felt like it was going to grow into the kind of love his parents had shared.

Now, knowing Willow for less than thirty hours, he already felt more of a connection to her than all the other women he'd dated combined.

What did that mean?

Right now was not the time or place to do anything about it. She'd just survived a horrific ordeal, she wasn't safe, and she had a lot to process once she got home. And he had a single purpose for his life right now, finally discovering the truth of what happened to his parents.

The timing was all wrong, but later?

After he had his answers and Willow had some time to deal with what had happened to her, would he do something about it then?

Staring into turquoise depths, the kind you could get lost in if you weren't careful, Cooper found that this woman made him want to throw caution to the wind and jump into things he would usually carefully consider first.

The question was, how did she see him?

Was he just the guy who saved her? Did she feel this current of strange electricity that seemed to buzz between them?

Or was he crazy for feeling anything for her at all?

～

July 12th
    1:10 P.M

"It's so different from home, isn't it?" Willow said as she stared out the window at the passing scenery. She'd been in Egypt for three days before she'd been caught by Professor Mahmoud. In that time, she'd visited the Pyramids of Giza, but that was it. She hadn't been there for fun, it was a work trip and she'd been dedicated to finding proof.

"It is," Cooper agreed from the driver's seat. "Do you ever travel for fun?"

"Fun?" For a moment Willow was kind of surprised by the word. No, she didn't travel for fun, hadn't really done anything for fun in the twenty-one years since her father's murder. Back then, she'd withdrawn into herself, not just pulled away from the people in her life but from her interests and hobbies as well. Then she'd been working hard at school and college, and then jumped right into focusing on her career.

In all those years, fun had just sort of fallen by the wayside until she didn't even recognize what it meant anymore.

"No. No traveling for fun," she told him. "What about you?" Over breakfast, they'd shared a little bit about themselves, so she knew Cooper was a former Delta Force operator who now worked for Prey Security, neither of which surprised her because she'd picked him as military the moment he walked into the professor's kitchen.

"Same. Traveled to a lot of places in my career, but never once for fun."

"That seems a shame. For both of us. Maybe we need to make some time for fun in our lives." As soon as the words were out of her mouth, Willow realized how they sounded. Like she was saying the two of them should have some fun together. That wasn't what she'd meant and yet ...

The idea didn't have any negatives that she could come up with.

She was attracted to Cooper, she respected him, and she certainly owed him her life, but more than that she actually liked him. He was a kind of serious guy, but every time he tossed a wink and one of those charming smiles at her, it made her heart melt, and her insides go all gooey. It definitely made heat spark between her legs, too. It had been so long since she'd been with a man that she barely even remembered what sex felt like anymore.

Intending to make herself clear, when she shifted her gaze from the sandy desert outside the window to the man in the driver's seat, those words died in her throat.

The way he looked at her ...

It didn't just make heat spark inside her, it basically doused her in a fiery touch that made her entire body long to combust.

Could he really be attracted to her, too?

Earlier, when he'd told her she was beautiful, although she'd melted at his words, she'd also coached herself to remember he was likely just being nice. He was a gentleman for sure, keeping his eyes on her face when he'd helped her undress then kept his back to her when he waited in the bathroom while she showered in case she needed help.

Maybe he wasn't just being nice?

Maybe he really did feel this attraction simmering between them, too?

"Why is it fun is the first thing that falls out of your life after something bad happens?" Cooper asked.

"It sucks, doesn't it? I don't even think I remember fun anymore. I don't think I remember joy either," she added. For some reason, she seemed able to talk to this man about anything. Even things she wouldn't dream of mentioning to the few friends she allowed into her life. She kept them at a distance, the protective barrier around her heart was secure because her heart couldn't handle another loss, but Cooper seemed to have found a little crack she didn't know existed and slipped through it.

"For the next couple of hours, we're going to fix that," he told her as he reached out and grabbed her hand. "For the next few hours, we're going to just be tourists. We're going to marvel at the Step Pyramid, then check out the Imhotep Museum, and then we're going to go back to Cairo, check into our new hotel, and you're going to eat a good meal and get a good night's sleep. For the rest of the day, there's going to be no thinking about Mahmoud or anything from our pasts."

"Sounds like a plan," she agreed. Thankfully, Saqqara was close to Cairo and a great place to go to blend in and just be tourists, which was their plan. They knew the professor had contacts everywhere, but they'd both agreed their best bet was to hide in plain sight. Egypt's oldest pyramids seemed like the perfect place to do that. A little quieter than the Pyramids of Giza, there should be enough of a crowd for them to blend in, but not so many people that they wouldn't notice immediately if they were being followed.

After parking the car, they both climbed out. Willow's body protested every movement, but she pushed through the pain. The painkillers Cooper kept giving her were helping, and the fact she'd got some proper sleep as well. Plus, she'd eaten some good food and was properly hydrated. All things considered, she was a heck of a lot better off than she'd been this time just twenty-four hours ago.

In just one day her entire life had changed around. She'd gone from being almost certain she was close to being killed, to being free and having her chance at destroying Tarek Mahmoud.

It was nice to have someone in her corner.

To not be fighting alone.

Honestly, she felt like she'd been living alone for so many years now that she didn't even know how to properly comprehend the idea that she now had a teammate.

She liked it though. Maybe more than she should.

"Did you get to see the Pyramids of Giza?" Cooper asked as he came around the car and took her hand.

For a moment, her brain short-circuited.

And not in a bad way.

Only he was touching her and little tingles of excitement strummed through her veins at the small contact. It was silly because, more than likely, he was only holding her hand because he knew she was still weak and a little shaky on her feet, but whatever the reason she welcomed the touch.

For once in two long weeks, someone was touching her with care and gentleness instead of inflicting pain and suffering. It was so nice, and usually, Willow wasn't even big on physical touch, her mind always mentally attempted to jerk away from it because it threw her back in mind to watching her dad being beaten to death. For some reason, the two were connected in her mind, and usually even the smallest of touches made her stiffen.

But not Cooper's.

Cooper's touch made her want to lean into it, soak up more of it, and maintain the connection rather than severing it as quickly as possible.

"Willow?"

Realizing she hadn't answered his question, she quickly scrambled to remember what it was. Oh, the pyramids, right. "Yeah, I actually saw them the first day. It was a long flight, I arrived early, couldn't check in yet, so I decided to go and see them. They were amazing, just standing there, staring up at them, I think it might be the coolest thing I've ever done."

"If you could go anywhere in the world, just for fun, where would it be?" Cooper asked as they walked closer toward the Step Pyramid.

"Umm ..." Willow trailed off as she thought. If she could go anywhere in the world, where would it be? There were so many amazing countries and so many wonderful cities, picking just one to visit was hard. There was one that topped her list though. "Rovaniemi in Finland. There's a Santa Claus village there that would be fun to visit. When I was a little girl, I loved Christmas so much, and my dad always told me one day he'd take me to where Santa lived. I know I'm all grown up now and no longer believe in Santa, but it would be so wonderful to go there. They have reindeer sled rides through the snow, and you could maybe see the Aurora Borealis. If I had to pick just one place to go to for fun it would definitely be that."

The fingers around hers squeezed. "That's nice. I hope you make it there one day."

"Me too. What about you? Where would you go?"

Instead of answering her, Cooper shifted his arm so it was around her shoulder, and angled her slightly so her body was more in front of his than behind. He also picked up their pace so that she almost stumbled, her aching body begging her to move slowly only.

"Think we're being followed," he whispered, his mouth above her ear, his breath warm against her skin.

"They found us? Already? How?" While she was sleeping, Cooper hadn't just organized clothes and makeup for her, he'd also organized a different vehicle. She had no idea how he'd managed it, but from what she knew of Prey from her friend Julia who was married to a man on one of their teams, she wasn't surprised. The men and women who worked there were smart, skilled, and resourceful.

But was Cooper smart, skilled, and resourceful enough to somehow get them out of trouble if they were being followed?

CHAPTER

Ten

July 12th
   1:29 P.M.

Damn.

This was the last thing they needed.

Cooper had weighed the odds, knowing that whatever road he chose came with risks. In the end, he'd decided that Tarek Mahmoud would be using all his contacts to watch airports and airfields, expecting that he would take Willow and immediately flee the country, they'd do the opposite.

Which seemed to have backfired on them.

Because now he was alone with Willow at the Step Pyramids of Saqqara, and they were being followed.

If it was just him on his own, he'd just take them out the first opportunity he got and then disappear. But Willow was injured, weak, tough yes, but the physical toll her ordeal had taken on her wasn't something they could just magically overcome.

"What do we do?" Willow asked, and he loved that she skipped right over panic and went straight to logic. It made things so much easier.

Not that she wasn't well and truly deserving of a meltdown, she'd been through hell, but right now, it gave them a better chance of surviving if Willow could hold it together.

"Right now, we do nothing," he told her, guiding her along with him as they headed closer to the pyramid. For now, there was the safety of numbers. If they stuck with the crowd, then it would be harder for whoever Mahmoud had sent after them to make any sort of move.

"Nothing?" Willow repeated, but she followed his lead and kept walking so it didn't look like he was dragging her along with him.

"Yep, our best bet for the moment is to just blend in." If they were caught there was every chance that Mahmoud would try to get him thrown in prison. Sure, Cooper knew he'd get out, he'd done nothing wrong, and Prey and Eagle Oswald's reach far outweighed that of Tarek Mahmoud. But in that time the professor would ensure Willow was killed.

They were on Mahmoud's home turf, and Willow was a walking advertisement that someone had been beating on her. There was every chance Mahmoud would use the injuries he inflicted to his advantage. Willow would no doubt tell anyone who would listen who had hurt her, but Mahmoud's reach was long, and Cooper was positive he'd have her declared incompetent.

Again, all it took was separating them for the professor to get his hands on Willow.

Not going to happen.

Not as long as he was standing.

Whatever it took, he was going to keep this woman safe.

"I won't let him hurt you again," he promised. It wasn't wise to make vows. Especially when he didn't have the upper hand. Unarmed but for a few knives that would do the job but only if he got close enough to the men following them, his weapon was out of ammo and he didn't have time to get more, he didn't have a good idea of the layout of the area, he had no backup, and he had an injured woman who was his responsibility.

But he'd worked with less.

Whatever it took.

"I know you won't," she said softly, resting her head against his shoulder.

Something warm shifted inside him at the simple touch. This woman got to him in the weirdest ways. It confused the hell out of him, but he wasn't going to fight against it. He was going to do what he had to do to make sure Willow got home safe and took down the professor, and then he'd see what happened.

No use worrying about it right now.

Now all that mattered was keeping her alive.

"I know you're strong, Willow. You're the bravest person I've ever met, but I need to know that you're going to do everything I ask you to do immediately and without complaint." He would do whatever it took, but he had to know that Willow wasn't going to be fighting against him. For them to stand a chance, he had to be confident that if he asked Willow to do something, she'd just do it.

"I won't be a liability," Willow said fiercely.

"Never thought you would be. But this is what I do, Willow. It's been my job my entire life. I might not be able to explain why I need you to do something, I might have to ask you to do something you're uncomfortable with. There can't be any arguing, even a couple of seconds delay can make the difference between life and death." It wasn't like he wanted to scare her more than she already was, but he also needed to ensure she realized the stakes.

"You don't have to worry. I know this is your thing, not mine. I promise I'll do whatever you need me to do without questioning you," Willow solemnly agreed.

"That's all I needed to hear. And, hey," he caught her fingers and squeezed them, "when I help you with your article, you can totally boss me around."

She gave a small chuckle, but when he tangled their fingers together, he could feel the tension radiating off her.

Unfortunately, there was nothing he could do about that.

If he could wave a magic wand, erase the bruises littering her body, wipe away the terror and fear she'd experienced, transport her back home where she would be safe, and put Tarek Mahmoud in a prison cell he absolutely would.

But he couldn't.

All he could do was work with what he had at the moment. Even if it wasn't a lot.

"You're really going to help me with my article?" Willow asked as they followed the other tourists along a wooden plank and through a narrow door.

They walked through the covered colonnade, Cooper hyper-aware of everything around them. With the time of year and the heat of summer in Egypt, more people were there than he would have thought, which both helped and made things harder.

What he needed was a quiet place to circle around and take down the men following them from behind. He could not do that when there were too many witnesses. While he wouldn't hesitate to kill anyone who was a threat to Willow, and he was confident Eagle could get him out of any mess, he didn't enjoy leaving a trail of bodies in his wake.

Until he got that opportunity, he'd just stick with the crowd. Not a great plan, but again, the best he had right now.

"Not walking away, Willow," he told her. Something inside him urged him to add a qualifier. Not walking away until. Only ... he wasn't sure what the until was. The sensible thing to do would be to say he wasn't walking away until she was safe, and Tarek Mahmoud was sitting in a prison cell.

But that didn't feel right.

There was something between them, he liked her, respected her, and wanted to get to know more about her. Crazy given they'd spent less than twenty-four hours in one another's company, but that was how he felt.

At the back of his mind—not that he'd ever given it a lot of conscious thought—was that if he was ever going to fall in love, he'd know it was that person when he met them. While, of course, he wasn't implying he loved Willow, he didn't even really know her, it was just that what he did know about her was enough to know that she could be someone he could fall in love with.

Which was not what he should be thinking about right now.

"I know we're being followed, but wow," Willow said, gazing at the pyramid across a sandy open space from where they were standing. "It really is amazing. I know we said that already, but standing in front of something like that makes you feel small, but not in a bad way."

Willow was right, seeing the pyramids was an awe-inspiring experience, and he wanted it to be only one of many that she got to experience over her life. He wanted her to be able to go up to Lapland, visit Santa, go on a reindeer-pulled sled ride through a snowy winter wonderland, and see the glory of the northern lights. To make all her dreams come true.

To do that he had to get her out of this alive.

His gaze scanned about as they continued to stroll along with the other tourists. Below them was a sandy maze of paths and rooms leading to small underground chambers. There had to be a spot down there he could separate from the crowd, get Willow hidden, and make a move.

"You ready to do this?" he whispered to Willow as he guided her over to the steps leading down.

"More than ready," she said, fierce bravery ringing in her tone.

"Plan is to head down, break away from the group, you hide, and I show the professor that he's messing with the wrong people."

In theory, it sounded easy, but as he knew all too well, all it took was one wrong move for everything to fall apart.

~

July 12th
    1:42 P.M

Her heart raced and her palms were clammy.

Willow prayed that whatever Cooper had planned worked out. Because if it didn't, neither of them would leave Egypt alive.

As she huddled in the sand, hidden behind a stone wall, she wished they'd come up with a different plan. Cooper had told her he believed them pretending to be tourists for a few days would give them a better chance at getting out of the country alive. She'd agreed. He'd also told her he believed that if he called for his team—made up of his three brothers and two stepbrothers—to fly out there they could make Professor Mahmoud believe Prey was coming after him, guns blazing.

Which put the two of them in more danger since they were there in the country.

At the time, she'd agreed with that decision, too. She knew the professor and had been watching him for almost a year, gathering intel, verifying sources, finding informants, and building her case so she could dismantle his plans before he built enough of an army to change the world as they knew it.

Now she wished they'd thrown caution to the wind and just tried to leave the country last night or had his brothers fly in to back them up.

Because she couldn't keep living with this rock of anxiety sitting heavily in her stomach.

It was supposed to be over now. She'd been rescued, she was supposed to be recuperating and working on her article because she was more determined than ever to destroy Tarek Mahmoud. What she wasn't supposed to be doing was hiding from men who no doubt were connected to the professor, terrified that she was going to be captured all over again.

There was no way she could survive that again.

Well, it wasn't so much that she couldn't mentally handle it again, she'd darn well do whatever she had to in order to fulfill the promises she made to her dad, but Tarek wouldn't be stupid enough to let her live. She was too big a threat and he knew that she actually possessed enough information on him to destroy him. Possibly even enough to get him jailed. Definitely enough for his fellow Allah's Warriors members to see him as more of a liability than an asset and take care of him themselves.

A soft thud had her straightening.

Fingers curled into fists, her chipped nails dug into the soft skin of her palms.

She really ought to have done something about them, she thought absently as she itched to sneak out of her hiding place and help somehow.

Sitting like this felt cowardly.

It wasn't her.

But she'd promised Cooper she'd do whatever he asked her to do without arguing, and what he'd asked of her was for her to hide and wait for him.

As much as she hated it, she'd do it unless she had no other options.

Just because she agreed that in this situation Cooper was the one with the skills and training to eliminate the men following them so they could get safely away didn't mean she'd sit there and let anything happen to him.

He had risked everything for her. Come back for her when he didn't have to, put his own goals on hold to help her take down the professor.

If it came down to it, she would absolutely disobey his orders if he needed her help.

There was no other sound but the ominous thud, and Willow subconsciously rocked backward and forward.

Maybe the thud was nothing?

Plenty of tourists were around even if this area seemed deserted. There were also a lot of stray dogs about. Most of them were sleeping in the shade, doing their best to avoid the hot early afternoon sun.

Most likely what she'd heard was nothing.

It was possible she could have convinced herself of that if she hadn't then heard the unmistakable sound of footsteps.

Quickly followed by a curse and then muted muttering.

The voices were too quiet for her to make out any of the words, but she could differentiate two distinct ones, so there were at least two people close by plus another who was more than likely the cause of the thud she'd heard.

According to Cooper, he'd identified five young men following them. From what he could see without making it obvious that he was onto them, they looked similar to the man who had followed him the day he'd confronted the professor about it. If she had to guess, she'd say that the men here today were young college guys that Professor Mahmoud had indoctrinated to his cause.

Where were the other two men?

Had Cooper already eliminated them?

Ideally, they'd love to take one alive to get answers, and even knowing who they were and what they did Willow would prefer to simply incapacitate the men rather than kill them, but she also understood they were fighting for their lives. Whatever they had to do to escape she wanted Cooper to do.

She hadn't allowed herself to think about it yet, but there was a chance she'd killed a man last night.

Again, if the man shooting at them when they climbed the fence and ran to Cooper's car was dead, it was because they were in a fight for their lives, but still, nausea swelled in her stomach at the thought that she might be a killer now.

Of all the things she'd suffered over the last couple of weeks, it felt like that was what would leave the deepest scars.

It fundamentally changed who she was as a person.

In ways that could never be completely erased.

The voices continued to murmur to one another and then she heard the sound of receding footsteps.

Letting out a breath she hadn't realized she was holding, Willow sagged in relief that they hadn't come this way. If they did, they would have seen her for sure. She wasn't really in a hiding place, more just tucked into a corner, totally visible depending on which way you approached the area.

Seconds ticked by.

Turning into minutes.

Sweat rolled down her back, and she wished she could remove the heavy jeans and long-sleeved T-shirt and replace them with a light, floaty sundress. But she had to cover up as much as possible to hide her bruises so she didn't stand out like a sore thumb.

Fear for Cooper grew with each passing moment.

It wasn't that she didn't trust him, or think he had the skills to take on five young men and win, it was just that she liked him, a lot, more than should be possible for how long they'd known each other, and she didn't want anything to happen to him.

If he died because of her ...

Willow couldn't even allow herself to think that.

"Well, well, well, if it isn't the little runaway journalist."

The words had her head jerking up and she saw a man standing atop the wall where she was hiding, looking down at her with a smirk.

There was no conscious decision on her part, Willow just scrambled away from him. If ever there was a time to disobey Cooper's rules, this was it.

The sound of feet hitting the ground behind her spurred or on, but a hand snapped around her ankle and dragged her back.

She fought.

Kicking with her free foot, swinging out with her arms.

It didn't do any good.

Knees clamped around her hips, and a hand closed around her throat, which was already still sore from Darius the previous night.

"Boss said whoever caught you could have some fun with you before we hand you over to him," the young man, who couldn't be more than twenty tops, sneered down at her.

The look in his eyes told her exactly what was going to happen to her.

It would forever be seared into her mind.

Greedy hands grabbed at her breasts, squeezing them painfully before moving to the zipper of her pants.

He was going to do it there?

Where some random tourist could stumble upon them.

Willow was torn between screaming for Cooper to help, and fear that if she did, the remaining men would use it as an opportunity to ambush him.

Yanking her pants open enough that his hand could slip inside, Willow did her best to clench her thighs together, but it didn't do any good. A finger prodded at her entrance, forcing its way inside her.

Bucking him off didn't do any good, and he swatted away her hands like they were nothing more than annoying pests each time she tried to hit him. Willow knew it was do something now or be raped at the world's oldest pyramid.

Instead of trying to brute force her way out of this, Willow reached out to grab a handful of sand, then threw it directly at the man's eyes.

He howled and pulled back, allowing her to scramble backward and put a little distance between them.

A snarl that sounded more animal than human was her first warning.

Then Cooper seemed to drop down from the sky like an avenging angel, even though she knew in reality he'd jumped off the same wall her attacker had. A single swipe of his knife across the man's neck ended his life.

"Are you hurt?" he asked, kneeling in front of her.

Shaking her head was automatic, in reality, she had no idea if she was or wasn't.

"We have to get out of here. I got all the others."

This time she nodded but made no attempt to move.

For now, she'd lost all control of her body.

"Come on, honey, you got this," Cooper whispered softly as he rezipped her jeans, then gently took her hands and pulled her to her feet. "We have to get out of here in case there are more of them around. If nothing else, we don't want anyone spotting us with a trail of dead bodies."

That she could agree with no matter how much shock was muddling her thoughts.

But it was already too late.

Before they could move more men appeared.

These ones weren't as young, and they had the air of seasoned soldiers.

Their chance of escape vanished like a puff of smoke.

CHAPTER
Eleven

July 12th
1:53 P.M.

"You try anything stupid, and I'll start shooting any tourists I see."

Impotent frustration rolled in Cooper's gut.

Best as he could see, there was no other option but to do what one of the men dressed in black had just ordered them.

The only weapons he had were no match for the AK-47s pointed at him and Willow. He might have eliminated the five young men following them, but they were child's play compared to this. Those men had been kids, untrained, unskilled, too eager, and too undisciplined.

But these men ...

They wore their training like armor, their skill evident in the calm way they held their weapons. There were at least half a dozen of them, maybe more he couldn't see. The chances of him taking them all on with a single knife without getting shot—worse without Willow getting shot—were as close to zero as it was possible to get.

"Drop the knife, and hands in the air," the same man, who Cooper had to assume was the leader, ordered.

It killed him to do it, but there were no other options.

At least not yet.

For the time being, he had to play along, make sure he wasn't eliminated as unnecessary baggage, make sure he stuck close to Willow, and protect her however best he could. If he fought now and got himself killed it wouldn't do Willow an ounce of good. All it would do was leave her once again powerless and vulnerable against a man who wanted—needed—her dead.

Slowly, he forced his fingers to uncurl, and the knife hit the sand with a muted thump.

Without it, Cooper felt naked. Of course, he could kill with his bare hands, but these men probably had close to the same level of training he did. They wouldn't be easy to catch unaware, and as long as they remained armed, his chances of getting close enough to do damage with his hands were slim.

"Good." The man gave them an approving nod.

Something dispassionate in them scared Cooper almost more than walking up to see Willow on the ground, a man's hand in her pants. Those kids had been driven by emotion. These men lacked all emotion. They were merely doing a job, one they would do to the best of their abilities.

"Now, hands in the air. Both of you," the man added with a glance at Willow.

Although she inched closer to him, breathing still harsh, fine tremors still wracking her body, she did as instructed, and honestly, he couldn't be more proud of her. No matter what was thrown at her, she handled it. It wasn't that she wasn't afraid, she wasn't a machine, she was a human being who got scared like any other, but she had the ability to push through, fight the fog of fear, and do what had to be done.

Not only did he respect the hell out of that, but it gave them a better chance.

While the leader and three others remained still, weapons aimed directly at them, two other men approached cautiously. Their grip was firm when they snagged his wrists and yanked them behind his back, but they were not overly aggressive.

They had to be mercenaries, probably former military, now in it for the money. At least he could rest easy that they didn't appear to have a sadistic side. Not that it meant they wouldn't hurt him, or Willow, or both of them, but at least they likely wouldn't go above and beyond.

Once their wrists were secured with plastic zip ties, they were both marched further away from the pyramid and toward two idling white vans. The back doors of one were open and they were shoved inside.

With their arms behind their backs, there was no way for them to break their fall. While he caught himself and rolled so no one part of his body took the brunt of the impact, Willow didn't know to do that and cried out as her already battered body bounced onto the floor of the van.

The door was slammed shut behind them, and Cooper was eternally grateful that no one had climbed in the back with them.

"Willow?" He pushed up onto his knees and awkwardly crawled toward the shadowy, huddled form he knew was her body.

"I-I'm okay," she stammered, and he saw her try to push up. Unable to get her body to cooperate, she slumped back down just as he reached her.

"Hold on, honey." Leaning forward, he lifted his arms and then brought them down hard on his backside. It took three tries, but the zip ties broke, and he rotated his shoulders, shifting his arms forward. Since they hadn't been bound long, there was the mildest tingling as normal blood flow returned but not the horrendous pins and needles he'd suffered in the past after being restrained that way.

"Did you get free?" she asked as he managed to snag an arm around her waist just as the idling vans took off sending them both sliding sideways. Now that he was free, he'd be able to protect her from getting tossed about and getting bruises on top of bruises.

"Sure did."

"Heard about how to do that but never seen it done, cool," she murmured as she snuggled into his arms. "Do you think we'll be able to try anything when we get wherever they're taking us?"

While Cooper would love for the answer to be yes, the truth was, he doubted there would be much they could do. They were outmanned and outgunned, and until he could get his hands on a weapon, nothing was likely to change that. Maybe when they arrived only one man would enter the van to drag them out. Maybe he could get his hands on the man's weapon if he had one, but even if he could, that didn't mean he could get himself and Willow out of this alive.

"You don't, do you?" Willow whispered.

Tightening his hold on her, Cooper shifted them both backward until they were in one of the corners. It was easier to brace them there, and he planted his feet on the floor, pressed his back into the corner, and tucked Willow between his knees.

"It's not impossible but the odds aren't in our favor," he agreed.

"If Professor Mahmoud didn't know for certain you were the one who saved me, he does now. I'm sorry, Cooper."

There was too much emotion in her voice, and he instinctively tightened his hold as though he could somehow forcibly eject it from her body.

"What the hell do you have to be sorry about?" he growled.

"You're here because of me. If you hadn't saved me, you might have gotten more information from the professor about your mom. Instead, you've been kidnapped at gunpoint, and ... and ... what if ... you have a family ... I don't ... if you don't make it home ... because of me ..."

Unable to take a second more of her pained rambling, Cooper grasped her chin between his thumb and forefinger and tilted her head up. It was dark in the back of the van, not nearly enough light to see her eyes, so when he dipped his head, he allowed his lips to hover above hers.

He heard her sharp intake of air.

Felt the warm puff against his lips as she let it out slowly.

When she didn't pull away, didn't tell him this was wildly inappropriate, he took that as permission.

That first taste was enough for him to be hooked.

Given where they were and what they were about to face, Cooper kept the kiss soft, sweet, and short. While he would love nothing more than to get lost in her sweet taste, he needed to keep a clear head, think, be able to focus, and take any chance that presented itself.

"Don't say that again," he whispered against her lips when he finally pulled back. "None of this is your fault."

"But you're only here because of me. Because I wanted to find enough evidence to bring Professor Mahmoud to justice."

"Which is not a bad thing," he reminded her. "I made the choice to save your life because I couldn't have lived with myself if I just left you there to suffer your fate."

A fate that might very well have caught up with her anyway.

There was no doubt that it was the professor who had sent these men after them. No doubt that the professor knew how dangerous Willow was and what she could do if he allowed her to live. And no doubt that he was now more than likely going to be collateral damage.

But if they were both about to lose their lives, if Willow was going to wind up dead anyway, then Cooper could at least take solace in the fact that he'd spared her taking her final breath all alone.

～

July 12th
   3:27 P.M

Every mile they drove felt like taking one step away from being saved.

Willow trusted Cooper implicitly. She believed that if anyone had the training and skill to get them out alive, it was him.

But she was also pragmatic enough to know how badly the odds were stacked against them.

Fear clogged every one of her pores, it seemed to seep down inside her body, attaching to her blood and making it throb as it flew through her veins. Her skin was clammy, her heart racing, and even though she kept trying to match her breathing to Cooper's she knew hers was much too fast.

As badly as she wanted to show Cooper that she could be strong and calm, be an asset to him rather than a liability, Willow knew she was failing.

What was so different this time around?

Last time she'd panicked of course, but she'd been able to pull herself together.

This time they'd been gone all of an hour, maybe, and she felt like she was going to fall apart.

Knowing if she did, she was putting Cooper's life in danger made it worse. Even though she was trying to use that knowledge to calm herself, it was doing the opposite. Making the panic worse, making her fear worse, making everything worse.

She didn't want him to die because of her.

Just because he said it wasn't her fault didn't change the facts.

And the facts were that if he'd left her at the professor's house, she'd already be dead but he'd be either safe in his hotel room or safely on a plane back home.

It *was* her fault.

When the van finally stopped moving, she pressed herself closer against Cooper's body. This would be the last time she'd feel a human touch that was meant to soothe and comfort her, that was soft and gentle. From here on out, when somebody touched her, it would be to cause her pain.

There were so many things she wished she could say to Cooper before they were both dragged out of the van, but her mind felt all tangled, and in the end, all she could do was tilt her face up and whisper her lips against his.

One last kiss.

One last moment of joy.

Maybe that would be enough to help her pull it together and last out whatever was coming. Maybe she could even find a way to make a deal to get Cooper out of there alive. After all, she was the one that Professor Mahmoud wanted. She'd told Cooper in the car what she knew about the professor, but he didn't have to know she'd already told him. If she lied and claimed that she had kept her evidence against Professor Mahmoud to herself then there would be no reason to kill Cooper.

Could she hold onto that lie under torture?

Only time would tell, but she would give it everything she had.

"You can do this, Willow. I believe in you. You are without a doubt the strongest and bravest person I have ever met. Don't forget that."

Before she could respond to Cooper's whispered words, bright light flooded the back of the van as the door was thrown open. Cooper's lips brushed across hers one last time as four men jumped into the van.

They hadn't talked much throughout the drive, and she hadn't been sure if Cooper was planning on making a move since he was free or if he was waiting to see what the odds were like when they got wherever they were going.

Obviously, four armed men against the two of them, her still bound because she hadn't had the strength to break the ties, meant the odds for them were non-existent.

"He's free, boss," one of the men called out as they saw Cooper's arms wrapped around her body.

"No big deal," Cooper said, lifting his arms so his hands were held palms out in a sign of surrender. "The lady's body is covered in bruises, I wasn't going to let her get tossed about, and she's still cuffed."

Somewhat cautiously, the four men approached. When they were close enough, two of them reached out and grabbed her shoulders, yanking her from Cooper's hold.

Willow clamped her lips together so she didn't cry out a protest at being taken away from him. It wouldn't do any good, and if the men suspected there was anything more between them than just that Cooper had rescued her, they would use it to their advantage.

There was more, wasn't there?

She wasn't imagining it?

No, she couldn't have. After all, he had kissed her first. There was something there even if she wasn't sure yet what it was. All she knew was that something on a soul level drew her to Cooper, and she absolutely would do everything within her meager power to get him out of this alive.

That helped her steel her spine as she was dragged out of the van. Her muscles protested every single movement, having stiffened during the drive. The pain in her potentially broken arm was almost unbearable from the awkward way her arms were pulled behind her back and bound.

But complaining or crying about wasn't going to help so she shoved the pain away and tried to focus. As she was walked toward a large sandy-colored house that blended in with all the desert sand, she scanned the area. Wherever they were it was remote. There was one road that she could see, then the long driveway they'd come down.

Instead of entering the house, they were led around it and toward a larger structure at the back. It kind of looked like a large warehouse or storage shed, and when they reached it, and she was shoved inside, she saw that it was completely empty save for a table and chairs down one end near a scant kitchenette and two lone chairs sitting in the middle.

Unfortunately, Willow didn't need a vivid imagination to figure out what the purpose of those two chairs was.

Behind her, Cooper was also led into the room, and they were both taken to the chairs. The men weren't gentle, but they weren't overly rough with her either as she was pushed into one of the chairs.

A hand on her back, between her shoulder blades, pushed her forward and she felt the slight scrape of a knife as it cut through the plastic ties. As soon as they fell away and her arms drooped forward, excruciating pain seared through the limbs as blood flow returned.

Determined not to show weakness by crying, she pressed her lips together and scrunched her eyes closed. Breathing through the pain as best as she could, eventually, it began to ebb, and once it did, she lifted her head to find that she'd already been cuffed, wrists and ankles, to the chair, as had Cooper.

His gray eyes reminded her of a thunderstorm as their gazes met.

In answer to his unasked question if she was okay, she gave a single nod. She was as okay as she could be given their circumstances.

Turning that stormy gaze on their captors, Cooper stared at them, waiting for them to make whatever move they intended to make.

Likewise, Willow also shifted her gaze from Cooper to the half dozen men surrounding them. Thankfully—or maybe not—Professor Mahmoud didn't appear to be one of them. Not that there was any doubt why she'd been taken. They knew her, knew she was the journalist after the professor, well the young men had known, and she assumed they had called in the professionals.

Wasn't like there were any other options. Were there?

Was it possible this was to do with Cooper's search for answers about his mother instead of her mess?

It didn't matter either way, they were in this together.

Together.

The word settled in her mind, pushing a calming strength through her body.

If they were in this together, she couldn't be the weak link. She had to hold it together just like she had before. If she could do it then, there was absolutely no reason why she couldn't do it again now.

One of the men that she recognized as the leader stepped up in front of her. Beady black eyes stared down at her, but she forced herself to stay still, not shrink under the weight of that stare.

"We can do this the easy way or the hard way," the man eventually said. "You tell us who you already sent your intel to and handle it, or things are going to get messy. Bloody," he added in a threatening voice.

Okay, so about her for sure.

She'd told the professor that if she got away, she'd see to it that she destroyed him, and it seemed he'd taken her at her word.

Meeting the man's gaze, she held it. "It's already too late for Professor Mahmoud. I suggest you let us go if you don't want to be taken down along with him. At least let Cooper go, all he did was rescue me, he doesn't know what I have on the professor or why I followed him to Egypt."

Even though she didn't look at him, Willow could feel Cooper's frustration rolling off him in waves. He didn't like her trying to protect him. Well, too bad. He'd risked everything to help her, and she would absolutely do the same thing.

Casting a suspicious glance at Cooper, the man then returned it to her. "You need to undo what you did. Contact whoever you told and tell them you were mistaken."

"Yeah, I'm not going to do that. Why would I?"

A slow smile took over his face as he reached out and placed one of his hands on the forearm of her possibly broken arm. "Because if you don't, I'm going to make things very unpleasant for you. Easy way or the hard way. Your choice."

There was no choice.

She had to do whatever it took to convince these men that Cooper knew nothing and was no threat to the professor. Even if that meant enduring more horrific pain.

CHAPTER Twelve

July 12th
3:40 P.M.

A sharp intake of air was the only sign Willow gave that anything was wrong.

But he'd heard it.

Heard the slight snap as one of the delicate bones in her finger was broken.

Rage, unlike anything Cooper had ever experienced, flooded his system. These men would pay for hurting Willow. Pay with their lives. Every single one of them. He would hunt them all down and rip them to pieces with his bare hands.

It wasn't until he heard laughter that Cooper realized he was growling at the men.

"Seems like he cares a little too much about a simple broken finger," the man said, clearly amused.

"Because he's a good man," Willow said, her breathing heavy, but determination flashing in her turquoise eyes. His little fighter was still standing, and while he absolutely hated that she was trying to protect him when it should be the other way around, he was so proud of her.

Again.

Even when he thought he was already as proud of her as he could be, she went and upped the bar again, proving that she was every bit the warrior he had trained to be and without the grueling training he'd gone through.

It was just who she was.

"He's a thief," their tormentor said. "He took something that didn't belong to him, now he has to pay the price for that."

"I don't belong to Professor Mahmoud," Willow snapped, sounding completely offended by the insinuation. "He kidnapped me, held me against my will, and beat me daily."

"You thought you could take him on, and he proved to you that you lost," the man said with a shrug.

"Only I didn't lose, did I?" Willow said, goading the man even though she had to know that would only make things worse for her.

"Seems like you did." The man pressed down on the hand that was still on Willow's almost definitely broken arm. Her face tightened, pain bracketing her lips as they were pressed into a thin line, but she didn't cry out in pain, and the determination in her eyes only grew.

"Because now you kidnapped me?" Willow asked. "Doesn't change anything."

Annoyance flared in the man's black eyes. "Tell me what you did."

"I'm sure you can figure it out," Willow shot back.

"You were only gone a few hours, less than a day, you could not have done anything drastic," the man said, although there was a thread of doubt in his voice.

Willow rolled her eyes.

Straight up rolled them like she wasn't cuffed to a chair, littered with bruises, with a freshly broken finger. Cooper didn't know if he wanted to cheer her on for her bravery or spank her pretty little backside for being so irresponsible as to invite their attacker to cause her more pain.

"Yeah, because there's no such thing as phones and the internet. I already did what I needed to do," Willow told their abductor.

With a snarl, the man grabbed the finger he'd just broken and twisted it viciously. Willow sucked in a pained breath, and even from where he was, Cooper could see tears of pain shimmering in her eyes, but somehow, she managed to stop them from falling.

"I told my boss to go ahead and publish what I already have if he doesn't hear from me in a week. It's already over," Willow said, triumph in her voice.

Cooper had no idea if that was true or if she was just playing their captors. He had lent her his phone, and she had contacted her boss after she'd told him what she knew about the professor and how he was radicalizing students at his university. Maybe she had told her boss that, or maybe she was bluffing, either way, Willow was right, it was already over for Professor Mahmoud. There was nothing to be gained by abducting them. Even if Willow was dead, it wouldn't stop the story from being published, and he had no doubt she knew enough to make the man's life hell.

"You may as well let us go, it won't change anything, and I don't care about you. You're just mercenaries, I don't even know if you've worked for the professor before. Maybe this is your only job for him, or maybe you're part of Allah's Warriors along with him. Either way, he's the head of the snake and the one I'm after. You don't have to go down with him, you can walk away now, let us go, and put as much distance as you can between yourselves and the professor so you don't go down with him. Doesn't matter how many contacts he has, he's not getting out of this."

Willow spoke so confidently, and that she could do it while in pain, spoke only of her strength. She believed in this fight, and she was going to keep fighting until she took her final breath.

He just had to figure out how to ensure that didn't happen today.

So far, there were no opportunities he could use. Given enough time, he could probably get free from the zip ties binding him to the chair, but to do that, he'd need them to be left alone long enough. If he could get free and get his hands on a weapon, he could get them out of there.

If he could.

But right now, he couldn't.

Which meant he had no choice but to watch as the enraged man standing before Willow clamped a hand around her neck, squeezing as he let out a string of what Cooper assumed from his limited Arabic were curses.

"You have ruined everything, woman," the man snarled at Willow, getting right in her face as it turned red, her body lacking the oxygen it needed.

"Can't kill her now," one of the other men said, stepping up and resting a hand on the man's shoulder. "Boss wants that honor himself."

While hearing that made his blood turn to ice, at least Cooper knew they had a little time for him to try to figure something out. Professor Mahmoud was likely already on his way, but he wasn't there yet, and that meant they at least stood a chance.

However small a chance he'd take it.

At least it was something.

Breathing hard, the man stepped away from Willow, looking down at her with furious disdain. "You think you're so smart."

"I'm smart enough to figure out what your boss was doing and gather proof," Willow said, voice raspy from a man's hand around her throat for the third time in less than twenty-four hours.

"Proof that my boss can make disappear," the man countered.

"I don't think so. Not this time. Not with me disappearing while in Egypt following him. That's too big a coincidence to ignore. There's no way to paint me as incompetent, or as having some sort of grudge, or even just crazy if I'm nowhere to be found."

Willow was right.

Unfortunately, Tarek Mahmoud was damned if he did and damned if he didn't. If he killed her, it only gave credence to Willow's claims. But if he didn't and he let her go, she would back up everything she had to say with the fact that only a guilty man would abduct her and try to kill her.

The man knew it too because he cursed again and then his fist flew toward Willow's head, connecting with her temple. Her head snapped to the side, and her eyes rolled back in her head as she passed out.

"You should have left it alone," the man told him. "Because now you're going to suffer the same fate as her."

With a final snarl in Willow's direction, the man turned and stomped away across the room, no doubt to call his boss and deliver the bad news that life as they knew it was already over, they were just waiting for the clock to countdown and their world to implode.

Looking at Willow's still form, slumped forward, held in place only by the cuffs on her wrists and ankles, Cooper couldn't have disagreed more. If this was how his life ended, he knew he would have made both his parents proud. Helping an innocent in need was who his mom and dad had been, and they would both have adored Willow.

With her determination to do what was right regardless of the danger it put her in, and her strength in the face of fear, she was everything anyone could want.

Which was why he had to find a way to get her out of this alive.

She'd tried to protect him, lied to try to save his life, he would give her no less in return.

Whatever it took, he was going to find a way to get her back home to her life even if it meant he died in Egypt.

～

July 13th
   1:05 A.M

Thankfully, they'd been left alone after the leader of their band of abductors had knocked her unconscious.

Willow had no idea how long she'd been out, but it was enough for Cooper to start panicking.

Since she didn't really think of the former Delta Force operator turned Prey operative as a panicker, she knew he was truly worried.

Not that he was the only one.

As they'd sat tied to the chairs in the big empty warehouse, they'd watched through the windows as the sun sank and the room grew dark as night fell. She thought the professor would have arrived by now. They couldn't have driven for more than two hours or so, possibly less, so they weren't all that far away from Saqqara, which was only a thirty-minute drive or so from Cairo.

Why wasn't he here?

What did that mean for them?

Despite her lies that Cooper didn't know what Professor Mahmoud was up to, no one had attempted to let him go. Maybe they'd set him free after they killed her.

No.

They weren't going to do that.

Whether she lied or not, they'd never been going to let him go.

They couldn't.

Whether he knew what had brought her to Egypt or not, he knew she'd been held against her will by the professor. That alone was enough for him to be killed.

A grumbling sound had her lips curling up into a small smile despite the direness of their situation. "Hungry?" she asked, looking over at Cooper who shot her a sheepish smile.

"I'd say no, but my stomach gave me away."

She huffed a small chuckle, wincing as the small movement aggravated the pain in her head. Blood had flowed down her face from the wound the blow that knocked her out had inflicted, and the feel of it sticky and crusty against her skin was almost as annoying as the pain itself.

At least there was one benefit to a concussion.

Nausea had stolen her appetite, and even though she hadn't eaten for hours, and before that had been half-starved for two weeks straight, the thought of food made her ill.

"I'm sorry," she whispered. Just because Cooper kept telling her that none of this was her fault she couldn't stop feeling otherwise.

They *were* here because of her.

That was just a fact.

How was she supposed to be okay with it?

Sure, it had been Cooper's choice to investigate when he no doubt heard Darius strangling and spanking her, but she had been the one who had allowed herself to get kidnapped in the first place. She should have been smarter, should have been stronger, should have done something differently.

"Don't make me say it again, honey," Cooper told her. "You know this isn't on you. You didn't force Mahmoud to join a terrorist cell. You didn't force him to start targeting young men at the university to convert them. You didn't force him to come up with a plan to plant radicalized young men in various places in our country and then coordinate an attack. And you certainly didn't force him to abduct and torture you. None of this is on you. The blame lies squarely on the shoulders of one man."

"Why isn't he here already?" she asked, even though she knew Cooper couldn't know the answer to that question.

"Don't know, but I'm going to count it as a blessing. He's already played with fire and almost gotten burned, I don't think he's going to drag things out this time."

Willow swallowed down a rush of bile.

She knew exactly what that meant and she agreed.

This time the professor wasn't going to keep her alive for weeks while he had his fun doling out daily beatings and watching her wither slowly away.

This time he was just going to get the job done.

Kill her.

Dispose of her body.

Try whatever he could come up with to mitigate the damage her article was going to cause.

It would be one thing if she was going to be the only one to suffer that fate, after all, this was her fight, but knowing that Cooper would suffer along with her was too much.

Tears leaked out of her eyes, and she didn't bother to fight them back.

It hurt too much knowing this man who had risked everything for her was going to wind up dead because of her.

"Shh, honey, don't cry," Cooper whispered, his voice soothing only this time it couldn't wash away the knot of terror lodged in her chest. "It'll probably be quick."

"Not why I'm crying," she said through her tears. "I'd take a long, painful death if it meant you got to live."

"You're crying over me?" Cooper asked like he couldn't comprehend that.

"Of course. You saved me and now you're going to pay the ultimate price for that."

"I'm not giving up yet," Cooper said fiercely, and as she looked at him through the tears filling her eyes, she could see new determination on his face. "As long as we're alive, there's still a chance."

A chance, maybe, but not a big one.

They were still cuffed to the chairs, the men were on the other side of the room whispering amongst themselves, with their weapons slung over the backs of their chairs. Any move they attempted to make would be seen and stopped before they could do anything. And even if they could somehow silently slip out of their bonds, they would never make it to the warehouse door without being shot.

Lapsing into silence, both lost in their own thoughts, Willow's head jerked up when she heard the loud, unmistakable sound of an approaching helicopter.

For a second, she wondered if somehow Prey had managed to dredge up their location and mount a rescue. That idea was quickly squashed when she saw the expression on Cooper's face.

This wasn't his people coming to rescue him.

Which meant it was likely a herald of Professor Mahmoud's imminent arrival.

So, it really was over.

Death was mere minutes away.

Maybe the professor would torture her a little first, try to find out exactly what she had on him so he could try to formulate a plan on how best to wriggle out of the charges that would no doubt soon be coming.

But even if he did, it would only delay her death by minutes at the most, and possibly not delay Cooper's at all.

When the men began to approach them, Willow was caught off-guard. She would have thought they'd head outside to meet their boss. The roar of the helicopter's blades was deafening, it must have been landing right outside the warehouse.

There was no way to protect her ears from the too-loud sound, so instead, she focused on trying to look strong and brave as the men stopped before them.

"End of the line," the leader snapped, a look of glee on his face. It was clear these men worked for the professor and weren't just a random group of mercenaries he'd hired for this particular job. Willow hoped whatever investigation was started because of her article wound up bringing these men to justice as well.

She wanted all of them to pay.

For Professor Mahmoud's entire house of cards to come tumbling down.

If it was the end of the line, at least Willow knew she could be proud that she had fulfilled her promise to her father. Her life had meant something, she'd taken what evil had been done to him and turned it into something good. Her article would dismantle a dangerous terrorist group. Sure, another would rise to take its place, but she had still done something good.

Instead of standing beside them, two of the men moved forward to cut the ties binding both her wrists and ankles to the chair, and Cooper's. Hands immediately clamped around her shoulders, pulling her to her feet and over toward the door.

She stumbled, partly because her limbs were numb, partly because she was in pain and dizzy from the concussion, but also partly because of shock. This was the room where she believed she would take her final breath, but it looked like she was wrong.

It looked like they were going to be transported in the helicopter because Professor Mahmoud hadn't entered the building, and they were being led out of it.

Transferring them someplace else allowed for a margin of error.

A chance.

Hope.

Rejuvenated, Willow didn't fight as the men dragged her out into the still-warm night and toward the helicopter, just a short walk away. She had to be ready, Cooper would be formulating a plan, she knew he would, so she had to be on her game ready to do whatever he needed of her.

Once already she'd prayed for help, to be saved, and God had delivered in the form of a sexy special forces warrior who had saved her from certain death. Tonight, again, she had to believe that a miracle could be waiting for them, all they had to do was figure out how best to use this situation to their advantage.

Because if they didn't, if they allowed this chance to slip through their fingers, there wouldn't be another.

CHAPTER

Thirteen

July 13th
1:20 A.M.

This was better than he could have hoped for.

Cooper flexed his fingers to ensure he got blood flowing as quickly as possible through his limbs because he was going to need them.

As soon as the time was right, he was making his move.

The helo was small, only room for the pilot and four passengers. With him and Willow being two of those, that meant there would be only two other men on board.

Odds he liked.

Fighting a grin, he allowed himself to be guided into one of the seats. Nobody bothered to hand him a set of headphones, the roar of the rotors was annoying and far too loud, but he wasn't complaining.

Not when it offered him the best chance he'd ever have of surviving this ordeal.

He had honestly believed that it was over. There was no way he could get out of the chair without getting caught, no way he could fight against a half dozen armed men, and no way he could get Willow out alive. Professor Mahmoud would eventually show up and their deaths would be quick.

Failure.

It had clung to him, permeated his being, and made him feel dirty. He was highly trained and had spent years in the field, he should be able to save a woman from a university professor.

And now he could.

Whatever risks he had to take would be worth it, so long as he got Willow out of this alive.

A man climbed in beside him, and then Willow was lifted onto the other window seat. While the sight of any of these men touching her made him see red, he shoved away those feelings and focused.

This was what he knew how to do.

Survive.

Fight.

Win.

Usually, he had a team at his back, and that definitely made things easier, but never before in his life had the stakes been this high. Willow was already important to him, and he wasn't going to let her down.

He couldn't.

Another man climbed into the front seat, but then all the others stepped back, away from the helo. For some stupid reason, they seemed to have believed that the game was already over and they had already been crowned the winners, but in reality, they hadn't even stepped foot on the field yet.

And now thanks to their stupidity, the ball was no longer even in their court. It was firmly in his and he couldn't wait to pick it up and make the first toss.

Whether it was stupidity or cockiness on their part, no one had rebound his hands, he was free, and if they thought that being in the air with two armed men in the helo was enough for him to just sit there like a docile little soldier, they were about to learn that they were sorely mistaken.

He liked these odds.

Loved them.

When they lifted off the ground, he felt adrenalin flood through his system as he already began to formulate a plan. There was every chance that he was going to wind up shot, but so long as a bullet didn't hit anything vital, and he was able to get this helo safely back down to the ground, he didn't care.

Time seemed to tick by slowly. Even though he wasn't wearing headphones, he could see the lips of the man beside him moving so he knew their babysitters were involved in a conversation. Distracted. Perfect. They weren't expecting any trouble and all he had to do was make his move quickly and efficiently.

Although he couldn't see her, there was the big body of one of their abductors between them, and it was dull inside the helo, Cooper could feel the energy pouring off Willow. She was smart, she knew this was their chance and he was planning something, and he knew he could count on her to do her part.

Over the loud roar of the rotors, there was no way he was going to be able to communicate verbally with her so he was going to have to hope she would be able to read in his facial and hand signals what he needed her to do.

Shifting slightly, he turned his head a little to see that she was looking in his direction. Their gazes met, he held it, and then looked down at the floor of the helo, hoping she would understand that when he made his move, he needed her to get down low.

Despite how they were acting at the moment, these men weren't stupid, and they knew the best way to ensure his compliance was to threaten Willow. That meant he had to make sure she was as out of the line of fire as he could get her.

She gave him a minute nod a split second before the man between them roughly shoved him back against the seat, shooting him an irritated frown.

Resting back against the seat, Cooper bid his time. They had to be far enough away from where they'd been held so that when he landed the helo they wouldn't see and come after them. But he also couldn't wait too long because he had no idea where they were being taken and how long it was going to take to get there.

After what he estimated to be about ten minutes of flying, he decided that was enough.

Time to make his move.

With lightning speed and pinpoint accuracy, Cooper snapped out his hands and grabbed the weapon resting uselessly in the lap of the man sitting beside him. He yanked it forward and up, slamming it into the man's face as he twisted his body and dragged the other one with it. Kicking out with his feet, he pushed the man from the helo, managing to keep hold of the weapon.

Praying Willow had understood his orders and followed them, getting herself down on the floor, he felt the sting of a bullet as it zinged past him, tearing through the flesh on his arm before hitting the seat behind him.

With a roar he lunged forward, ramming the weapon into the face of the man in the passenger seat of the helo.

Immediately, he slumped forward, and Cooper wasted no time in relieving him of his weapon.

Then he pointed one at the pilot.

Keeping the weapon steady, he clambered over the seat and into the passenger seat, ignoring the other man's slumped body, but snagging his headset and putting it on.

"Land the helo now," he ordered the pilot.

"I ... I have orders," the man babbled. It was obvious that he wasn't trained the same way their captors had been. This man looked ready to pee his pants if he hadn't already done so.

"Your orders have changed. Put us down," he commanded as he glanced into the back to see that Willow was now sitting on the seat, her eyes wide. There was no other headset he could give her since the man he'd kicked out of the helo had taken his with him, and he needed this one, and for the pilot to keep his.

When he arched a brow at her, asking if she was all right she gave him a shaky nod. Since he didn't need two weapons right now, and he didn't like the idea of her being vulnerable even if he had things under control, he passed her the other assault rifle. Her hands shook as she took it, but she held onto it and he saw the determination he was familiar with in the blue depths of her eyes.

Just as he took the first proper breath he'd taken since he realized

Willow was definitely being held against her will at Professor Mahmoud's house, Cooper sensed it.

Movement.

He was a split second too slow responding, and an arm clamped around his neck.

Willow screamed, maybe he heard it or maybe he just imagined it, he wasn't sure, but he was sure of the fact that he, too, had gotten a little too cocky. He'd thought the other man would stay unconscious or at least be too woozy to attack.

Stupid.

A mistake that could undo everything he'd just done.

Ramming the weapon in his hands back, he felt the other man grunt as it connected with his ribs, but he held on tight. There wasn't much room for him to fight, and he needed the pilot alive and uninjured to get them safely down.

Giving the man another jab to the ribs he felt the hold around his neck loosen a little.

Then all hell broke loose.

Willow lunged forward swinging the assault rifle he'd given her at the man's head. It connected if the further loosening of the arm around his neck was anything to go by.

But then the man reached for Willow.

They tussled over her weapon as Cooper turned with his, intending to end this now.

Just as he fired at the man, Willow's gun went off, peppering the control panel of the helicopter with a spray of bullets.

The man attacking him slumped over, a red dot on the center of his forehead indicating that Cooper's bullet had struck its target.

No longer was the man a threat, but now they had bigger problems.

The helo was shrieking at them, the pilot panicked as he tried to regain control of the machine that was now spiraling right toward the ground at a sickening pace.

July 13th

1:33 A.M

They were going to crash.

Willow knew it with absolute certainty.

Just because she wasn't wearing a headset and couldn't hear much of anything above the constant roar of the rotors, she could tell from the way they were falling, the way they'd tipped sideways.

She'd tried to help but she'd only made things worse.

Cooper had been fighting against the other man who had risen almost from the dead to attack him. There wasn't enough space for him to properly fight off the attack and she had no idea if the pilot was also armed.

So, she'd thought she could just knock out the man attacking Cooper.

But he'd reached for the weapon she brandished more like a club, they'd fought over it and she knew it was those bullets from the weapon she was responsible for that had fired into the helicopter's control panel.

They were going to die, and it was all her fault.

A scream fell from her lips as they lurched sideways, and she was thrown toward the open door where Cooper had thrown the other man guarding them.

Frantically, she threw her hands out, scrambling to hold onto anything within reach so she, too, didn't go flying out that door. Just because they were quickly losing altitude didn't mean they were close enough to the ground to survive the fall.

Somehow, she managed to catch onto a seatbelt with her bad arm. Pain screamed through the limb from her broken finger to the likely broken bone in her forearm, but she couldn't let go.

If she did, she'd fall right out the door.

Whimpering, she clung with all her might to the seatbelt that was the only thing keeping her alive.

In the front, the pilot was frantically pushing buttons. From the way he moved, he knew nothing he could do would save them. The helicopter was damaged, it was going down, he'd already lost control over it and that meant their fate was sealed.

The miracle that had seemed within their grasp when her gaze met Cooper's and she'd read his instructions to get down when he made his move, had now shimmered completely out of reach.

Her grip on the seatbelt loosened when the helicopter tipped further to the side.

There was no way she could hold on much longer.

Cooper looked over at her, their gazes met, and she locked onto it like a lifeline. In that one look, she tried to convey how deeply sorry she was that he was going to die because of her. While she would leave behind nothing but a few friends who would miss her but quickly move on, he was leaving behind an entire family of three brothers, a sister, two stepbrothers, and a niece who would all grieve his loss for the rest of their lives.

It wasn't fair and she wished she could undo it somehow.

She also tried to convey her gratitude for how hard he'd fought for her. It was only because of him that she'd stood a chance.

At least she'd achieved what she set out to do when she arrived in Egypt. She and Cooper might be dead in a few seconds, but at least Tarek Mahmoud was going to go down in flames as well.

Another tilt of the helicopter as it hurtled toward the ground had her tenuous grip on the seatbelt faltering.

No longer could her broken arm hold her entire body weight.

As though in slow motion her fingers slipped.

Then she was falling.

Next thing she knew, pain exploded inside her body, and the world around her disappeared.

Maybe seconds, maybe minutes, maybe hours later it was back.

Pain.

Consuming her.

Beating through her blood, reaching out to every extremity.

It was so bad that maybe she passed out again.

All she knew was that she was floating in a black haze of agony that made functioning impossible.

Alive.

Even through the pain, she was cognizant of that fact.

Somehow, she'd survived the fall.

By the time her hand lost its grip, they must have been close enough to the ground that she hadn't been killed on impact.

Cooper.

Fear shoved aside a good amount of pain as she focused on the brave man who had fought so hard for both of their lives.

Had he survived, too?

"Cooper?" she called out. Even to her own ears, her voice was insubstantial, a hint of sound in the otherwise quiet night.

She had to find him, had to help him, he had to be alive, he had to be.

She didn't want to live if he hadn't.

Limbs trembling with fear, pain, and exhaustion, Willow had to battle against her own body to get it to cooperate with her.

It took almost everything she had left in her to shove up onto all fours. She swayed, darkness encroaching on the corners of her mind, but she pushed it away.

She had to get to Cooper.

It was a single-minded chant inside her head, it was all she could focus on.

"Cooper?" she called out, her voice a little stronger this time.

There was no answer.

Just silence.

Mocking silence.

Reminding her of what it felt like in the underground cell the professor had kept her in.

But this wasn't the cell, she'd gotten away from him because of Cooper. Because he'd risked everything for her.

Now he needed her to get it together and be there for him.

With more determination than she realized she possessed, Willow managed to get to her feet.

It was dark, but there was enough light from the moon and stars that she could see the helicopter's wreckage lying around twenty yards away from where she'd landed.

With her gait awkward and unsteady, she ran toward it.

Had to get to Cooper.

Had to find him.

Had to help him.

He needed her.

The smell of gas in the air was strong and grew even stronger the closer she got to the wrecked helicopter.

A body was hanging partway out the passenger side door.

Terror lodged in her throat.

Cooper?

From the way it lay and the angle of the spine, Willow already knew whoever it was was dead before she dropped to her knees beside it.

Please don't be Cooper.

Please let him be alive.

With a badly shaking hand, she reached out and turned the face toward her.

Relief almost stole consciousness from her.

It wasn't Cooper.

It was the man who had tried to kill them.

"Not Cooper, it's not Cooper," she babbled to herself, sounding dangerously close to hysteria even to her own ears.

Just because this wasn't his body didn't mean that he had survived.

Gagging as she went, Willow crawled over the man who had been intent on taking her to her death, and into the helicopter.

It was dark inside, and there was a hissing sound that she wasn't cognizant enough to figure out what it meant, but instinct told her it wasn't good.

Two figures lay inside.

Neither was moving.

Assuming the one slumped over the controls was the pilot, Willow shifted toward the other.

As she moved, a shaft of moonlight illuminated the face enough that a sob caught in her throat.

It was Cooper.

He was so still and blood streaked his face.

As badly as she wanted to see if he was alive, she was paralyzed. In this second, she had hope, but if she reached out and touched him that hope could be ripped away from her.

But she had to know.

Had to know if he was still with her or if she'd lost him and he was already gone, leaving her all alone.

When her fingertips brushed against his skin, she found it still warm. It was a good sign but given that they might have only crashed mere minutes ago, not necessarily an indication that he was still alive.

Slowly, her fingers swept down from his cheek to his neck, searching for a pulse.

There.

A slight fluttering against her fingertips.

A pulse.

Willow cried out in relief as she flung her arms around Cooper's still body. He hadn't left her yet, he was still alive.

Alive, but in what shape?

She had enough first aid knowledge to know that moving him could be dangerous, but also enough knowledge to know that if she left him where he was, and the helicopter drenched in gasoline exploded, he would go up along with it.

She had to get him out.

It was the only way to keep him safe.

For now at least.

Reaching down, she found his hands and curled hers around them. Pain screamed up through her broken arm, but she had to ignore it.

Had to get Cooper out.

It was all that mattered.

That first attempt at moving his much larger body didn't just send pain firing through her injured arm but through her entire body. Her chest felt like it was on fire, and every inch of her protested.

Not stopping.

I won't stop until Cooper is safe.

Please, Daddy, give me enough strength to get him away from the wreckage.

Slow going though it was, somehow, Willow managed to drag Cooper's body onto the dead man's. She stumbled as she went, losing her footing and landing hard on her backside. Cooper's body fell with her, landing on top of her, his weight crushing her already weak body.

Tears burned her eyes.

She didn't have enough strength left to push Cooper's body off her and get back up.

You have to.

Don't be a baby.

If you don't do this Cooper will die.

Fear of losing him was enough for her to summon what strength she had left and push with all her might until she was able to roll Cooper to the side and scramble up onto her knees.

They were out of the helicopter.

It wasn't enough though.

They needed to put distance between them.

If the helicopter caught fire now, they'd catch fire, too, because she wasn't leaving Cooper's side no matter what.

Breathing heavily, she staggered to her feet and reclaimed her grip on Cooper's hands.

Each step was excruciating.

Willow lost count of the number of times she fell.

Each time she forced herself to get back up.

Forced herself to keep moving.

The helicopter grew smaller.

The darkness around them seemed to grow larger.

Or maybe that was just because her hold on consciousness was weakening.

The next time she stumbled, Willow knew she'd reached the inevitable.

She wasn't getting back up.

She was too weak, too exhausted, her body no longer had enough steam to move.

A red fireball suddenly streaked through the night.

The helicopter exploded.

With all she had left to give, Willow threw her body over Cooper's to protect him as best she could and succumbed to the darkness pulling at her mind.

CHAPTER

Fourteen

July 13th

2:17 A.M.

There was roaring in his ears.

Cooper couldn't figure out where it was coming from.

Everything was all jumbled inside him.

He couldn't seem to figure anything out.

He had no idea where he was, what had happened to him, and why something was lying on top of him, pinning him to the ground.

Or why he hurt so badly.

But he knew he had to figure it out.

There was something in his mind, poking at him, trying to stir him awake, trying to force him to figure things out.

Only he didn't want to.

He wanted to slide back into the peaceful slumber he'd been in before the roaring started.

Just as he was drifting away, allowing the darkness to pull him under one word screamed inside his mind.

Willow.

It was like a physical shout.

Like there was somebody inside his head screaming her name.

Not just once, but over and over again, like a chant he couldn't ignore.

Willow needed him.

That much he was sure of.

Once he latched onto that thought, everything else came tumbling back.

Being followed at the Step Pyramid, being captured, driven in the van, watching helplessly as one of their captors snapped her finger like it was nothing but a twig. The helicopter, the fight, knowing they were going down and there was nothing he could do about it.

Then ...

Nothing.

He didn't remember hitting the ground, but it was evident he'd somehow managed to survive the crash.

Had Willow?

Fear propelled him through the darkness clogging his mind and body, and he jerked fully awake.

The black, inky sky stretched out above him, and for a second, Cooper was confused. He should be inside the wreckage of the helicopter if he survived the crash.

Only he wasn't.

He was outside.

Had he fallen out the door before they hit the ground?

If he had, then what was pinning him down?

A glance at his chest answered that question for him.

Blonde hair spread out across his neck, tickling his skin.

Willow was lying on top of him. But they hadn't been together when they crashed. She'd been in the backseat. He'd watched in horror as her grip on the seatbelt had loosened and she'd fallen out the door.

He remembered vividly screaming her name and trying to scramble over the back seat to get to her. Even if he'd fallen out of the helicopter before it hit the ground, she'd fallen first, there was no way he could have hit the ground, and then she landed on top of him.

No way.

Lifting his head, Cooper looked around, but the helicopter was nowhere in sight.

Then he spotted it.

Red and orange dancing flames.

That was when it clicked.

The roaring that had awakened him had to have been the helicopter exploding. He was in it when it crashed, he was positive of that. Which meant the only reason he wasn't in it now, wasn't currently dead or burning to death, was because of the small weight resting against his chest.

Willow.

She'd saved his life.

She must have regained consciousness first and pulled him from the wreckage, anticipating that it might go up in flames.

Relief had tears welling in his eyes. Cooper hadn't cried since the day he was thirteen years old and learned his mother had apparently committed suicide in her cell so she didn't have to face the consequences of her betrayal of her country.

He'd cried then and he wasn't ashamed to admit he shed a tear or two now.

If Willow had dragged him from the wreckage, then she was alive. Against all odds, they had both survived the crash.

A miracle.

No other way to describe it.

Carefully, he reached out and smoothed Willow's hair. His body moved as he'd ordered it to, even if it hurt, so he had to assume he had not just survived but managed to do so without life-threatening injuries. Willow, too, because she'd dragged him a good hundred yards or so away from the remains of the helicopter.

"Willow, honey, can you hear me?" he asked as he shifted her body slightly so he could sit up. This woman never ceased to amaze him. Not only had she pulled him out of the wreckage and a safe distance away from it, but when the helicopter had exploded, she'd thrown her body over his before passing out.

Warmth spread through him. Willow was a keeper, that much he knew for certain. As uncertain as their future was it was nice to have that one thing to hold onto.

And he did hold onto it as he moved onto his knees and lay Willow's still form out before him. There was fresh blood on her face, and he noted several rips in her clothes that were also sticky with blood. As he ran his hands up and down her body, searching for anything he had to be immediately concerned about, he was beyond grateful when he didn't find anything.

Settling his fingertips on the wrist of her unbroken arm, he checked her pulse. It was exactly how he'd expect to find it given the trauma she'd just been through, but the very fact that it beat beneath his fingers was a testament to how lucky they had been.

"Willow?" he called her name again, brushing locks of hair away from the blood on her face.

There was no answer, and as badly as he wanted to be staring into her turquoise eyes, he accepted that she'd used up whatever strength she had after the crash by saving his life. Right now, her mind needed to protect itself and her body, and to do that, it had to shut down and allow itself some time to recoup.

"Thank you, honey. I won't ever forget what you did for me." Leaning down, Cooper brushed his lips to her forehead. No matter what happened between them, he wanted Willow in his life, even if he could only have her as a friend. She was strong, brave, loyal, determined, and someone he counted himself lucky to know.

Since there was nothing he could do for her right now, Cooper struggled to his feet, his own body longing for the respite of unconsciousness, but he had to check out the wreckage to see if anything was salvageable.

Just because they had survived the crash didn't mean they were out of the woods.

Or out of the desert.

Their situation was still precarious. They were both injured, both bleeding, and infection was a major concern. Willow had already been hurt before the crash, her body had already pushed up to and beyond its limits. Then there was the fact that as soon as the sun rose it was going to get hot. Really hot. Dehydration was their biggest concern right now. Injured as they were, it could take them out in less than a day. Lost as they were, they couldn't just sit around, no one was coming to rescue them, and no doubt, once the helicopter didn't show up, Mahmoud's men would be out searching for it. Which meant they had to move, water or not.

Heat was radiating off the wreckage as he approached it. He could see one body partially hanging out of the helicopter, it was likely the man he'd been fighting with when the gun went off and took out the helicopter's controls. That still left the pilot, but what were the chances that all three of them had survived the crash and escaped the wreckage before it exploded?

Not high.

Still, he rounded the burning remains and saw the body of the pilot still in his seat.

One worry out of the way. At least no one would be coming after them for at least a few hours.

If Mahmoud's men came looking for them while it was still dark, the burning wreckage was a dead giveaway to their location. There was nothing he could salvage from it. It was burning too badly for him to see if there had been water on board, or even a first aid kit which might have bandages and antibiotics.

There was one thing he could do though.

Scooping up a handful of sand, he threw it at the closest dancing flames. Slowly, Cooper circled the plane over and over again. Gathering as much sand as he could to douse the flames. It was hard, tiring work that made only a tiny bit of difference at a time, but eventually, he began smothering some of the flames.

"Cooper?" Willow's terrified voice called his name, and he turned to see her staggering through the dark toward him.

He was moving before he even realized it.

Snatched her into his arms and crushed her against his chest as soon as she was within reach.

Burying his face against her neck he inhaled deeply. Beneath the coppery scent of blood, and the heavy scent of gas in the air, he could smell Willow's sweet scent. She was there, she was alive, she was in one piece, and he hadn't lost her, although he'd come damn close time after time.

"You weren't there when I woke up," Willow whispered as she pressed against him as though she could meld their bodies together if she tried hard enough.

"Wanted to see if I could salvage anything."

"Could you?"

"No. The flames were too strong. Was just trying to douse them so it's not a flaming arrow pointing right to us."

"I'll help. If we work together, maybe we can put them out, and it'll buy us a little extra time."

When she went to pull back, Cooper tightened his hold on her. That right there was exactly why he had so much respect for Willow, why he didn't care that feelings were springing to life so quickly.

Beaten and battered as she was, exhausted and no doubt in agony, she was right there volunteering to help. They were in this together. As rough as this whole mess was, as much danger as they were still in, as badly as he wanted to take her, clean her up, bandage her wounds, make sure she wasn't in pain and got the rest she so badly needed, he was glad that she was by his side.

Right where he wanted to keep her.

This wasn't a woman he wanted to let go of, he liked having her by his side, and he was going to make sure nobody snatched her away from him.

Whatever he had to do he was going to slay all the dragons standing between him and a shot at a future with Willow.

~

July 13th
    3:31 A.M

Exhaustion tugged at every fiber of her being.

It clung to her just as the sand did.

Coating her body in a fine sheen of sweat that seemed to get heavier each time Willow leaned over and scooped up more sand to throw on the dwindling flames.

After what felt like hours of kicking and throwing sand onto the wreckage of the plane, to say her body was aching would be the understatement of the century. Adrenalin had long since worn off, and it had taken with it the mask that had initially covered some of her pain.

Now it screeched at her like an angry bird, making sure she knew she was pushing her body beyond what it could handle every time she moved. She was barely able to move now, but there were a few lingering flames, and she certainly wasn't going to leave this all to Cooper, he had to be hurting just as badly as she was.

They were in this together.

That's what she'd told him earlier and that's what she believed.

For better or worse, they would fight side by side against their common enemy.

Right now, Willow couldn't allow herself to think about what happened next. About what would happen if they managed to get out of Egypt alive and dismantled Allah's Warriors taking Professor Mahmoud down along with it.

There was every chance that Cooper would just walk away, after all, he owed her nothing. He'd helped her and got a boatload of trouble for his efforts, if she was him, she'd be grateful to get rid of the burden she represented.

Only ...

That wasn't how Cooper looked at her.

Each time she caught him staring at her, she could have sworn that burden was the last thing she saw in his gaze. Respect was there, maybe a little bit of awe, deeper things, too, like tenderness and affection. Maybe he didn't want to walk away as soon as he knew she was out of danger.

Maybe he wanted to stick around.

"Okay, honey, time to call it quits." Hands circled her shoulders, gently massaging the tight muscles around the back of her neck.

With a sigh of contentment, Willow sank back against Cooper's sturdy frame. Other than the blood and tears to his clothing, you wouldn't guess he'd just been kidnapped and in a helicopter crash. He looked so strong, so confident, his movements were sure and smooth, he was something else, and she found she liked watching him, even when all he was doing was kicking sand on a smoldering wreck of a helicopter.

"You think they know the helicopter didn't arrive by now?" she asked. Out there it was hard to keep track of the time. The sky was still inky black, stars twinkled merrily like they weren't shining down on death and destruction. The moon was moving across the sky like it always did, but she didn't know enough to figure out how to approximate time based on its position.

"I'm guessing they do."

"You think they're already looking for us?"

There was a slight pause, and his hands tightened their grip on her. "My guess is yes, they're assembling a search party and heading out here now to try to find us."

A shiver rocketed through her, and the overheated feeling she'd had while they threw sand at the smoldering helicopter suddenly disappeared leaving her feeling icy cold.

Of course, she'd known they'd be looking for her.

Professor Mahmoud *had* to look for her if he wanted even a chance at saving himself. What she'd told the mercenaries was true. She'd used Cooper's phone to call her boss, given him the passwords to the drive that held all her work files, and instructions to go ahead and put it all together in an article in a week if he didn't hear from her again. That same intel would also be sent to the appropriate authorities.

Regardless of whether she lived or died, the professor's life as he knew it was over.

Not that he'd stop coming after her.

Not until either he was dead or she was.

Revenge would eat away at him, even if he was battling charges, he would need to see her punished. Even if it wound up painting him in a worse light. He placed no value on women, and to be bested by one would be more than he could bear. In his mind, at least if he punished her and took her life, he would regain some of his standing and respect amongst the warriors.

"Hey, we're alive, and right now that counts for a lot," Cooper reminded her as he turned her around so she was facing him. "Don't lose hope now. We can't be all that far from where we came from, we can walk our way out of the desert."

Although she nodded in agreement, anxiety settled heavily in her stomach.

Sure, they *could* walk out of the desert and back to civilization. It wasn't out of the realm of possibility. But they were both injured, and as soon as the sun came up the temperature would rise, high and fast, and they had no water and no real likelihood of finding any.

Their situation wasn't just dangerous, it was precarious.

"I'll get you out of here, Willow. That's a promise."

There was so much determination behind those words that, despite all her doubts, she nodded again, this time a little more forcefully.

Cooper was right. They couldn't give up now. It was nothing short of a miracle that they were alive. That they'd survived the crash defied all odds. Giving up now would be almost disrespectful to the universe that had handed them this chance. A chance they couldn't waste.

"Okay," she agreed. "We give this everything we have. No giving up. If anyone can find their way out of the desert, then it's us for sure."

"That's my girl." The smile he beamed down at her warmed her, melting away a little of the icy fear that still clung to her body along with exhaustion. What warmed her more were his words.

He'd called her his girl.

A slip of the tongue or something he meant and had consciously decided to say?

Willow was too cowardly to ask.

Instead, she just leaned forward, pressed her cheek to Cooper's solid chest, tucked her head beneath his chin, and wrapped her arms around his waist. Maybe it made her selfish, but she was glad he was there with her. Of all the people who could have seen her in the professor's house, she was so grateful it was a man with enough honor and integrity to do something about it.

"We need to rest for a while," Cooper said, one of his hands absently stroking the length of her spine while the other palmed the back of her head.

"Shouldn't we start walking?" If the professor's men were already going to be heading out to search for the missing helicopter, they needed to put as much distance between themselves and the wreckage as quickly as possible.

"It's dark and we're both exhausted and hurting. If we try to walk now, we're likely to stumble, trip on the rocks, lose our footing in the sand, and hurt ourselves more. There were no lights around as we were going down, wherever we are, we're not close enough to a village that anyone should have reported the crash, which means, they've got no idea where to start looking. We need a couple of hours rest. We can afford this break," he added as though knowing she needed a little extra reassurance.

As badly as her body begged her for rest, Willow couldn't help but feel like they needed to just run as far and as fast as they could get from the helicopter.

But this was what Cooper did.

He'd been in Delta Force and now he worked for Prey Security. If he believed they could afford a couple of hours to rest and recharge, she shouldn't be arguing with him.

"Okay," she agreed, her eyes already growing heavy just at the prospect of sleep.

When he scooped her into his arms, Cooper killed the protest she'd been about to utter by feathering his lips across hers. "Shh, honey, don't argue with me. Let me carry you. Better to only have one set of footsteps leading away from the helicopter anyway. That way, if wind doesn't blow sand over our trails they at least won't know right away that we both survived."

"Don't want you to hurt yourself, I can walk," she told him, even though she burrowed into his embrace and rested her head on his shoulder, which made for a surprisingly comfortable pillow.

Carrying her a short distance from the wreckage, over a small hill that would provide them a little cover should Professor Mahmoud's men show up quicker than they thought, Cooper then sank down to sit in the sand. He kept her on his lap, his arms firm like steel bands around her, but she felt the softness to his hold.

"I'm glad I didn't lose you," she whispered sleepily, no longer able to fight off the darkness tugging at the corners of her mind.

"I'm glad I didn't lose you either," Cooper whispered back, and she felt his lips touch a kiss to her temple.

A smile was on her lips as she drifted off to sleep. They weren't safe, they might not survive the trek across the desert, but she had Cooper by her side, and somehow, that made everything better.

CHAPTER

Fifteen

July 13th
 5:28 A.M.

A scant couple of hours later, Cooper had to wake Willow.

She hadn't gotten even close to enough sleep. Her body would take weeks to recover from the physical and psychological trauma she'd been through, and two hours on the sand in the desert wasn't even enough to take the edge off her exhaustion.

But the sky was beginning to lighten, streaks of color painting beautiful pinks, reds, and golds across the expanse above them, and he knew that they had to get walking. In reality, spending these last couple of hours resting wasn't the smartest thing to do if they wanted to give themselves the best chance of getting out of there.

Only when it came to Willow he couldn't think clearly.

Torn between doing what he'd do if he was out there alone, or if he'd been with either his Delta team or Charlie team, which was get walking, get as much distance between them and the crash site, and doing what was in Willow's best interest. In that moment it was rest. She was running on empty, she'd given everything she had, and walking was out of the question for her at the time. While he would have carried her, he was wiped out, too, covered in bruises and gashes, body aching and screaming for rest, he wouldn't have been able to carry her indefinitely.

So sleep it had been.

Two hours was the best he could give her because now what was in Willow's best interest was to get them the hell out of there.

"Hey, honey," he murmured, stroking a lock of hair off her face, and touching a kiss to the side of her head. He was such a goner when it came to this woman, she'd blasted into his life like a hurricane, tossed him up, thrown him about until he lost all sight of anything but her.

Giving a small groan, Willow burrowed deeper into his arms, and he couldn't help but smile. She was adorable half asleep like this, all warm and soft and pliable. What would it be like to wake up with Willow in his arms when they'd spent the night in a real bed, after making love, falling asleep sated and safe?

There was no use denying he wouldn't love to find out, but now wasn't the time to focus on anything but their lives and their safety.

Later.

When they were out of danger he could see if she'd be interested in going out on a date with him.

"Come on, honey, you have to wake up."

"Don't wanna," she muttered, pressing her face against his neck.

Cooper chuckled. "I know you don't, honey. But the sun is rising and we have to get walking."

Another groan tumbled from her lips, but she lifted her head, blinked sleepily, and gave him a soft smile that shot like an arrow straight into his heart. "Did you get any sleep?"

"Dozed a little." It was all he could allow himself. While they'd both been kidnapped in Saqqara, and they'd both been in that crash, he was still streaks ahead because these were just the latest in a series of traumas Willow had endured over the last few weeks.

"I wish we could have had a proper bed to sleep in and about a week of uninterrupted time so we never had to get out of it," Willow said wistfully.

We.

A slip of the tongue, or had she meant she wanted to see him again after this ordeal ended?

"Hold onto that, honey," he told her as he framed her face with his hands and touched the softest of kisses to her lips. "You're going to need something for motivation to keep putting one foot in front of the other."

The truth was, they had hours at the least, possibly days' worth of walking to find their way out of there. Cooper wasn't sure they could do it. If he was on his own, he'd give himself a reasonable chance, but Willow was so weak. They'd already been concerned about cracked ribs, there was no way, if they'd only been bruised before, that they weren't broken now. Plus, there was the broken arm, and the finger one of their abductors had snapped, and bruises littering her body. Cooper didn't doubt that she would give this one hundred percent, but she couldn't give more than was in her.

Willow's face was serious as she looked back at him. Her gaze moved slowly from his lips to his eyes, and he felt something flow from her turquoise depths, he just wasn't sure what exactly it was he was feeling.

"Don't worry about me having motivation to keep walking, I have the best motivation in the world. I have to pee," she added without giving him a chance to respond to what she'd said, to ask what she was using for motivation.

"Sure thing." Gripping her elbows, Cooper stood, his body protesting every movement, each muscle screaming in pain, and brought Willow up with him.

The small, pained gasp was the only indication he knew she was going to give him that she was in agony. His heart urged him to sit her right back down, make her stay still so she didn't hurt herself worse, and just wait there and pray for a miracle.

His head reminded him no miracle was coming.

If they wanted to be rescued, they were going to have to do it themselves.

Breathing in short, sharp pants, Willow had scrunched her eyes closed, and he knew it had to be taking everything she had not to sink back down.

Torment plagued him.

He wanted to help her but ... there was nothing he could do. He had no medical supplies, no water, and no vehicle he could just stick her in and drive her out of there. He had absolutely nothing and it tore at him in a wave of helplessness that felt like it was going to pull him under and toss him around in a sea of despair he might not be able to fight his way out of.

If Willow herself hadn't been the one to break the spell that felt like it trapped them both in place, Cooper wasn't sure what he would have done, but he was sure it would have been led more by emotion than his training.

"Pee, right, I'm just going to hobble over there and take care of business," she said, giving him a tight smile and jerking her good hand at the other side of the small hill he'd used for protection while they rested.

How she managed to keep going after everything she'd been through he had no idea.

The woman was the Energizer bunny. While she maybe wasn't jumping about with spunk and sass, she just didn't give up no matter what life threw at her.

Taking care of business was a good idea, and once Willow disappeared, Cooper moved slightly away and did the same. Just as he was zipping back up, he saw Willow walking slowly but determinedly toward him and he felt a rush of tenderness sweep over him. As soon as he had her safe, he was going to fuss over her like she'd never been fussed over before. He would make sure her every need and want were taken care of.

"Ready to start walking?" Willow asked as she held out a hand.

"Ready." Cooper closed the distance between them and curled his fingers around hers, giving a slight squeeze. Despite the pain bracketing her mouth, and the fatigue in her eyes, she offered him a smile that warmed his chest.

Those first few steps were silent, but they hadn't gone more than half a mile before Willow broke it.

"So, I'm a little jealous that you have so many siblings. I always wanted a brother or sister, but after having me, my mom had complications and couldn't get pregnant again. What was it like growing up in a house with so many kids? Was it pure craziness?" she asked, a hint of wistfulness in her tone. If she'd had a sibling to help support the load after her dad's death, he was sure it would have been a lot easier to bear. Cooper knew he wouldn't have survived the aftermath of his parents' deaths without his siblings and stepsiblings. They were a family, and they always had one another's backs no matter what.

That's what he wished for Willow going forward. That she'd have a team there beside her, supporting her, watching over her, helping her not because she wasn't capable of going it alone, but because she shouldn't have to.

He wanted to be the one to give her that.

To be her teammate, to give her back a family after she'd so tragically lost hers when she was so young and needed them so desperately.

"The best kind of crazy," he told her as he tightened his grip on the hand that felt so small and fragile in his own. For now, they were teammates, and when they got home, he would fight for a chance with her. If friendship was all she wanted while she healed, then that's what he'd give her, he'd be the best friend she ever had. And when she was ready, he'd give her more. Give her everything.

But for now, hand in hand, they were going to face whatever was coming.

～

July 13th
    11:44 A.M

How had this ever seemed doable?

As Willow forced her body to take the next step, the one after, and the one after that, it felt less and less like she was capable of walking through the desert and back to a town or village.

Not just much less.

Impossible.

But as impossible as it felt she didn't have a choice.

One thing she knew for certain was that if she couldn't walk any further then Cooper would carry her until he collapsed from exhaustion. And if it came down to it, he would sit there with her in the desert under the blazing hot sun until she died.

Until he died.

That wasn't something she could allow to happen.

So, she had to keep walking. Had to keep finding strength she was sure she didn't have. Had to keep putting one foot after the other.

Sweat poured down her back. She'd tucked her broken arm inside her long-sleeve T-shirt, but it did little to stop it from throbbing with each step she took. Her head thrummed with a constant pounding headache that was likely a mixture of the head injuries, dehydration, and exhaustion. Even breathing hurt. If her ribs hadn't been broken before, the crash would have fractured them, which meant even if she stopped moving and could make the rest of her body rest, she had to keep breathing which meant she was never free of that pain.

After going on three weeks now since she'd been kidnapped, Willow barely remembered what it felt like *not* to be in pain.

It had consumed her for weeks and all she wanted was one tiny little break from it.

Only instead of getting a break, things just seemed to keep getting worse.

When Cooper rescued her from that little underground cell, she'd been naïve enough to believe that everything would be okay. They'd lay low, pretend to be tourists, let the dust settle a little, then get out of the country and return home. She'd write her article, Professor Mahmoud would be arrested, and she'd move on to her next story.

Naïve.

But not a mistake she'd make again.

Not after they'd been caught, tortured, almost died, and were now left to wander in the desert in the scorching heat. There was no way she would ever again be naïve enough to just believe that things would work out.

When her foot struck something, likely one of the many rocks lying beneath the layers upon layers of sand, Willow didn't have the energy to catch herself before she fell.

Her good arm cartwheeled, but it didn't help her regain her balance.

Instead, she landed hard.

Pain shot up her knees and into her legs when they struck rock, and she slumped forward, her bad arm getting squashed between her body and the ground as she toppled over.

A muted cry fell from her lips, and she would have been able to hold in her tears, only Cooper was right there. Crouching beside her, he gathered her up, righting her then sinking down to sit beside her, settling her between his spread legs and guiding her head to rest against his shoulder.

All she wanted was to keep walking. She didn't want to be the weak link and didn't want Cooper to lose his life because of her.

That's the only reason her tears fell.

They weren't necessarily tears of sorrow, although she was sad thinking that this was how Cooper's life might end. It was more from frustration. She'd come to Egypt to do the right thing, it shouldn't end this way.

It wasn't fair.

Sure, she knew life wasn't fair, she'd learned that lesson a long time ago when she stood at her front door and watched grown men beat her dad to death. But this was going so far beyond fair that it was hard to comprehend.

Willow wanted to have the strength to walk out of there and do what she'd set out to do, and now she was forced to confront the reality that she might not be able to do it.

"It's okay, honey," Cooper soothed, his hands gently stroking up and down her arms.

It wasn't though.

Not even close.

In fact, it was as far away from okay as it could be.

But Cooper was a good guy. He'd saved her life, he'd fought for her, and he didn't even know her. And now he was going to stay with her no matter what. He wouldn't leave her alone, not for anything, and that terrified her.

When she tried to struggle back to her feet, Cooper's fingers curled around her biceps, easily holding her in place.

"We have to keep walking," she protested, trying to force her way out of his hold.

It didn't work.

Cooper's hands held firm, his touch careful not to squeeze too hard on her bruised body, but they were still an unbreakable hold. "No, honey, we need to rest for a few minutes."

"We're not moving fast enough." Willow knew it was her fault, and she would give anything to change it, to have more strength, more stamina, and power through regardless of her injuries.

"We're moving as fast as we can."

"I'm sorry," she said, her voice catching on a sob she somehow managed to stuff back down before it could fully erupt.

"You don't have to apologize, you're giving this everything you have."

"It's not enough."

"It's all we can ever do, Willow."

Darn him for being so noble, honorable, compassionate, and kind. She wanted him to just ditch her and get himself out. After all, this was her mess not his.

There was only one thing she could do right now.

If she didn't give him permission, he wouldn't do it.

He was too caring, his heart was too big, and she wasn't going to allow it to get him killed. Not on her account.

Just because she hadn't known Cooper for long didn't mean this was hard to do. In fact, it was surprisingly easy. She might be signing her own death warrant, but she'd save Cooper's life and that was all that mattered.

It made this more than worth it.

Stopping fighting against his hold, Willow sank back against his chest, willing to take this one last moment to soak up the warmth and comfort of his touch. Because this was it. As soon as she said the words, it would all be over.

"Cooper?"

"Yeah?" There was a slight hint of trepidation in his tone like he somehow knew that whatever she was going to say, he wouldn't like.

Time to spit it out. The sooner she said it, the sooner he could get himself to safety. "You have to leave me behind."

His entire body went stiff.

The hands that had been smoothing up and down her arms stilled.

In fact, his chest barely rose and fell.

Seconds ticked by and he didn't say anything. Willow would have thought that he hadn't heard her, but she knew he had.

"Cooper? You know I'm right. I can't do this." Those words tasted bitter on her tongue. If there was one thing she hated, it was admitting failure. Normally, she wouldn't, but these weren't normal circumstances, and the stakes were higher than they had ever been before.

This was a matter of life and death. Cooper's life. Her death.

"You *can* do this," he countered vehemently, and the fingers on her biceps tightened until she winced, and he immediately loosened his hold. "You can do this, Willow, I don't want to hear you saying you can't."

"You think I like saying it?" she whispered. She hated it but it was true. Refusing to accept reality wasn't going to help either of them, least of all Cooper, and that was all she was focused on right now.

"I won't leave you," he said fiercely.

A sad smile curled her lips up. "I know you don't want to, but you have to, Cooper. I'm too weak, and the sun ... it's too hot ... I feel like I'm burning alive. Each step ... it's agony. Maybe I can go a little further, but I can't walk out of the desert. You can, Cooper. You have to. Please. I don't ... I don't want you to die because of me." Tears started falling down her cheeks in a torrent and she didn't even bother trying to hold them in.

"Oh, honey." Cooper shifted her so she was facing him, sitting on his lap. His hands framed her face, and his thumbs caught her tears. "There is not a chance in hell I am walking out of here and leaving you behind."

"But you have to," she wept.

"I don't have to. We keep moving forward together. I wish I had water for you, I wish I had shade, I wish I had painkillers and a bed so you could get the rest you need. I wish I could just transport you out of here and back home where you're safe. But, Willow, listen to me because I'm only going to say this once."

His hands stilled and he waited until she met his gaze squarely.

"We are in this together. We live together or we die together. It's as simple as that."

CHAPTER

Sixteen

July 13th
2:47 P.M.

For as long as he lived, Cooper would never forget that Willow had been prepared to sacrifice her own life to give him a chance at surviving.

If he hadn't already been falling hard and fast for her, that would have pushed him over the edge.

But he was falling, and reality was quickly crashing down around him.

When he'd dozed for those couple of hours early this morning, and he'd been thinking on what their next move was, he'd rated their chances of making it to a town or village as maybe eighty percent. It would be hard, but they hadn't been in the air all that long, so he didn't think they could have been overly far from civilization.

Hour by hour those odds were dropping.

Their injuries and the heat were affecting both of them, but he was in a much better position than Willow, and he was starting to genuinely believe that there was every chance she actually wasn't going to make it.

Thirst clawed at him, the temperature alone would have dehydrated them even if they'd had water. They would have had to be constantly guzzling down bottles of the stuff to keep enough water in their systems.

No water in the desert equaled certain death.

There was no way they could walk fast enough to get out of there before that happened. On his own, Cooper was sure it was doable, he wasn't as badly injured, and he could move a whole lot faster.

But for Willow ...

The truth was, her body was just too weak.

Which meant he now gave them a less than ten percent chance of surviving this ordeal, mostly because he wasn't ready yet to accept that this was hopeless.

Because once he did there was no going back.

One thing he knew for certain, though, was that he wasn't walking out of there and leaving Willow behind. If she wasn't going to make it there was no way in hell he was going to allow her to die alone in the desert.

No damn way.

If she died, then he'd have to make a choice. Try to walk out carrying her body or bury it in a layer of sand so it wouldn't be found if Tarek Mahmoud and his men searched this area, and leave some sort of marker so he could come back to it later. And he sure as hell would come back.

One way or another, he would bring her home.

Beside him, Willow suddenly cried out and dropped to her knees, her good hand scrambling to reach for her calf as tears streamed down her cheeks.

Tears were good, they meant there was still some water left in her body.

On the other hand, they were bad because Willow knew how to keep her emotions in check, and if she was at the stage where she was crying then she wasn't doing well.

"What's wrong, honey?" he asked anxiously as he knelt beside her, reaching for her good hand.

She batted it away and began to rub at her calf muscle. "C-cramps," she forced out as she clenched her teeth together.

Just what they needed.

They were creeping toward a medical emergency he didn't have the tools to deal with.

First, it was heat cramps, then it would progress to heat exhaustion, then following that would come heat stroke. Something she wouldn't survive if he couldn't get her out of the heat and get some water into her.

Helplessness crushed heavily upon his shoulders. It wasn't that he didn't want to help her, his entire body screamed at him to do something productive. But he couldn't. He could literally do nothing to help Willow, and it was killing him.

Forcing his fingers to uncurl from the fists they'd formed, he gently shifted her hand away from her legs. "Here, honey, let me do it."

Teeth still clenched, Willow sank back to lie against the hot sand. Heat was everywhere, it surrounded them, it was in the ground, it was in the air, the sun shone relentlessly on them, and there was not a single tree to give them a little relief.

Massaging her cramps wasn't going to do a damn thing to help her. This wasn't just an overuse problem that working out the kinks in the muscles was going to solve. The only thing that would relieve her of the pain was water.

Right now, he would sell his soul to the devil himself for a bottle of the stuff.

Or for a village to appear on the horizon.

Anything.

Literally, anything that would prevent him from having to stand helplessly by and watch Willow die while he was powerless to do anything about it.

"I'm sorry, Willow," he whispered forlornly. If he was going to have any chance of processing her impending death, he needed her to know how sorry he was that he couldn't save her.

Lifting her head just enough to look at him, her brow furrowed as she asked, "For what?"

"Not getting you somewhere safe, for all of this." He waved a hand at the desert surrounding them on all sides and their mortal enemy the sun.

"None of this is your fault," she said softly. Although he could feel the tension in her body, and knew the cramps had to be excruciating, somehow she managed a smile for him, and it had tears burning the backs of his eyes.

How was she so strong?

He knew she knew what was coming, it was why she'd tried to convince him to leave her behind. Yet even staring death in the face she was being so damn brave. She was still walking alongside him even as he had to slow his pace until they were barely crawling along. They alternated between him carrying her and her walking a little on her own, but they weren't making anywhere near enough progress to outrun the inevitable.

Cooper's fingers tightened on her leg as though he could somehow force the cramps from her body. "I should be able to do ... something," he hissed in frustration.

"Like the impossible?"

"Damn the impossible. I want to make it possible. I won't let you die out here," he roared into the empty desert.

Pushing herself up into a sitting position, Willow's hands covered his, gently easing them off her cramped muscles, then entwined their fingers together. "That's exactly why I'm falling for you," she murmured.

His gaze darted to her face in shock.

Relief that he wasn't the only one who felt this pull drawing them closer momentarily wiped away a little of his fear that he was going to lose Willow before he ever had a chance to make her his.

"I know I've only known you a couple of days, but I've never felt for another man anything even close to what I already feel for you. I just ... I wanted you to know." Her gaze dipped and she didn't need to finish that sentence. Didn't need to say she wanted him to know because she more than likely wasn't going to survive this.

Framing her face, Cooper crushed his lips to hers. This time, it was no sweet, delicate kiss, this time he poured everything into it. These feelings he was developing for her, his helplessness, his regret, how badly he wanted to have a chance with her. All of it. Because this might be his only chance. Willow was deteriorating quickly, and hours might be all he had left with her.

"You're not the only one," he told her when he finally pulled back enough that he could see her face. "I feel it, too. It's crazy, but it's so strong. It's like my soul is screaming out for yours."

Tears trickled down her cheeks as she nodded. "I wish we would have gotten a chance."

"We still have it, it's not gone yet," he said fiercely. While he might not be able to give Willow's body the water it needed, he could make sure she didn't give up. That he could give her. For weeks, she'd been fighting this alone, but she wasn't alone anymore, and he could fight hard enough for both of them.

"Cooper—"

"No. I won't let you give up. Not yet. Not while we're both still breathing." Maybe he couldn't stop the inevitable from happening, but he'd sure as hell give it the best chance he could and fight with everything he had.

Scooping her into his arms he started walking again.

There was no way he was going to just sit there and watch her die right in front of him.

He was going to get them both out if it killed him.

While he might last longer than Willow, death was certain for both of them unless he could find help.

"Talk to me," Willow said, exhaustion lacing every word as she rested her head against his shoulder. "Tell me anything, I don't care what, I just like hearing your voice."

That was something he could do.

Temporarily buoyed by having a practical task to do to make things at least a little better for Willow, Cooper did his best to shove all thoughts of the fact that Willow might not even make it to sunset when the temperatures would fall a little, and just started talking.

~

July 13th
5:13 P.M

Why wouldn't the world stop spinning?

She wasn't even walking on her own, she was over Cooper's shoulders in a fireman's carry, and yet it felt like the world had sped up until it was like one of those crazy fair rides where you got whipped around in circles until it felt like you were going to throw up.

In fact, Willow did feel like she was going to throw up.

Nausea churned in her stomach, and she was sure that if anything was in there, she would have already embarrassed herself in front of the man she liked by vomiting all over the sand.

So, she supposed it was some small mercy that she hadn't eaten in over twenty-four hours.

Why couldn't the sun give them just a tiny break?

What she wouldn't give for clouds to form, blocking out some of the sun's rays and giving her and Cooper a respite from the relentless heat.

Unfortunately, it was still hours until the sun would set and give them a little relief. Not that the temperature drop would be enough to save them, but maybe it would at least slow down the progression of dehydration and heat stroke enough to buy them a few more hours.

It was clear Cooper wasn't going to give up.

He was going to walk himself into an earlier grave by his determination to power on even though he, too, was struggling with the same effects she was, just a little slower.

She was worried about him.

Maybe she should be more worried about herself. She was the one who was more quickly succumbing to dehydration and heat stroke, but she had a feeling her death was going to do terrible things to him. Willow absolutely one hundred percent wanted Cooper to live even if she didn't, of course she did, why wouldn't she? But she didn't want him carrying around a weight of guilt for not saving her. That was no way to live.

All she wanted for Cooper was for him to be happy.

To find the answers he needed about his mom so he could get some closure and focus more on his future and less on his past. To find someone to love him as much and as deeply as she would have if they'd had the chance to get to know one another properly and allow these tiny little feelings to grow into something more.

When Cooper stumbled, barely managing to regain his footing before they both hit the ground, Willow knew she had to do something.

Had to make him stop and rest for a while.

Make him see reason.

"Cooper, stop," she said as insistently as she could manage through the blaring headache that had taken up residence between her temples and the dizziness that made her feel like she was still moving even as she registered Cooper had stopped.

"What's wrong?" he asked, panicked, as he crouched down and laid her out in the sand.

It felt much too hot against her already overheated skin, and it was hard not to get sidetracked thinking about how wonderful it would be to sink into a nice cool bath and be surrounded by cold rather than hot.

Heaven.

That's what it would be, but it wasn't something she should be focused on right now.

Not when Cooper needed her.

This might be her last chance to have a cognizant conversation with him. Already it was getting harder and harder to focus, and she didn't know how long she had left, she just knew the end was coming faster than either of them wanted.

"Honey?" Cooper's hand brushed over her forehead, lingering a little before sweeping around to cradle the back of her head in his palm. "Damn, honey, you're so hot."

Helpless frustration was radiating off him in waves, and Willow felt a swell of grief inside her. They could have built something wonderful between them, she was sure of it. Given a chance, they could have fallen in love and lived a long and happy life together.

Instead, they were both likely going to die in the middle of the Egyptian desert.

Shock stole her breath for a moment when she tried to lift her hand to caress Cooper's stubbled jaw only to find that she didn't have the strength for even that simple task.

"What's wrong?" Cooper immediately demanded, picking up on her distress.

"I can't ... lift my hand ... I'm so weak ..." she murmured, finding she barely had the strength to talk let alone move.

She was deteriorating even quicker than she had realized.

How much longer did she have left?

It was still hours until sunset, and even then, the temperature wouldn't drop low enough to be cold. If they were lucky, they might hit the high sixties, which would certainly be a whole lot nicer than now, but it wouldn't be enough to undo the damage the sun had caused.

Tortured gray eyes stared down at her, so tumultuous, so stormy that if she'd had any tears left in her, they would have cascaded down her cheeks.

"I'll keep carrying you, honey, all you have to do is focus on breathing and staying with me."

That was the problem.

Cooper was pushing himself so hard to compensate for her lack of strength that he was going to push himself into an earlier grave. He had to pull back a little and prioritize his body's needs. Willow didn't want to take her last breath knowing that Cooper was going to quickly follow her into death.

"No," she insisted as firmly as she could manage.

"No what?"

"No more carrying me. You need to rest. Tonight, when it's dark, you'll be able to walk faster then, use up less of your body's dwindling reserves of water," she explained. This next part was a lie, but she said it anyway. "Maybe I'll be able to walk better when the air isn't so hot."

In truth, there was no way she was going to be able to walk more than a handful more steps before her body was officially done.

Any steps she did manage to force her body to take would be slow and unsteady. The cramps were bad, they equaled the throbbing in her head, and the only thing that was worse was her body's pleas for water.

Pleas she couldn't satisfy because she had no water to drink.

Part of her wished that she'd just died in the crash. At least it would have been done and over with. This was like prolonging the whole thing and the ending was still going to be the same.

She wished she could make Cooper understand that.

Her fate was already sealed. Unless a magical oasis suddenly appeared out of nowhere, and she was able to guzzle down as much water as she wanted then bathe in it and cool her body down, she wasn't going to live.

This wasn't her giving up, it was simply accepting reality.

The quicker Cooper accepted it the better off he'd be.

At least then maybe he could start making decisions that were in his best interest instead of worrying about her. Willow couldn't deny it felt nice to know she mattered to him enough he still wanted to believe that she could be saved, but not nice enough to know it was going to cost him his life.

"The dark is only going to make it harder for us to see where we're going, easier for us to trip and fall," Cooper reminded her.

That might be true, and it might have mattered this morning when they started out on this journey, but not now.

Now it was the sun and their exertion that was killing them. She'd rather risk them falling on the rocks that were everywhere beneath the sand, it was the lesser of the two evils they faced.

"I know earlier you didn't want to hear it, but—"

"No," Cooper growled at her. The sound might have terrified her if she didn't know him well enough to know he'd never hurt her. Now it just made her smile sadly at him.

"Cooper, you have to accept the inevitable," she said softly. This wasn't a conversation she believed she'd ever have with another person, that she'd have to talk about her impending death calmly and factually felt surreal. But she had to do what she had to do.

"It's not inevitable," he snapped.

Summoning what she had left, Willow managed to lift her hand off the ground and brushed her fingertips across Cooper's jaw. "It is. I'm dying. Without a miracle, I'm not going to survive. We both know that. You have to accept it, because ... I don't want you to die, too." A sob caught in her throat. "Please. I don't want to die knowing I'm going to be the cause of your death. You still stand a chance if you leave me behind. But if you wait much longer then you seal your own fate."

Gripping her shoulders, Cooper gave her a small shake, and she bit back a moan as pain sliced behind her eyes. "Get this through your head. I am not leaving you behind. Not now, not ever. I will get you out of here."

His harsh words were softened when he briefly rested his forehead against hers, but then he was standing, gathering her into his arms, and walking again.

Stubborn.

That's what he was.

And while she admired tenacity and determination, this time those qualities were only going to wind up getting a man she cared about killed.

She was going to get a man she cared about killed.

And Willow had no idea how to stop it from happening.

CHAPTER

Seventeen

July 13th
    10:03 P.M.

@stop hereIn his career in Delta Force and at Prey, Cooper had seen a lot of atrocities.

He'd heard the screams of the dying, stared into cold, dead eyes of evil men, and rescued children from certain death.

Nothing was harder than this.

Sitting helplessly under the clear inky sky, dotted with millions of glittering stars twinkling merrily like they weren't watching an innocent woman die.

And Willow was dying.

As much as he'd love to hang onto denial, pretend it wasn't happening, that a miracle was suddenly going to come blasting through the night, Cooper had to accept reality.

Over the last couple of hours, Willow had continued to deteriorate. Her speech had become slurred, she'd become confused and agitated, fighting against him as he tried to carry her.

By the time the sun had sunk low in the sky and then disappeared altogether, it had taken his last shreds of hope along with it. Acceptance had sunk in and now all he could do for Willow was stay by her side, hold her head on his lap, her hands in his, and make sure she wasn't alone as she passed.

It wasn't enough.

Never in his life had he wanted to save someone as badly as he did this woman who had blasted into his life and wriggled her way under his skin with her bravery and strength. She was a fighter, and even now, she was hanging on. While her breathing was too fast, and her pulse beat a harsh staccato beat against his fingertips, each time he touched them to her wrist, she was still alive.

For now.

But would she still be alive when the sun rose again, baking them with its inescapable heat?

Cooper feared she wouldn't.

Even if she was, there was nothing else he could do for her. Unless water and shade suddenly sprung up out of nowhere, he didn't have the tools necessary to save her life. Another hour or two and even that wouldn't be enough. Once her body got past a certain point there would be no going back, even if he managed to find them a safe haven.

"Come on, Willow. Hold on for me. I know I'm asking the impossible, but I can't let you go. I need you to fight," he pleaded as he brushed his knuckles across the hot, dry skin on her cheeks.

There was no way he wasn't going to blame himself for Willow's death. What he could have done differently, he had no idea, nor did it matter. He'd failed her.

Bright lights suddenly broke through the darkness, and Cooper's head snapped up.

Someone was coming.

Salvation or certain death?

Those were the only options.

It was either Tarek Mahmoud's men who had finally managed to track them down, or a random person who could transport them to a town or village.

Carefully easing Willow's head off his lap, he quickly moved away from her, wanting to put a bit of distance between them. If it was the professor's men, he could always lie and say Willow had already died and he'd left her body behind. There was a chance they'd search the area anyway, and even if they believed him and only took him, it wasn't like Willow was strong enough to walk out alone. But it might give her a couple of extra hours and who knows what could happen in that time.

Knowing he could be signing his own death warrant, Cooper also knew he had no choice but to wave down the vehicle. If it was Mahmoud, then all that would happen was he'd hasten their deaths by a couple of hours, but if it was anyone else then he still had a chance to save Willow's life.

Running toward the approaching vehicle, he shouted and waved his arms, praying that he wasn't making a mistake.

The vehicle slowed, it was make-it-or-break-it time.

Body tense, weak as he was, mouth dry as the sand surrounding them, sunburn on his exposed skin, dying for a drink of water, the beginnings of muscle cramps hindering him, Cooper was ready to pounce if these were Mahmoud's men.

No way would he go down without a fight.

"Coop?"

His twin brother's voice was the last thing he expected to hear in the vast desert.

"Connor?" he asked, barely able to believe what he was hearing. Was this the equivalent of a mirage? Was he losing it, too?

More figures climbed out of the vehicle. He recognized every single one of them. Connor, Cade, Cole, Jax, and Jake. His brothers. His team. Here. In Egypt.

"What are you doing here?" he asked, frozen in shock.

"Jumped on a plane when you didn't check in yesterday," Cade explained.

Yesterday?

Was it really only a little over twenty-four hours ago that they'd been caught at the Step Pyramid in Saqqara? Forty-eight since he'd rescued Willow from that underground cell?

It felt like a lifetime.

While he wanted to know how his brothers had found him, it wasn't what was most important right now.

"Willow," he said, turning and running back toward where he'd left her. His knees hit the sand beside her and his hand immediately reached for her neck. Relief slammed through him as her rapid pulse thumped against his fingertips.

Still alive.

He hadn't lost her yet, and now he actually had a chance of saving her life.

There was no need to make sure his brothers had followed him, he knew they would. Knew they had his back. Hell, they'd jumped on a plane and managed to track him down in Egypt.

"What happened?" Cole asked as he knelt beside Willow and immediately reached for her wrist to check her pulse. Cole was a medic, and never traveled anywhere without a fully stocked first aid kit.

"What didn't," he said wearily. "We got caught by Mahmoud's men. They took us to a warehouse and broke Willow's finger when she wouldn't give them what they wanted. They were transporting us on a helicopter to meet with Mahmoud who was going to kill us."

"Tell me you didn't," Cade said, voice tight.

"I did."

"You crashed a helicopter?" Jax asked incredulously.

"Well, it wasn't on purpose, but it did get us away from them. Willow is suffering from dehydration and heat stroke." His voice had a pleading quality that he knew his brothers wouldn't have missed. But thankfully no one called him on it.

"How long as she been unconscious?" Cole asked as he began to rifle through his medkit.

"She'd been fading all day, but she passed out about an hour or so ago, hardly stirred since," he answered as he reached out to grab Willow's good hand, clutching it tightly between his.

"We have to get her temperature down," Cole said. "Get all the water we have in the truck," he ordered the others.

While Connor, Cade, Jake, and Jax ran off to do as Cole ordered, Cooper stared helplessly at his little brother. "Tell me it's not too late," he begged.

Cole's dark eyes met his, the truth was plainly written in them. "We'll do everything we can for her, okay?"

Cooper nodded because what else was there to say?

Help had arrived in enough time to save him, but maybe not to save Willow.

"Let's strip her clothes off," Cole said, but sat back and allowed Cooper to be the one to remove the long-sleeve T-shirt and jeans he'd bought for her, baring her pale, bruised skin to the moonlight.

His brother's jaw tightened as he took in the bruises littering almost every inch of Willow's body. "She went through hell," he snarled.

"She did."

"She survived it. She's a fighter," Cole added as he pulled out an IV kit and started setting it up. "We're going to pump fluids into her and get her temperature down. Start washing her down," he ordered as the guys returned with several bottles of water. "Don't worry about saving any, we can get more when we get to a motel. I'm giving her fluids intravenously, so keep a bottle or two for Cooper, the rest is best used to cool Willow down."

"We've got icepacks in here, too," Jake said.

"Neck, groin, and armpits for those," Cole ordered. "You, drink first." His little brother pointed a finger at him then the bottle of water he'd just set down on the sand beside him.

"Willow needs—"

"Willow is getting what she needs," Cole countered. "Right now, you're also dehydrated and need water. Just because it hasn't progressed as quickly doesn't mean you aren't also in the early stages of heat exhaustion. Rest. Drink. Trust your team to have your back and hers."

Trust wasn't the problem right now.

There was nobody in the world he trusted more than his brothers and stepbrothers—and his little sister, but right now Cassandra was safe at home—but they weren't miracle workers, and in the last forty-eight hours Willow had become important to him.

Knowing there was still a good chance he could lose her, that help had arrived too little too late, made it almost impossible to breathe.

What was he going to do if she didn't make it?

~

July 14^(th)
  8:08 P.M

She was cool.

That was the first thing that struck Willow as her groggy mind swum through the thick, foggy swamp it was stuck in and back toward consciousness.

Other than one side of her body which was toasty warm, the rest of her was cool almost to the point of being too cold.

Blinking open confused eyes, it took her a moment to realize that she was no longer surrounded by endless blue sky and sand in every direction. Instead, there were walls painted a light gray, with darker gray curtains covering the windows. It was hard to tell what time it was because she couldn't see the sky, but whenever it was and wherever she was it was a whole heck of a lot nicer than the desert had been.

Shifting slowly, Willow was pleased to see that her pain had dulled until it was more of a nuisance than anything else, and for the first time in what felt like forever she wasn't dying for a sip of water.

Where was she?

As she turned her head, she saw Cooper's big body laid out beside her, fast asleep. He must be the source of the warmth, and she smiled as she looked at him. Peaceful for the first time since she'd met him. The gash on his head had been stitched and his face was clean, she felt clean, too, and it finally sank in that they'd been rescued.

They'd gotten their miracle.

Tears stung her eyes, and as much she wanted to wake Cooper and celebrate, he needed the rest. If he felt safe enough to go to sleep in a bed beside her then wherever they were was a secure location.

It wasn't until she realized she needed to pee that she heard hushed voices.

Panic immediately followed.

Voices meant people.

People could mean danger.

Heart racing and pulse thundering in her ears, Willow tried to reassure herself that there was no way Cooper would go to sleep if they weren't safe.

It didn't work.

Carefully, she lifted her head, wincing at the pain between her temples, even dulled it was enough to almost tear a groan from her lips. Somehow, she managed to keep it in and scanned the dim room.

There.

On the opposite side from the bed.

Men.

Five of them.

Big, scary-looking men.

They were sitting around a table and didn't appear to realize she was awake.

Did she need a weapon? Chances were there were none around and she could hardly drag Cooper out of there with her. Heck, she could barely hold her head up, she was in no condition to either run or fight.

As though sensing her growing distress, one of the men looked over at her, and her heart felt like it beat its way right out of her chest.

The man.

He looked exactly like ... Cooper.

Brow furrowing in confusion, she looked beside her, but Cooper was still there, fast asleep.

There was no way he could be in two places at the same time.

Had her mind finally snapped?

Was this just all some pre-death delusion?

Rising slowly, the man held up his hands, palms out, and cautiously made his way toward the bed where she lay. Behind him the other four men also turned in her direction, and Willow whimpered and pressed herself into the pillows.

They didn't look like a delusion, and this didn't feel like some hallucination. Two of the other men also looked like Cooper and his double, who was still making his way toward her.

"Shh," he soothed as he approached. Other than the fact that his eyes were blue instead of gray, he looked exactly like the man lying asleep beside her. "It's okay, Willow. I'm Connor, Cooper's twin brother.

Behind me are Cade and Cole, and Jax and Jake. Did Cooper tell you who we were?"

Giving a shaky nod, her gaze darted between Connor, the others, and then Cooper. "H-how did you f-find us?"

Last she knew they'd been out in the desert, she'd been no longer able to walk, and Cooper, stubborn man that he was, had been carrying her, then everything had faded away. Try as she had she'd been unable to hold her eyes open any longer, and even though she knew that as soon as she lost consciousness that could be it for her, she might never wake up again, she hadn't been able to stop it from happening.

"Cooper's watch has a tracker in it. We tracked it to the desert, but then lost the signal. We were driving around looking for you guys when we found Cooper waving us down," Connor explained.

"You were lucky we found you when we did," one of the other men told her as he also approached the bed. "I'm Cole. May I?" he asked, nodding at her arm which she now realized had an IV running from her elbow to a bag that was looped around the top of the bedpost.

Tentatively, she nodded and forced herself not to tense when he perched on the edge of the mattress beside her. Cooper's warm body was still pressed against her side, and it was a testament to how exhausted he was that he hadn't woken yet.

"Just going to check your pulse, okay?" Cole asked, waiting until she nodded her assent before his fingertips pressed against the inside of her wrist. "You're doing better," he told her with a smile a few seconds later.

"You guys saved me. Us," she added, looking down at Cooper. "Thank you."

"That's what family is for," Connor told her with an easy smile.

"How long have we been here?" Willow asked.

"Going on twenty-four hours since we found you two," one of Cooper's stepbrothers replied, only she wasn't sure which. He must have seen her confusion because he gave her a warm smile. "I'm Jax. That's Jake," he said, pointing to his brother.

"Twenty-four hours?" Had she been asleep that long?

"You weren't in good shape when we found you," Cole explained. "We started cooling you down with water and got an IV with fluids going then got you into our truck. Put you in a cold bath when we got here to the motel, but it took several hours before your temperature dropped enough that I was satisfied you were going to be okay. Came pretty close to having to risk a trip to the hospital."

"I'm glad you didn't have to, it would have put targets on all your backs." Willow dropped her head, unable to meet their gazes any longer. "I'm sorry for almost getting Cooper killed."

She could only imagine how much they must resent her.

If it wasn't for her, their brother would have taken the intel he got from the professor and headed safely back home to his family. Instead, he'd almost been killed several times over and they'd had to hop on a plane and fly halfway around the world to rescue him.

"Look at me." The hard voice offered no option to disobey, and when she lifted her gaze, she found Cade's dark eyes drilling into her. "None of that talk. It's not your fault and you don't apologize for someone else's actions. You did nothing wrong. Cooper's made it clear that you're important to him, he wouldn't let himself rest until we knew you were out of danger. If you're important to him then you're important to every single one of us. Got it?"

Sure her mouth was hanging open in shock and she was staring at him with wide eyes, Willow found she couldn't do anything else but nod.

When she looked around at the other men, she found they were all nodding in agreement, and she couldn't help but feel she'd just kind of been adopted into this family she didn't know just because of a man she'd known a couple of days.

"Is Cooper okay?" she asked, looking down at his still sleeping form.

"Better than you," Cole answered. "Nothing broken, a couple of cuts that needed stitches. In addition to the dehydration and heat stroke, I stitched your head and another few cuts I was worried about. Strapped your arm which is almost definitely broken, and splinted your finger. Cheekbone is also broken and I'm pretty sure you have at least a couple of cracked ribs. You also have more bruises than I've ever seen on a person before."

"Professor Mahmoud liked having his own personal punching bag," she said softly.

The protective energy in the room surged, and despite everything,

Willow chuckled as she looked at the big, burly men surrounding her who looked like they'd give anything to get their hands on the professor.

"Umm, this is a little embarrassing, but I have to pee," she announced.

Cole grinned at her. "Music to my ears. Means your body is hydrated again. After you go, we can take the IV out."

Disconnecting it from the port in her arm, he helped her swing her legs over the edge of the bed and kept a steadying hand on her arm until the spinning in her head stilled enough that she wasn't going to fall over.

As she hobbled into the bathroom, Willow wondered what happened when they got home. She and Cooper had admitted there were feelings there, but that didn't mean they would work out. What if once the adrenalin was gone, and they were no longer in danger and running for their lives, he decided he was no longer interested in her? What if he was just one of those guys who had a savior complex and once she didn't need saving anymore she lost her appeal?

CHAPTER

Eighteen

July 14th
8:20 P.M.

There was no longer a body curled up at his side.

The realization was enough to snap Cooper from sleep to find the bed beside him was indeed empty.

Jerking upright, it took his brain a little longer to process things than it did for his panic to kick right on in. Taking in the motel room, and his brothers standing around the bed, his panic eased only marginally.

They might be out of the desert, but that didn't mean everything was magically fixed.

It had taken them hours to get Willow's temperature down enough that Cole was satisfied she was improving. Along the way, there had been half a dozen times they'd come too close to needing to risk it all and take her to the hospital.

Once he was sure she was going to be okay he'd finally crawled into bed beside her and allowed himself to crash.

Had that been a mistake?

Had something happened while he was asleep?

While he knew his brothers would never lie to him, he also knew that if something had gone wrong, if Willow's condition had suddenly taken a turn for the worse, they would try to cushion the blow and deliver it in the gentlest way possible.

"Relax, bro, before you have a coronary," Cole told him before Cooper could open his mouth and demand to know what they'd done with Willow.

Even if she'd passed away, they should know that he didn't want her alone.

Not even for a second.

"She's in the bathroom," Connor explained.

"The bathroom?" he repeated, relief slowing his heartbeat to a more normal rate. "And you let her go alone?"

Jax chuckled. "Don't think your girl wanted an audience while she peed, dude."

There was no embarrassment that came with his brothers referring to Willow as his. While they had all agreed that their priority was finding the truth about what happened to their parents, they all still knew they were allowed to have their own lives outside of that.

So far Cade had been the only one to ever have a relationship serious enough that it turned into love. While they all had their suspicions that his daughter's nanny's quite obvious feelings for him weren't as nonreciprocal as Cade pretended they were, none of them had ever gone for it with a woman.

Well, he was going to go for it with Willow.

Not giving this thing with her a chance would be the biggest mistake of his life. He'd already gotten a taste of what it would be like to live without her when he'd thought she was going to die, and he didn't want a repeat.

"She can't be strong enough to be up and about on her own," he rebuked his brothers as he climbed out of the bed. It wasn't rocket science. He'd told them, in great detail, what Willow had been through. Didn't they have a brain between them?

"I think that woman is strong enough to do anything," Jake countered.

Before Cooper could agree with his stepbrother's assertion, the bathroom door opened, and Willow limped out. With most of the dirt washed off her face, and a little color back in her cheeks, she looked a million times better than she had when he'd left her side to run toward the approaching vehicle.

Her eyes widened when she saw him standing there, and it felt like the rest of the world faded away as their gazes locked. He had no idea how long they stood there staring at one another, but the next thing he knew she was moving toward him and he was closing the gap between them, snatching her off her feet and into his arms.

Where she belonged.

"We're alive," she whispered, pressing her face against his neck.

"Thought I lost you," he admitted, burying his face in her hair and breathing in her scent, letting it invade his nostrils and then his body, reassuring him that she was alive and as well as could be expected after what they'd been through.

"You didn't lose me, I'm right here." The arms she had wrapped around his neck tightened and she lifted her face and shot him a brilliant smile before touching her lips to his.

Cooper was sure the kiss was supposed to be quick, chaste, but he immediately tangled a hand in her long, blonde locks and deepened it. His tongue sweeping inside her mouth, in a fiery kiss that under other circumstances would lead to a whole lot more.

But now wasn't the time.

Willow might be awake, but she'd almost died, she was weak, and injured, had to be in pain, and likely still exhausted.

A mewed protest fell from Willow's lips when he pulled back, and clear desire shimmered in her turquoise eyes.

"Later," he promised as he touched a kiss to the tip of her nose.

"Definitely later because right now, with all of us watching, would be totally weird," Cole joked, making them all laugh.

Shifting his hold on Willow so he was cradling her against his chest, Cooper carried her over to the table where it was clear his brother's had been hanging out and sat, settling Willow in his lap. There was no way he wasn't going to keep her as close to him as physically possible until they'd eliminated the threat hanging over her head.

They might have made it out of the desert, but they were far from safe.

So long as he was alive and free, Tarek Mahmoud was a danger to Willow. She had the ability to destroy him and even if he couldn't stop it from happening, the professor wanted to ensure he got his revenge on her.

"Let's take your IV out," Cole said, pulling up a chair beside them.

"Here. Drink some water," Cade said gruffly, taking a bottle and unscrewing the lid before handing it over to Willow who took it with a smile.

If his older brother's gruff manners put her off, Willow didn't show it. While he cared fiercely about the people in his life, Cade wasn't one to sugar coat things, or handle them with care, unless they were talking about his daughter. But he'd accepted Willow as one of them, as had all his brothers, and Cade would treat her as such.

"You should eat something, too," Cole said as he reached for her elbow and removed the needle, replacing it with a ball of cotton wool and a Band-Aid.

Scrunching up her nose, Willow gave a small shake of her head, even as she sighed. "I'm not all that hungry, I know I should be but I'm not. You're right though, I should eat."

"You almost died," Cooper reminded her. As much as he hated to say the words, they were true. Willow had been through so much, she wasn't just going to magically bounce back to full strength. It would take time, a lot of it, before she was fully recovered. "Baby steps. Why don't you try some fruit, that should be light on your stomach."

"We have oranges," Jake said, holding one out to Willow. "It'll help with hydration, plus lots of vitamins and minerals."

"Thanks," Willow said, accepting the piece of fruit.

"Let me check your eyes first," Cole directed, pulling out a penlight.

"I'll cut the orange for you," Cooper told her, there was no way she could hold it and cut it with a broken arm and finger.

"You're doing as well as could be expected," Cole announced after checking her pupils and then taking her pulse. "I'd feel much better if a doctor checked you out, and a couple of your wounds are going to need to be watched for infection, but as long as you take some time to rest and recover you should be okay."

"I don't have time," Willow reminded them as she took the piece of orange he held out and took a bite. "Professor Mahmoud is still out there and he's not going to just back off. He must know by now that we weren't in that helicopter when it crashed. Maybe he'd be prepared to let Cooper go, but he's not going to feel the same about me. I won't stop until he's held accountable for what he's done," she said with the glint of determination in her eyes that he'd come to recognize as being innately Willow Purcell.

"We were thinking we'd sneak you out of the country," Connor said. "He knows you have Cooper as back up, but he doesn't know you now have all of us. Once you're back home you can finish up your article and hand over everything you have on him so far to Prey. Eagle would be more than happy to bring down a man like Tarek Mahmoud, I'm sure of it."

"Actually," Willow said slowly, dragging out the word as though she knew what she was about to say he wasn't going to like.

If it was anything other than getting herself as far away from danger as possible and having a twenty-four seven bodyguard then she'd be right.

Her safety was his number one priority.

"Actually what?" he asked tightly.

"I have a plan to catch the professor," she said, meeting his gaze squarely even as he could read the apology in it.

"A plan?" Jax asked.

"One that I'm sure will work," Willow said.

"What is it?" he demanded, harsher than he should have, but anxiety had already raged to life inside him.

"I play bait."

~

July 14th
  8:34 P.M

. . .

"You what?" Cooper asked, voice low and dangerous.

Willow fought the urge to shrink down, to pacify the obvious fear billowing off Cooper.

It was a new experience for her. She had basically been on her own since she was eight years old. Maybe her mom was physically present but that was it. Not only wasn't she emotionally and psychologically present, but she didn't take care of any of her parental responsibilities.

So, Willow had learned to do it all herself.

Learned to become self-sufficient.

Even as an adult, she rarely found herself relying on other people except for the most basic things like doctors, dentists, mechanics, and pilots. Any skill she couldn't do herself she sought out an expert, but that wasn't working as a team, that was just them performing a skill she didn't have.

This was the first time she had a team at her back.

The first time someone else's opinion mattered to her as much as her own.

But just because she didn't want Cooper to be angry, didn't want him to be scared, she also didn't want to let a dangerous man walk free when she absolutely did have the skills needed to do something about it.

Writing the article wasn't enough.

Sure, it might wind up ruining Professor Mahmoud's reputation and hopefully get warrants put out for his arrest. But the professor had a huge head start. He knew he was at risk and would have gone to ground. He had enough resources and enough people backing him to stay under the radar indefinitely.

Unacceptable.

This was the fastest and most efficient way to get Mahmoud to show his face, with the best odds at working.

To that end, Willow straightened her spine and met Cooper's gaze squarely. "I play bait. We all know there is no way the professor will pass up a chance at snatching me."

Silence echoed around her.

None of Cooper's brothers said anything. It was clear even to her that they were letting this one be Cooper's call.

Only it wasn't his call.

It was hers.

"I'm not asking permission," she added. "I'm telling you what I'm going to do."

"Unless I have Cole sedate you and we throw you on a plane back home," Cooper muttered under his breath.

"Dude," Connor groaned with a roll of his eyes.

Willow's lips quirked up. "It's okay," she told Cooper's twin. "I know he's just joking. He'd never do something like that to me knowing what I've just been through. He's just scared. I am, too, Cooper. But we all know I have to do this. I will literally never be safe again if we don't make sure that Professor Mahmoud is taken care of."

The hand that rested on her hip tightened its hold on her, his fingers digging into her flesh almost to the point of pain. His other hand rubbed tiredly at his eyes. They were both wiped out and needed proper rest, but they only had a short window of time if they were going to make a move and end this once and for all.

"I'm not just scared, Willow. I'm terrified to let you anywhere near that man," Cooper said. The hand that had been rubbing at his eyes moved to palm her cheek, fingertips whispering across the bandage taped to her temple. "I don't want to lose you."

"And I don't want to lose you. But if we don't do this, I could lose everything. Including my life. I'd rather deal with this now while I have a whole team at my back." Her gaze roamed the room to include everyone. These men might be Cooper's family, but they knew she was important to their brother and that meant Willow was confident they would do whatever it took to have her back.

"You got it, sister," Cole said, grinning at her.

"I don't disagree that if we don't take this opportunity to get Mahmoud, we might not get another, but I think I should be the one to play bait," Cooper told her.

Fear gripped her heart in an icy hold.

The same fear she knew was pulsing through Cooper's body.

They both wanted a chance to explore what could be between them, but one huge Egyptian professor-sized bolder stood in their way.

Lifting her good hand, Willow stroked her fingers through Cooper's short hair. "I love that you want to put yourself between me and danger. It's been a long time since anyone cared enough to do that. But, Cooper, we both know that Mahmoud might be prepared to let you go to protect himself, he's only after you because you got in his way by rescuing me. There is no chance in hell he'll pass up an opportunity to take me."

"Willow's right," Cade interjected, and she shot him a grateful smile. He was definitely the scariest of the five other men surrounding her, but Cooper had told her a lot about his family in the hours they'd spent walking through the desert, and she knew the oldest Charleston brother would do anything for his family.

"Course I am," she teased, cracking a small smile out of Cooper.

"I don't like this," he said, and she could hear every drop of the raw terror in his voice.

"I don't particularly like the idea either. But it's the right thing to do. It gets a dangerous man in custody, and it gives you guys an opportunity to question someone who might have more answers about your mom, and your dad," she added, glancing at Jake and Jax. "It's killing two birds with the one stone. There's no other way I can think of that will get us the same results."

"I hate that you make too much logical sense because I don't want to be logical right now." Cooper wrapped his arms around her and crushed her against his chest. "I just want to wrap you up in cotton wool, tuck you into a nice, warm, comfortable bed, and make sure you get the rest you need. I want to slay all your dragons so you never have to put your armor on again. I want to stand between you and anything that wants to hurt you and take every single one of those bullets so you never feel pain again."

Tears blurred her vision, and she pressed closer, soaking up every ounce of Cooper's support. That he could already care about her so deeply after such a short time was nothing short of a miracle, and Willow prayed like she'd never prayed before that they got a chance to shoot for their happy ever after.

"Thank you," she whispered through the tears rolling down her cheeks.

When she lifted her head to meet Cooper's gaze, she found it tortured. His stormy gray eyes reflected everything he felt for her to see. Respect, admiration, fear, tenderness, affection, and attraction.

It was the last that had her blood heating.

Her gaze dropped to his lips and a groan rumbled through his body.

The only kisses they'd shared had been while they were fighting for their lives.

Now they were free, nothing stood in the way of them exploring their mutual attraction, except ...

"We're going to let you guys have some time alone together," Connor announced, and she could hear the guys moving about even though she didn't tear her eyes from Cooper's lips.

"We have both the rooms next door, if you need us, you know where to find us," Cole said, and Willow gave a short nod as desire hummed through her body.

"Yeah, thanks," Cooper said, tearing his heated gaze off her for a moment. "I mean it. Thanks for everything. For hopping on a plane and flying out here, finding us, not giving up, and for saving Willow. I can't ever repay you for that."

"Pfft, as if we want payment," Jax said.

The closing of the door signaled that they were alone, and Willow wasted no time in crushing her mouth to Cooper's. Right now, she didn't care that there was a terrorist wannabe with a personal vendetta against her, or that her body still throbbed with a myriad of aches and pains. She didn't care that she was still exhausted or that the feel of sand still clung to her skin even though it had all been washed away.

All she cared about was this.

Him.

Cooper Charleston, who had set aside his own quest for answers to save her life, and stuck by her when he could easily have handed her and her problems off to someone else. Willow knew how lucky she was. Another man might have left her to her fate, walked away because it didn't concern him.

But not Cooper.

That wasn't who he was.

He was honorable, had a big heart, loved fiercely and completely, and wouldn't walk away no matter how tough things got.

Now she just had to pray that her plan to play bait worked so she got her chance at happiness. A chance she hadn't even known would exist for her, hadn't even cared about anything other than fulfilling her vow to her father.

A chance she would now do anything to make come to fruition.

CHAPTER
Nineteen

July 14th
8:53 P.M.

He couldn't get enough of this woman.

Even though she was sitting on his lap, her arms around his neck, her lips millimeters from his, her body soft and pliable, and his to enjoy for the night, to treasure, it wasn't enough.

Cooper needed more.

Needed forever, and he knew how precarious forever was right now.

As badly as he needed to rage against Willow's plan to play bait, to refuse to go along with it, to tell her she was on her own if she wanted to stupidly put her life on the line, he knew he could do none of those things. Willow needed to do this, and if he tried to stop her and squash her spirit, the chance he wanted with her would slip through his fingers.

This was who she was.

It was who he'd fallen for.

Her strength, bravery, and determination to do what she believed was the right thing to do. How could he possibly ask her to be someone that she wasn't when the person that she was was so utterly, mind bogglingly amazing?

"Cooper?" Her voice held a thread of vulnerability as she said his name, a hint of doubt he needed to erase.

"I want you so badly I can't think straight," he admitted, dotting kisses to her lips between each word. "And I'm so afraid I'm going to lose you."

An understanding smile curled her plump lips up. "You won't lose me. Want to know why?"

"Why?"

"Because I have the very best team watching my back. They would never let anyone hurt me."

The confidence in her voice carved out some of the fear sitting heavily in his chest and replaced it with a sliver of that confidence. "I would die before I let anyone lay a hand on you."

Terror flared in her turquoise eyes. "I don't want you to die. I don't want anyone to die. Well, I'm not adverse to the professor's death." A tiny smile erased a little of the terror in her eyes. "But tonight, I don't want to think about anything else. Tonight, I just want you."

"You have me, honey. Tonight, and every night for the rest of our lives."

Wrapping an arm around Willow's waist, Cooper stood. Her legs immediately locked around his hips, pressing her hot center against the hard ridge in his pants. Burning desire laced his veins, he'd never felt such a deep need for a woman in his life. It was like a craving, this clawing feeling that if he didn't get inside her soon he was going to die.

Tonight had to be gentle though. Willow's body was a roadmap of the trauma she'd endured these last few weeks, and even though he was positive she would argue the case, it couldn't handle rough right now.

Not that he cared.

He wanted her any way he could have her.

Hell, he wanted her *every* way he could have her.

But tonight was their first time and it had to be special.

Carrying her over to the bed, Cooper set her on her feet and touched a brief kiss to her lips before licking and nibbling his way down the slender column of her neck. He paused at the point where her pulse was fluttering and let his lips linger there, drinking in the reassuring knowledge that she was alive.

So many times in the last few days he could have lost her.

But she was still there.

Still standing.

Nothing short of a miracle.

While he trailed kisses down to her collarbones, his fingers found the hem of her T-shirt and pulled it up and over her head. Since she'd been unconscious when he dressed her earlier, he hadn't bothered to put on a bra or panties, although his brothers had packed both in the bag they'd brought for Willow, so her beautiful breasts were bared for him to admire.

Not even the bruises mottling her skin could hide their beauty.

Dipping his head, Cooper bent his knees enough that he could take one pebbled nipple into his mouth and suckle on it. Willow moaned, her head falling back, her fingers tangling in his hair, holding him in place like he had any intention of moving any time soon.

When he finished lavishing attention on one breast he moved to the other. Swirling the tip of his tongue on her nipple had Willow's body trembling and he filed that information away to use when he got her naked.

By the time he finally tore his lips away from her pert breasts and kissed a line down her stomach, Willow's eyes were dark with desire, and he was so hard it took all his restraint not to just strip her and bury himself inside her.

Instead, he forced himself to take his time, savor every second, live in the moment.

His thumbs hooked into the leggings she was wearing, and he took them down with him as he knelt before her. As much as he despised seeing her body littered with black and blue marks, each one was a testament to Willow's strength and bravery.

"Do you know how amazing you are?" he asked, looking up at her.

Her fingers were still in his hair and softly played with the strands. "I'm determined."

"You're the most incredible woman I've ever met," he corrected. "I want to give you the world."

"I don't need the world. I just need ..."

"What?" he prompted when she didn't continue.

"I don't want to be alone anymore," she whispered.

"Oh, honey, that is one thing I can promise you without a shadow of a doubt. You will *never* be alone again. Not ever," he vowed as he nudged her legs apart.

"Cooper," her fingers tightened on his hair, "I've never ... no one's ..."

His eyes lit up as desire licked at his skin. "So, I'm going to be your first."

"What if ...?" Willow's gaze darted away before steadfastly returning to meet his. "What if I don't like it?"

"Then I'll stop. But trust me, honey, you are going to love it," he promised as he buried his face in the apex of her thighs and breathed deeply. "So sweet, so perfect," he murmured, nudging her legs further apart.

Since she made no move to stop him, his tongue darted out and he swept it along her center, making Willow moan.

The sound was enough to snap some of his control and he dove right in and feasted. Each moan, each sharp intake of air, each time her fingers tightened in his hair, it spurred him on. He licked and suckled, alternating between thrusting his tongue as deep inside her as he could get, and lavishing attention on her bud.

Willow's legs began to tremble, and he gripped her hips, holding her in place, and upped the pace.

"Cooper, I'm ... oh ..." She gasped. "I'm ... I can't ... I'm going to ..."

"Let go, honey, I'll catch you when you fall," he whispered, his lips still around her bundle of nerves, and when he sucked it into his mouth and swirled the tip of his tongue around it just as he'd done earlier with her nipples, she fell apart for him.

Not letting up until he'd drawn out every last drop of pleasure from her, by the time Cooper pulled back, Willow's cheeks were flushed, her eyes closed, and the sweetest smile on her lips.

Now she knew she could let go with him, that she was safe.

Scooping her into his arms as he stood, he carried her the last few steps to the bed and laid her down. As he stripped out of his clothes, and sheathed himself with a condom, Cooper couldn't take his eyes off her.

Damn, she was perfect.

Everything about her.

"Inside me, Cooper, want to feel you," she murmured, opening her eyes and smiling up at him.

"Can't wait, honey," he said as he climbed on the bed, stretching out on top of her.

Entering her in one thrust, Cooper stilled, enjoying the feel of her tight body around him, her heat, the fluttering of her internal muscles. It felt like coming home.

Slowly he began to move, thrusting in and out with as much restraint as he still had left. Willow moved with him like they'd been doing this all their lives. Her legs hooked around his hips, drawing him deeper, and he found her lips, kissing her with every drop of emotion he felt.

Balancing his weight on one hand, his other slipped between them, touching her where their bodies joined, building her quickly toward another orgasm because he sure as hell wasn't coming alone.

The second she cried out, her internal muscles clamping around him as pleasure tore through her body, Cooper let go, let his own release gather him up and toss him around in a whirlwind of ecstasy.

They were both breathing hard by the time they floated back down to earth. Willow's eyes were soft as she looked at him, and he touched another kiss to her lips before easing out of her. Disposing of the condom, he went into the bathroom, ran a washcloth under warm water then returned to the bedroom and cleaned Willow up.

Then he pulled the covers down, lay beside her, drawing her into his arms, and tucked them both in. "Sleep time now, honey," he murmured as he touched a kiss to her temple.

"Are you staying here all night?" she asked, voice already turning sleepy.

"Wild horses couldn't drag me away," he promised.

Maybe wild horses couldn't drag him away from the woman snuggled against his side, but there was somebody who could.

Tonight, he got to sleep with his girl in his arms, but tomorrow morning she was going to play bait for a dangerous man who had already tried to kill her several times over, who wouldn't hesitate to do it if given the chance.

All it would take was for one tiny thing to go wrong and he could lose her forever.

~

July 15th
   9:23 A.M

This seemed like a much better idea when she sat safe in a motel room surrounded by six strong, skilled warriors.

Now ...

Now Willow was thinking maybe this wasn't her best plan ever.

Saying goodbye to Cooper before the guys dropped her off had felt wrong somehow. Almost like she was tempting fate. That her stubborn determination to bring down Tarek Mahmoud whatever the cost was going to wind up costing her far more than she was prepared to pay.

Only it was too late to back out now.

After spending the night sleeping peacefully in Cooper's arms, they'd woken early, made love again, then showered together and gotten dressed. When she put back on the dirty, blood-stained clothes she'd been wearing when the helicopter crashed, she'd gotten her first fore-shadowing that something felt wrong.

But she'd brushed it off.

Even though things felt wrong, and she wished she had Cooper and his brothers at her back, Willow still knew her plan was solid. This was the best way to ensure they got their man. If they didn't, she didn't want to be responsible for what Allah's Warriors would do if they were left to freely indoctrinate young men and then follow through with their plans.

This was for sure the right thing to do, so why did it feel so wrong?

Glancing around, Willow tried to check if anyone was watching her, but nobody was around.

What if she was wrong about this?

What if there weren't any of the professor's people around here?

The entire plan depended on someone spotting her and getting word to Professor Mahmoud. While she and Cooper had been having sex and sleeping tangled together in one another's arms, the rest of the guys had been busy planning. Normally, Willow would feel guilty for sleeping on the job, she should have been there, helping work through the details, but this time she knew the best thing she could do for all of them was rest.

Even with the few hours of sleep, she was running on one step away from empty.

It would take her weeks to fully recover from this ordeal, but at least she was no longer dying of thirst. The guys had pumped her full of painkillers so the throbbing in her head, and her arm, and her chest, and pretty much every single muscle in her body, was dulled to a more manageable level.

Still, the sun felt too hot against her already sunburned skin, and the filthy clothes felt stiff and scratchy against her body. As much as she wished she could have stayed in one of the outfits they had packed for her, that would give away the fact that she'd been rescued.

For this to work, it had to look like she'd wandered alone in the desert since the crash and then taken refuge in the first building she found.

The guys had located what would have been the closest village to where the helicopter crashed. It sucked to know that she and Cooper had walked in the wrong direction, and had they come this way, they might have found help before things became so dire and she almost died.

Still, if they'd come this way then maybe they wouldn't have met up with his brothers when they did and been caught and captured for real.

Before the sun rose this morning, she'd said her goodbyes to Cooper and his brothers about a half mile from the property at the closest edge of the village to where she would have come if she'd walked out. Then she'd hidden out in there, used her bloody T-shirt to pretend to use the well water to clean herself up a little so it looked like she'd stumbled upon the place quite at random.

Then she'd sat there, huddled in a corner, and waited for the sun to rise so she could "sneak" away. All that time she'd imagined what it would have been like if she really had found this village alone, how scared and hurt she would have been, and how terrified she'd be found. Just because she was determined to fulfill her vow to her father and do good with her life didn't mean that sometimes she wasn't afraid.

She got scared plenty.

She'd been terrified while being held hostage by Tarek Mahmoud. She'd been terrified when she and Cooper were caught. She'd been terrified when she realized the helicopter was going to crash. She'd been terrified when she crept toward Cooper in the wreckage unsure if he was dead or alive.

And she was terrified now.

Just not enough to back out of the plan.

So instead of standing stock still looking around like her head was stuck on a swivel stick, Willow made herself keep walking.

Walking was the last thing she wanted to do. Her aching feet protested each step, and her muscles screamed at her to let them rest and recover. But she couldn't do that. She had to keep walking through the town, had to play this like she would have if she hadn't met up with Prey's Charlie Team.

Which meant walking and then finding someone to make contact with.

Hopefully before she had to figure out who she would have trusted enough if she'd been in the position she was pretending to be in for real the professor's men came for her.

Willow was so afraid she was going to mess this up somehow. Not only were lives on the line because of what Professor Mahmoud and his people had planned, but the lives of a man she cared deeply about and his brothers were also at risk if she made one wrong move.

It had killed Cooper to stand back, to let her go, to drive away and leave her behind even if she was wearing a tracking device sewn into the hem of her shirt. So long as the professor believed she really had just walked out of the desert there would be no reason for him to check to make sure she wasn't wearing anything.

The problem was, Willow was all too aware that all it would take was for one tiny thing to go wrong and this would have a very different outcome than they hoped.

"You can do this, Willow. Don't go and give up on yourself now. You promised your dad you would make your life mean something, and you have every motivation in the world to do this and then get home safely."

That was true.

Everything she had always wanted but never allowed herself to admit was all wrapped up in that six foot two package of lean muscle and huge, warm heart that was Cooper Charleston.

Now that he'd opened her mind to what she could have, of what could be waiting for her on the other side of this mission, she wanted to grab hold of it and refuse to let it be ripped away from her.

But it could be.

Far too easily.

As she kept walking, getting closer to the center of the village, there started to be people out on the streets. Willow was aware of every curious, suspicious glance thrown her way, and as badly as she wanted to shrink away from those scrutinizing looks, she couldn't.

She wanted to be spotted.

Had to be if this was going to work.

The village was small, and she was starting to lose hope that there would be anyone who was part of Allah's Warriors. What were the chances that they had someone in every village in the entire country?

Slim to none.

But this village *was* one of the closest to the crash site, and by now the professor had to know that both she and Cooper had survived the crash. He'd be looking for them, and she had to believe that he would be watching all the towns and villages they could reach.

The eyes on her made her skin prickle uncomfortably and she wished that one of those sets of eyes belonged to Cooper. She'd feel so much safer if he was within eyesight of her, but he wasn't. If any of the professor's men spotted him close by but not with her, they would tip their hand.

So, he was probably a couple of miles away. Sitting with his brothers, waiting for the tracker she wore to indicate she was no longer walking so he could follow. Follow but not intervene until he confirmed that Professor Mahmoud was with her.

This had been her plan, and she couldn't back out.

Couldn't be weak now.

Not when she was so close.

Keep walking, that was all she could do. If this didn't work out, she wanted to know she had done everything within her power to get the professor. At least when she got home and wrote her article, the world would know who he really was, and he'd be a target of every agency of every country across the globe.

Just then, she heard an engine rev and tires squeal as a white van rushed up beside her.

Four men jumped out of it, grabbing at her even as she screamed and backed away.

Hands closed around her arms, lifting her off the ground.

Zip ties were secured tightly around her wrists.

A bag was thrown over her head.

And her body connected with the floor of the van with a bone jarring thud that had her moaning in pain as she was tossed inside.

Looked like playing bait had worked because she'd just been kidnapped.

CHAPTER
Twenty

July 15th
   10:10 A.M.

"We shouldn't have let her go off alone," Cooper said into the quiet car.

It was more than just his need to keep the woman who'd come sneaking into his heart when he wasn't looking safe, it was something else.

Something felt wrong.

He couldn't put his finger on what exactly it was that was bothering him.

While he'd never been a fan of this plan just because, on principle, he wasn't ever going to like anything that was Willow walking willingly into danger, he'd gone along with it because he'd agreed this was the best way to get what they needed to keep her safe long term. Just because he didn't like something didn't automatically make it bad or wrong, and Willow was right when she'd said this was the quickest and most efficient way to bring Mahmoud in.

There was no way that the man could resist getting his hands on Willow to punish her.

Not even self-preservation would keep him in hiding.

His brothers had been meticulously working out the details of the plan while he and Willow slept last night, and when they'd climbed into the car in the early hours of the morning, he'd been confident they could pull this off without a hitch.

Now he wasn't.

Nothing had outwardly changed. They were still sitting in the vehicle, parked out in the desert not all that far from where they'd dropped Willow off. They'd tracked her to the barn where she was going to pause and stay for a bit, then they'd watched as she started walking.

Being forced to sit there and twiddle his thumbs while Willow trudged slowly along in the heat, following her progress on the screen, had left him antsy. He didn't want to be sitting doing nothing, safe and sound in the vehicle, while Willow was out there alone. He should be with her. Watching her back. Hell, he should be carrying her because they all knew she wasn't strong enough yet to be out there walking, possibly for hours.

But over the last few minutes something had changed.

Now he didn't just feel antsy he felt like a million fire ants were crawling all over his skin.

His gut was screaming at him that something wasn't right, but he didn't know what specifically was wrong.

Only that he needed to get to Willow.

"You know this was the right move," Cade said, his voice calm, borderline disinterested. Just because Cooper knew his older brother would move heaven and earth for anyone in their family, or their Prey family, and since he was with Willow now it made her one of them, didn't mean his attitude didn't irk.

What right did any of his brothers have to be so calm while he was an anxious mess?

"Feels wrong," he muttered, absently rubbing his chest because it felt too tight. He wasn't used to anxiety like this on a mission. Of course, he always worried about the safety of his team, they weren't just his colleagues but his family as well, and Cade had a kid at home who'd already lost her mom, so he always worried a little more about his big brother. But he was never consumed with fear like he was in this moment.

Because never before had the stakes been this high.

His brothers were his family, he loved them unconditionally, they'd all been there for each other through the hell of their teenage years. But Willow was his future. She had the power to complete him in a way he hadn't even known that he needed to be completed. She filled holes in him that had scabbed over but never completely healed.

Now she could be gone.

"It feels wrong because you care about her," Connor said sympathetically. Leave it to his twin to be on his side no matter what.

As grateful as he was that none of his brother's had questioned his sudden and completely unexpected obsession with the woman he'd saved from certain death, he needed them to grasp just how deep those feelings already ran.

They needed to understand that losing Willow would break him in a way that losing their parents hadn't.

"It feels wrong because something isn't right," he corrected. Cooper just wished he could put his finger on what exactly that was.

"This just because you're into her?" Jake asked, his assessing brown eyes studying him in that calm way he always did. Jake was a quiet man, he thought more than he spoke, he always assessed every situation, noticing the tiny details that others often missed. Not only was Jake an asset to Charlie Team, but he was an asset to their family as well. Cooper couldn't have picked better stepbrothers than Jake and Jax, and he saw them as his brothers as much as those who shared his DNA.

"No. I can't explain it ... I just have this gnawing feeling in my gut," he replied.

"What do you want us to do about it?" Cole asked.

"Want us to get closer to her? Get eyes on her?" Jax asked.

Yes.

That was exactly what he wanted.

Maybe if he could get her in his line of sight, he could figure out what had him tripping out.

Before he could say that, the dot on the screen suddenly started moving at a much faster rate. It was what they'd been waiting for but now it didn't seem so good.

It meant that Willow had been taken.

It meant that they'd gotten what they wanted.

It meant they could finally stop sitting around and actually do something.

Finally end this, follow the dot that would lead them to Mahmoud and take the man into custody. Or kill him. Which is absolutely what Cooper would prefer. The man had hurt Willow, littered her soft skin with so many bruises that she was more multicolored patchwork quilt than human being right now. The man deserved death. Ideally, a long, slow, painful one.

"Show time," he said, forcing a grin because the knot in his gut didn't fade.

If anything, if felt worse.

While he should be feeling relief that he was finally heading off after Willow and would soon have her back in his arms where she belonged, his nerves were ramping up.

Cade was sitting in the driver's seat, and started up the engine, taking off in the direction that Willow was moving.

Had they hurt her when they grabbed her?

Fear for what she was going through pulsed through his body. Just because she'd signed up for this didn't mean Willow wasn't going to be scared when Mahmoud's men kidnapped her.

"Won't be long," Cole consoled him, slapping a hand on his back.

"Bet anything that Mahmoud is already in the area. Shouldn't take them long to get Willow to him," Connor added.

However long it took it would be too long.

Every second that he didn't have her safely on his lap, his arms wrapped around her, his face buried in her hair, inhaling her sweet scent, it hurt. A physical ache inside him.

"Hold on, bro." Jax nudged him and shot him a reassuring smile.

Sand flew up and surrounded them as Cade floored the gas, and a few minutes later they were turning onto a road. Fields lined either side of the narrow dirt road, interspersed with the occasional small hut of a house.

Where were they taking Willow?

Was Mahmoud really close by?

Could Cooper really have her back in his arms soon?

Hope started to edge away a little of the fear that had settled over him. At least now this wasn't all on Willow's shoulders. They'd track them to wherever she was being taken, get confirmation that Mahmoud was there, then strike. It should be easy enough, the same thing they'd done dozens of times before over their careers. Just because the stakes for him were higher than ever didn't mean he would allow it to affect him.

This would go down without issue.

It had to.

Because if one tiny little thing went wrong, he would lose Willow and the future he could have had with her.

Just as hope pushed away more and more of his fear, clearing his head, calming him, allowing him to settle into the zone, prepare himself to do what he knew how to do, they rounded a corner and his world all but screeched to a halt.

The road before them was blocked.

A truck was parked in the middle of it, and surrounding it were what had to be at least two dozen cows. They were wandering aimlessly about, filling the space from the field on one side of the road to the field on the other.

Leaving them no access.

There was no way they could get past.

Which meant there was no way he could get to Willow.

Which left her alone and helpless in the hands of a man who would risk his own safety for a chance to make her pay for attempting to bring him down.

∼

July 15th
 11:03 A.M

The guys are coming.

Cooper is coming.

You did this once already you can handle it again.

Willow kept repeating those thoughts over and over again as the van she'd been thrown into careened down the road.

She wasn't alone in the back. The four men who had jumped out of the vehicle to grab her had gotten in with her. They sat around her, talking and laughing every time her unprotected body was tossed about. With her hands restrained behind her back and the bag over her head, she was helpless to do anything to stop herself from sliding across the floor of the van each time it turned a corner, braked, or accelerated too fast.

Her Arabic wasn't the best, she knew some basics but not enough to make out everything they said.

Not that she needed to.

Their tones were ones she'd heard plenty of times before as a young woman.

It seemed like the game plan had changed.

Before, when he was keeping her held hostage, Professor Mahmoud hadn't allowed any of his men to touch her in a sexual way. She'd believed it was because they viewed her as a dirty westerner, she was the enemy, and they hadn't wanted to contaminate their bodies by joining them to hers. That fit in with the propaganda she'd learned about Allah's Warriors, they believed in abstinence as a way to draw closer to their god.

But the way the men were speaking now sounded like the professor was about to give them free reign to use her body as they wished.

Icy cold dread settled into her bloodstream, pumping its way through every inch of her until she shivered uncontrollably.

Cooper will get here before they touch you.

Unless the professor was further away than they believed and Cooper and his brothers had to wait for confirmation before coming in to rescue her.

Terror spiraled inside her and Willow could feel herself losing whatever control she had on her emotions. Before she could devolve into a full on panic the van slowed and came to a stop.

Time was up.

They'd arrived.

Now all she could do was pray that the professor was already there waiting for her. If he was then this would all be over in minutes. Well before what she feared was about to happen ever got a chance to get off the ground.

Still laughing and chattering amongst themselves, the four men dragged her out of the van along with them. With her arms bound, and still no vision, if they weren't holding her up then Willow was sure she would have stumbled at least a dozen times.

After a brief walk, she was taken inside a building. The slightly cooler air was a relief. With the bag over her head not only couldn't she see, but her much too fast panicked breathing only made it hotter beneath the rough material, increasing her fear.

Doing her best to control it, she found it so much harder than it had been before.

Maybe it was because now if she died, she'd be leaving a hole in someone's life whereas before she'd felt untethered to anything.

"Well, well, well," Professor Mahmoud snickered as she was shoved down onto something soft, a mattress by the feel of it. "The prodigal daughter returns."

It took everything Willow had to give to hold it together as the hands on her shoulders shoved her backward, and more hands grabbed at her ankles. The only reason she didn't lose it completely as she was twisted so she was lying flat on her back, and the unmistakable sound of duct tape filled the air was because she knew Cooper would be coming any second now.

The professor was there. It wouldn't take the guys with their gadgets long to get visual confirmation, then they'd be breaking down these doors and killing everyone inside.

Bloodthirsty or not, Willow wanted Professor Mahmoud dead and she didn't even care if that made her a bad person, which she didn't believe it did.

"No one is going to save you this time, Ms. Purcell," Professor Mahmoud said, and she could feel him close beside her even before he snatched the bag off her head revealing his smirking face.

Yeah, that's what you think.

Doing her best to keep her face impassive, Willow pressed her lips together and merely returned the man's stare until his brows knit together in irritation.

"Your friend is dead, died in the crash, but you know that don't you?" Professor Mahmoud leaned over her until the hot stench of his breath invaded her nostrils. "He's not coming to your rescue this time, and you are going to end up just like his mother did."

That revelation caught her attention, and she shoved away her fear. She had to gather as much intel as she could for Cooper because she was pretty sure that neither the professor nor his men were going to be alive much longer.

"What do you mean?" she asked.

Tossing his head back, he laughed. "Always the reporter, aren't you, Ms. Purcell? I guess it doesn't hurt to tell you since you won't be alive much longer. My wedding day wasn't the first time I'd met Caterina Charleston. I met her for the first time six years earlier. A night I remember very well." His hand dropped, caressing her neck before sweeping lower to palm one of her breasts. "Very well," he added with a chuckle, the hand on her breast squeezing painfully tight.

Her breathing accelerated, and she tugged on her bonds even as she attempted to command her body to stay still. These men would pounce on her fear and use it to their advantage.

Cooper is probably right outside this very second. Just hold on a little longer.

"She was tied up much the same way you are right now," Professor Mahmoud continued. "Only with a little less clothing on."

Straightening abruptly, he nodded to one of his men who approached her with what looked like a box cutter.

Instinct had her flinching and all the men in the room—over half a dozen of them—laughed.

There was nowhere for her to go, no way for her to fight as the man sawed at her clothing, nicking her dozens of times as he cute her clothing off her until they hung in rags between her body and the mattress.

Tied spreadeagled as she was, there was no way for her to close her legs or cover her private areas. They were on display for every one of these disgusting men to ogle, and even though she'd been so strong every other time she was in the professor's presence, this time she couldn't prevent a couple of tears from escaping.

Come on, Cooper. What are you waiting for?

Smiling in delight at her tears, Professor Mahmoud cupped her center, one of his fingers forcing its way inside her body. He added another, and then another, tearing at her dry skin as he laughed at her vain attempts at expelling him from her body.

"I hear being raped to death is one of the most horrific ways a woman can go," he said, then crushed his lips to hers in a bruising kiss.

They were both breathing hard when he pulled back, although for very different reasons. While he might be turned on, she was one step away from a full-on panic attack.

"We'll be back, Ms. Purcell. We must go and pray before we come back and enjoy your body."

The men trailed after him as he left the room, and Willow just lay there, frozen in terror.

Cooper had to be close by, she got that he and his brothers hadn't been able to follow the van close enough that they'd be spotted, but she'd been there several minutes now, they had to be outside.

The problem was, if she waited for them to rescue her it might be too late.

She had no idea what was involved in this prayer time the professor and his men were going to engage in, but she'd seen the hunger in their eyes and knew it wasn't going to last long. They were eager to get to work violating her body, and tied up as she was, she couldn't stop them.

Waiting wasn't an option.

She had to take charge of her own fate.

Tugging on the tape that was wrapped around her wrists and ankles, binding her to the bedposts, she tested its strength. It hadn't been wound too tight, and there was a chance she might, given enough time, be able to work herself free.

Time was the one thing she didn't have, though.

Then she spotted it.

The box cutter.

Lying just an inch away from her right hand. Her good hand.

How could they have been so stupid as to leave it right there?

Were they really that drunk on lust that they'd make such a potentially idiotic mistake?

Stretching her hand as far as she could, she ignored the pain in her muscles, something she was, thanks to the professor's violent beatings, quite good at now. Her fingertips brushed across the box cutter, but not enough to get a hold of it.

Tears of frustration burned her eyes.

She had to do this.

Flat out.

There was no other option.

There were a thousand reasons why Cooper and his brothers hadn't stormed the house already, but whatever they were, if she just lay there and waited for them it would be too late for her. That she was certain of.

If she wanted to live, she had to fight for herself, same way she always had to.

And she did want to live.

For whatever reason Cooper wasn't already there by her side, it wasn't because he didn't want to be, that she knew for sure.

Trying again, she strained as hard as she could, pulling on the tape, and it gave just a little. Enough that her fingers were able to scoop the box cutter off the mattress and into her hand.

There was no time to enjoy her brief victory, she was still nowhere close to being free.

Sawing at the tape was awkward and the blade slipped, cutting her skin more times than she could count.

But Willow didn't give up.

She couldn't.

Relief had her crying out when she finally cut through the tape enough that her arm came free. It felt heavy, blood flow returning slowly, but there was no time to wait and nurse it. She had to keep moving.

Reaching across her body, Willow made quicker work of sawing through the tape on her left arm. Once it was free she sat up. Her head spun, the room along with it, but she blinked away the fuzziness and went to work on her ankles.

Slippery with her blood, the box cutter continued to slide between her fingers, adding more tiny wounds to her already battered body.

Determination was the only thing keeping her moving, and it paid off when the last bit of tape came free.

Shoving off the bed, Willow wavered for a moment and then ran to the window, searching the area outside for any signs of Cooper and his brothers.

She found none.

Maybe they were around the other side of the building.

Wherever the house was that she'd been brought to, there were other houses around so the guys would have been able to follow more easily without fear of being spotted. They had to be out there, just plotting the best way to get inside, get her out alive, and the professor and his men caught or killed.

There was a smaller building not far from the room she'd been left in, if she could get to it, she could hide in there until she spotted one of the guys.

Thankful she was on the ground floor. Willow eased the window open and climbed out.

Unfortunately, that was where her luck ended.

Just as she started creeping toward the small building, she spotted Professor Mahmoud and his men praying to their god on their knees in the sunshine.

Of course, it was too much to hope that they wouldn't spot her.

They did, and as she broke into a run, she heard feet pounding the ground behind her.

"Going somewhere?" the professor growled as an arm wrapped around her neck, yanking her backward and pinning her in place as something cold touched her temple. Willow didn't have to look at it to know it was the barrel of a gun.

So close yet so very far.

CHAPTER
Twenty~One

July 15th
  11:38 A.M.

Seconds had never felt so long in his life.

They literally felt like eternities.

Every single one of them.

Sixty in just one minute.

Minute after minute.

It was over an hour since the tracker Willow was wearing began to move faster indicating she was no longer walking but now in a vehicle, and Cooper was more than ready to lose his mind.

The only thing keeping him clinging to sanity was the knowledge that Willow needed him.

Needed him to be not just in the game but at the top of his game. Anything less and she might not walk out of this alive.

If she even was still alive.

No.

He couldn't let himself think that.

Surely the delay of moving those cows out of the way wasn't enough that they'd lost their window of opportunity. Mahmoud wanted Willow dead, but not to the extent that he wasn't going to taunt her first. He thought he'd won, and he was going to make sure he rubbed that in her face before no doubt inflicting a long, slow, painful death on her.

Hold on, honey. I'm coming.

Please, baby, hang on.

Fear like this was crippling, and his hands were physically shaking as he followed his brothers.

The house where Willow's tracker indicated that she was being held was in a small community. There were other houses within eyesight of it which meant it was easier for them to approach without being immediately noticeable. But on the other hand, it meant that a shootout was going to draw unnecessary attention.

Attention that could wind up slowing them down and getting Willow hurt.

It wasn't until they scaled a fence, and his feet landed on the ground inside the property where Willow had been brought that Cooper finally felt a sense of calm settle over him. This was what he knew how to do. What he was good at. The stakes may be higher than they'd ever been before but that just meant there was zero room for error.

Almost there, Willow.

Hold on just a little longer for me.

Out on a small patch of lawn were around a dozen men. They were all down on their knees, and from the looks of it they appeared to be praying.

What did that mean?

Good news for Willow or bad?

Cooper wished he could at least lay eyes on her. Then he'd be able to reassure himself that he hadn't failed, that he wasn't too late, that she was still alive, and he could do what he'd promised her he'd do.

Because if he did fail, if that small delay had cost Willow her life, he didn't think he'd ever be able to move forward. Willow had never had anyone in her life to watch out for her since she was an eight-year-old little girl, and she'd watched in horror as her father was beaten to death right in front of her for crimes he hadn't committed.

"Cooper, you get inside the house, find Willow. The rest of us will take out the men," Cade's voice came softly through the comms. His older brother was a natural born leader, and it was only because Cade had a little girl at home that he wasn't Charlie Team's leader. When they'd all agreed to join Prey about three years ago, Cade turned down Eagle's offer for team leader and instead suggested Cooper fill the role. He'd always been proud his big brother had thought this was a job he could handle, and he'd done his best to lead the team the way Cade would have.

But today he was happy to allow Cade to take over.

His nerves could not handle the additional responsibility when his entire being was screeching at him constantly to get to Willow.

Diverting away from the others, while they headed to the front of the building where the men were, Cooper headed to the back. The house was quiet, too quiet as he approached it. The backdoor stood wide open and much like the house where he'd first spotted Willow huddled in a corner, a kitchen took up the majority of the back end of the building.

The kitchen was empty, so he crept through it and began to clear the other rooms on the ground floor. While he would have loved to have flown the drones they had with them, gather more intel without revealing their presence, the fact that they'd been delayed had changed everything. They no longer had the luxury of staying hidden while they confirmed Professor Mahmoud was there, they had to act now or risk being too late to save Willow and possibly too late to capture Mahmoud before he went to ground and was never spotted again.

Holding it together well considering the circumstances, that all fell away when Cooper entered a smaller room off the wide hallway toward the front of the house.

That's when he lost it.

The room was mostly empty other than a bed and a dresser.

Lying on the bed were clothes.

Willow's clothes.

The ones she'd been wearing when they were caught and crashed the helicopter to escape.

The ones she'd put back on this morning when they'd prepared to drop her off and use her as bait.

Now they lay on the mattress, cut to pieces.

A roar echoed inside his head, and for a moment, Cooper wondered if he'd just cost all of them their lives by screaming out loud. Then he realized the agonized howl was trapped inside his mind.

Willow had been there.

They'd stripped her naked while she was bound to the bed if the scraps of duct take left on the bedposts were anything to go by.

She'd been there but where was she now?

Was she already dead? Was that why the men were outside? Were they having some sort of celebration that they'd killed one of their enemies?

He'd been so sure that whatever Mahmoud had planned for Willow would take time, but obviously he'd been wrong.

He should have trusted his gut. It had been screaming at him that Willow playing bait was too dangerous, and all morning he'd known that something was wrong. He'd allowed himself to be talked out of listening to his instincts because everyone believed those instincts were compromised by his feelings for Willow.

Attention drawn to the commotion happening outside, Cooper moved to the window, saw it was open, and a tiny tendril of hope lit inside him.

Was it possible Willow had been the one to open it?

All the other windows in the house were closed except this one. Could she have escaped?

Renewed by hope, Cooper jumped out it and once he'd gone a few yards forward he could see his brothers fighting the men who had been praying. In an attempt not to alert everyone in the area with gunfire, his brothers were using a combination of their hands and knives to eliminate each threat.

Desperate for answers, Cooper rushed into the fray, grabbing the closest man still standing and slamming him down to the ground, holding the blade of his K-Bar to the man's neck.

"Where's Willow?" he growled, low and dangerous.

The man sputtered but stared defiantly up at him.

Everything around him faded away.

He would get answers, no matter what it took.

Pressing the blade just deep enough to draw blood, he repeated his question. "I know she was here, where's Willow?"

The man swallowed hard, forcing his neck deeper into the blade. "I ... she ..."

"She what?" he roared.

"We ... the professor ... he promised us ..."

"Promised you what?"

"That we could share her," the man blurted out. "That we could use her however we wanted until she died."

Time felt like it stopped.

Horror burned inside him.

Of all the deaths he'd pictured over the last few hours, Willow being raped to death hadn't been one of them.

Something had happened though. Because Willow was no longer in the bed where the men had put her. She had to have gotten free somehow, so where was she? And where was Mahmoud? He wasn't there with the others.

"Where is she?" he demanded.

"She escaped. Came out the window. The professor went after her, told us to keep praying, we need to give thanks that God handed our enemy over to us, give thanks that he would allow us to touch her without becoming dirty because she is a sacrifice to our god," the man babbled as tears streaked down his cheeks. Not really a man, more like a kid, he couldn't be more than early twenties if that, maybe even late teens.

Not that the kid's age would give Cooper even an ounce of guilt over what he was about to do.

Plunging the blade of his knife deep into the man's neck, he yanked it free as he stood, his attention already moved on from the kid who would have participated in raping his woman until she bled out and died.

Around him was a sea of dead bodies, but the two people he wanted to find were nowhere to be seen.

"We'll find them," Jax assured him.

"They can't have gone far," Cole added.

Scanning the area, Cooper tried to go slow when all he wanted to do was spin in wild circles and run and scream Willow's name until he got a response.

There.

Over by a small outbuilding.

Movement.

Trusting his team to have his back, he took off toward the small building.

As he got closer, his heart dropped.

Hidden between a tree and the side of the building were Willow and Tarek Mahmoud. The man had her pressed against his body, using her as a human shield, with a weapon held to her temple.

~

July 15th
    11:42 A.M

Everything was happening too fast.

Her already aching head was spinning.

All Willow needed was a moment to gather her thoughts, pull herself together, and figure out a way that they all made it out of this alive, but she didn't have that luxury.

Just as Professor Mahmoud had grabbed her, shoving a gun against her temple and telling his men to get back to praying, a commotion had broken out behind them. Like the true coward he was, the professor hadn't rushed forward to help his men, instead, he'd pulled further back into hiding, taking her along with him.

As much as she wanted to call out, because Willow knew without a shadow of a doubt that it was Cooper and his brothers out there, doing what they did best, she was afraid to make any move that would put them any more at risk. They were outnumbered, and while she was confident they would still come out on top, she wasn't going to make it harder for them.

Besides, she was confident of something else, too.

While Professor Mahmoud badly wanted her to die as punishment for trying to take him down, he also wanted to live.

She was his best bet at walking out alive. Although she trusted the guys to do what they knew how to do, and knew they would never allow the professor to walk out with her, Willow also knew if it came down to it, she would sacrifice her life if it meant that Professor Mahmoud also lost his.

Cooper's voice wafted over to her before she saw him.

She heard him order someone to tell him where she was, and it took all her willpower not to call out to him.

The weapon that pressed to her temple was motivation enough to keep silent.

If she wanted this to work out the way it should, she had to play this smart, not allow her fear to make her impulsive. She was sure a moment would come, but she had to wait for it. Right now wasn't that moment.

Footsteps pounded across the ground and then a moment later she looked into those stormy gray eyes that had become her anchor.

Cooper was there.

Her world settled.

Everything was going to be okay so long as he was with her.

"It's over, Mahmoud," Cooper said, his weapon trained on the man cowering behind her, using her as a human shield in an attempt to save himself.

Behind Cooper, she could see all of his brothers. They all wore fierce expressions, but there was a confidence in their eyes that she could feel was lacking in the professor. They knew what they were doing, they had done this kind of thing dozens of times before. Professor Mahmoud, on the other hand, was used to convincing young men that their purpose was to fight against their country and destroy it. Something he did from the safety of his university world, this was all foreign to him and she knew he knew it, too.

"Your men are all dead," Cooper continued, taking another step closer, his weapon never wavering. "There's no one coming to help you. Put down the weapon and let her go."

"If I let her go you shoot me," Professor Mahmoud said. While his voice wobbled, the weapon pressed against her temple remained steady.

"Trust me, knowing what you did to her while you were holding her captive, and knowing what you were going to do to her if we hadn't shown up, there is nothing that would make me happier than shooting you and watching you bleed out slowly. But in the end, all I want is for you to pay for what you did, and if that means you sitting in a prison cell for the rest of your life then I'm up for that as well."

"I'm not going to prison," Professor Mahmoud shouted like he had more than two options.

"Well then, pick the body bag. Personally, I don't care either way, but one thing is for certain," Cooper said, his voice dark and menacing, "you are not walking out of here with my girl, so make your choice."

"I-I have to g-get away," Professor Mahmoud wailed, and for the first time the weapon held to her head began to waver just the tiniest bit.

All Willow needed was one little chance.

In her hand, she still held the box cutter. She was not stupid enough, even in the haze of fear, to put down a weapon and leave it behind. If the gun moved away from her temple, even just an inch, she could use the box cutter to get the professor to loosen his hold on her.

Then all she had to do was drop to the ground and let Cooper and his brothers do their thing.

"Why do you have to get away, Tarek?" Cooper asked, a measure of calm to his voice she knew he wasn't feeling because she could see the anger and terror for her raging in his eyes.

"Because otherwise they'll kill me," the professor mumbled.

"Who?" Cooper asked. "Who will kill you?"

"It wasn't supposed to go this way," Professor Mahmoud keened, ignoring—or not even hearing—Cooper's question.

"What wasn't supposed to go this way, Tarek? How was it supposed to go?" Cooper asked.

"I didn't want to reach out to you," Professor Mahmoud babbled. "It was dangerous. Stupid. They made me. It was supposed to divert attention away from them, put it on me. I was just supposed to give you a tiny bread crumb, not enough to give you anything that you would be able to use to prove what happened to your mother. I said it was stupid. That you'd never be able to figure things out anyway, but I was outvoted."

The professor was starting to sound panicked, and Willow got the feeling that the man was devolving. And quickly.

She needed to look for an opportunity to make her move.

Right now, Cooper was restricted in what he could do because the professor was using her as a human shield, and with the gun to her head it was too great a risk for him to try much of anything.

This was on her.

If she wanted to live to have the chance with Cooper that she so desperately wanted, she was going to have to get herself out of this mess.

"Tell me names, Tarek," Cooper ordered in a voice that brokered no arguments.

"I can't," Professor Mahmoud wailed. "They'll kill me."

"*I'll* kill you," Cooper said matter-of-factly. "So, pick your poison. There are only three options. You do something stupid and get yourself killed right here and now, which I'll say is my personal favorite. Or you put that weapon down and let me take you into custody. If we go that way and you're prepared to tell everything you know, then we'll make sure whatever prison you wind up in you're protected. Or we can take you into custody and leave you wide open to whatever attack comes from your friends."

Behind her, Professor Mahmoud's body began to shudder. He wasn't just afraid of whoever he'd been working for, he was flat out terrified.

She needed to amp up his fear.

Cooper and his brothers were an intimidating bunch, and right now they were the biggest threat because they were right there and itching to kill him.

If she could push him over the edge, she was sure she could get that gun away from her head long enough to act.

This was not the way she wanted to deliver this information to Cooper or his brothers, but desperate times called for desperate measures. Sending up a quick prayer for forgiveness for blindsiding the man she was falling for, Willow said the words she knew would break Cooper's heart.

"He raped your mom, Cooper, probably with these men he's scared of," Willow told him as gently as she could.

The anger radiating off the six armed men staring at them flew up several dozen notches and she got exactly what she'd hoped for.

Professor Mahmoud's shaking increased.

The pressure against her temple disappeared.

Willow's fingers tightened around the box cutter.

Slamming the blade down, it sank into the professor's thigh, causing him to howl as he stumbled backward, raising his weapon so it now pointed at her and the men behind her.

Still between Professor Mahmoud and Charlie Team, Willow lifted the blade again, this time plunging it down into his neck.

With a surprised gurgling sound, the professor dropped his weapon. It fell with a thud at his feet as his hands flew to the blade buried deep in his neck.

He yanked it free but that only sped up the process.

The professor sunk onto the ground.

Cooper shouted behind her.

She heard footsteps once again thundering closer.

Blackness encroached on her vision.

Overwhelmed, her mind and body had reached the end of the road.

Everything swirled around her and then disappeared altogether as unconsciousness took over.

CHAPTER
Twenty~Two

July 15th
11:46 A.M.

Never, no matter how long he lived, would Cooper ever forget the sight of a weapon held against the temple of the woman he was falling for.

Ever.

That image was burned into his mind's eye for all eternity.

Now he reached Willow's side just as her knees buckled and she dropped.

Thankfully, he was close enough to catch her before she hit the ground, and quickly swung her into his arms.

Just when he thought he couldn't be any more impressed with his girl, she decided she had to one up herself. Willow had saved herself. She'd set up Mahmoud to be distracted for a split second and then struck when the opportunity presented itself.

She was everything.

The words she'd spoken just before she struck the professor hadn't sunk in yet, but they would. There would be time to be horrified and devastated by what his mother had gone through, there would be time to figure out how that played into what had happened to her and who had set her up to take the fall.

But that time wasn't now.

This time was to take care of the precious bundle he cradled in his arms.

"Mahmoud is bleeding out, no way to save him," Cole said from where he was crouched beside the dying man. There was a hint of frustration in his little brother's voice that Cooper knew had nothing to do with Willow saving herself by killing the professor, and everything to do with the fact that they now had more questions than ever and no way to get any answers. Professor Tarek Mahmoud had held the answers they sought in the palm of his hand, but those answers were going to die along with him.

"Good riddance," Connor snarled, glowering down at the professor, whose hands had fallen by his sides and who's eyes were taking on the glassy, empty look of death.

"Wish we could have gotten names out of him, but that's one hell of a woman you have there," Jax said, shooting an appreciative smile Willow's way.

"She hurt?" Cole asked as he straightened and came to touch his fingertips to Willow's neck.

"There's blood all over her, but I think most of it is Mahmoud's. There was some blood on her fingers before she stabbed the professor," Cooper replied. There were still scraps of duct tape wrapped around her wrists and ankles as well, and since she was naked, he could see dozens of small wounds dotted around the tape, probably caused when she cut herself free.

Naked.

That hadn't even hit him yet.

He'd been too focused on the gun at her head.

"Here."

Looking over his shoulder, Cooper saw Cade approaching with a blanket in his arms. While the rest of them had been standing around watching the professor bleed out, his big brother must have returned to the car and retrieved the blanket to wrap Willow in. Why was he not surprised that of all of them, Cade was the one to note this seemingly small thing but one that would be huge to Willow, and take steps to rectify it?

Cade was always taking care of all of them, he just did it with a perpetual scowl on his face.

"Her hands are a mess, and I'll have to check them out more closely when I clean them, but nothing looks too deep," Cole pronounced as he set Willow's hands on her stomach.

"We need to decide how we're going to handle the fallout," Jake reminded them all. "We're here with Prey's blessing but still have a dead world-renowned Egyptologist. Are we going to take responsibility for the kill? Willow's article hasn't run yet, and I'm sure she's going to want to include everything that he did to her in it."

"She'll keep our names out if we want her to," Cooper immediately interjected. None of them would stand in the way of everything Willow had achieved, she deserved to take all the credit, but he knew she'd also respect whatever they decided.

"Never doubted she would," Jake assured him. "I was just thinking it could work to our advantage to have it known that we're onto whoever Mahmoud was working with. If we claim involvement in what went down then we make it harder for them to try to take us out because it would paint too big a bullseye on them, draw too much attention their way. At the same time, it would make them nervous, maybe make them slip up. Could be the only way to get the answers we all need."

That all made sense, and Cooper knew they were going to have to sit down and talk about all of it.

But not now.

Now he had to focus on Willow.

"I'm fine with whatever you guys choose. Right now, I just want to get Willow home," he told his brothers as he started walking toward the vehicle.

Priorities.

The word had been echoing in his mind from the moment he stepped foot in Egypt. When he'd come there it was for the express purpose of getting whatever intel he could out of Mahmoud. As soon as he'd spotted the figure draped in black sitting in the corner of the professor's kitchen, his priorities had been torn. But as soon as he rescued Willow, and got to know her, those priorities had shifted once again.

Now they were the woman he held tight against his chest.

This was what his mom would want him to do. As much as she would be proud of all of them for fighting to clear her name—something he still intended to do—she also knew that what mattered most in life were the people you loved.

As he slid into the back seat of the SUV, Willow moaned slightly, and as he settled her on his lap her eyelashes fluttered against her cheeks. Dark bruises of exhaustion were painted under her eyes, blending in with those caused by fists. The mottled blues, blacks, greens, and yellows gave her a washed out, sickly look, and he was overcome by a need to just lock her away someplace safe for the next few months, so she had nothing to worry about but recovering and regaining her strength.

"Cooper?" she murmured, struggling to get her eyes open all the way.

"Right here, honey." Dipping his head, he pressed a kiss to her forehead. The sight of blood on her soft skin made him nauseous and he tucked the blanket tighter around her to cover as much of it as he could.

"Professor Mahmoud ... is he ... dead?" she asked, finally managing to pry open her eyelids and look up at him.

"Yeah, honey, he's dead. He can't ever hurt you again," he assured her. While he would have settled for taking the professor into custody, would have made sure he was personally in charge of the interrogation so he got the answers on his mom his family needed, Cooper was glad things had worked out as they had. Willow deserved to be able to recover without the added weight of knowing her tormentor was still out there somewhere.

"I ... killed him." Her throat worked as she visibly swallowed down her emotions and her eyes had a sheen of tears.

"I know, honey, you were magnificent."

His words seemed to surprise a laugh out of her and some of the horror disappeared from her gaze along with the tears swimming in those turquoise depths. "Thank you," she murmured as she snuggled closer. "Can't seem to keep my eyes open."

"Then don't, honey. Your body knows what it needs, don't fight it. Sleep," he urged.

"Are you ... I'm not sure ... what happens now?" she asked vulnerability evident in the way she kept her face tucked against his neck.

"Now, we drive to the airfield, get on a plane and fly back home. You go straight to a hospital where a doctor will check you out. You'll take as long as it takes to allow your body and your mind to heal. And I'm guessing you write your article and show the whole world just how magnificent you are and how you singlehandedly brought down an entire terrorist cell."

"And what about you?" she whispered.

Hooking a finger under Willow's chin, Cooper nudged until she lifted her face and looked up at him. "I'll be right there beside you every second."

The anxiety melted away, and Willow gave him a small smile. "Good."

"The only thing that changed is that I somehow respect and admire you even more," he told her. "Unless anything has changed for you?"

Her brows knitted together. "Why would it?"

"Because I almost didn't get to you in time." There was no way to wipe away the knowledge of what would have happened if he and his brothers hadn't shown up when they had, and he still had no idea what might have happened to her because they were delayed.

"Did you get to me as quickly as you could?"

"Damn straight."

"Then nothing has changed for me. I just want to go home with you," she said with a sleepy sigh as her eyes fluttered closed.

Home with you.

No words had ever sounded so perfect.

～

July 18th
   6:55 A.M

. . .

Today was the day.

After three days of working on her article every chance she got between doctor's visits, debriefings with agencies where she shared everything she knew about the professor, and sleeping, today was the day her article was released into the world.

She was proud of it, not only had she managed to gather the intel she needed to ensure that the professor would have to pay for his crimes, but she'd actively participated in making him pay and managed to write an article she was pleased with. True to his word, Cooper had helped, and there was a chance she may have even been a little bossy with him while he did so.

More than that, her trip to Egypt hadn't just ticked professional goals, she'd also met the man she was already convinced she was going to spend the rest of her life with.

Right now, he was asleep beside her in his bed at his house. Since her apartment was tiny and she used it only as a base while she spent most of her time traveling and working on articles, they'd kind of set up at his place. Cooper hadn't wanted her to be alone and she wasn't all that keen on the idea of being without him anyway, so when she'd been discharged from the hospital it had felt natural to come there.

Everything with Cooper felt natural. It was like finding a piece of yourself you hadn't even realized was missing.

Just having him by her side had made these last couple of days so much easier. He'd been right there with her at the hospital while she was poked and prodded, her arm x-rayed and casted, tests and scans performed, and fluids and antibiotics pumped into her. And he'd been right there with her while she told her story over and over again, repeating everything from what first put the professor on her radar to how she'd taken his life.

Maybe that hadn't quite sunk in yet.

While she knew it was the right thing to do, it had saved her life and those of Charlie Team, it still settled uneasily in her stomach to know she had killed someone.

"You're thinking too loudly," Cooper grumbled from beside her as he rolled her over so she was lying on top of him. "It's too early for thinking."

That made her giggle. "It's almost seven in the morning. I bet you get up hours before this to do PT."

"No PT today though, honey, just you and me, and that means it's too early for thinking." His serious gray eyes looked up at her. "You doing okay? Today's the day your article comes out."

"I'm doing all right," she assured him, and it was mostly true.

Willow wasn't naïve enough to think there weren't going to be bad days coming. So far, she'd had enough to do to keep her mind occupied so it didn't wander, but sooner or later, it was bound to creep toward darker thoughts. Small, hot, dark cells, and fists and feet striking her body, all of those things would have to be processed, but for the moment, she was as good as she could be given the circumstances.

"I'm mostly talked out though," she added. Cooper had insisted on making sure she didn't keep anything bottled up, encouraging her constantly to talk about whatever she was feeling whether it be anger, fear, helplessness, or anything else. He'd shared his own emotions with her and reminded her regularly that keeping things trapped inside would lead to problems later on.

"What do you want to do then? Want to celebrate today with a big breakfast? Or we could call my brothers and sister, see if they want to come over and hang out? We could go out and do something just for fun, or we could just stay inside and chill out, you definitely deserve that. Whatever you want, honey, today is your day."

How she'd spend the rest of the day Willow had no idea.

What she'd spend the next hour doing she knew for sure.

"Right now, I just want you," she said, sliding a hand between their bodies to stroke along his length. It jerked at her touch and a smile lit her lips, she loved knowing how badly Cooper wanted her because she felt the same way about him. Like she could never get enough of him even if she spent the rest of her life in bed with him.

"Mmm, that I think we can make happen."

Before she knew what was happening, Cooper had flipped them over so she was on her back and he was balanced on his hands, staring down at her with desire dancing in those gray eyes she found herself getting lost in every time she looked at them.

"Way too many clothes," he teased as he pushed the T-shirt of his that she was wearing up to bare her breasts to him. Since that was all she was wearing, it gave him an unobscured view of her body.

For a moment, Willow had to fight the urge to cover it. While she wasn't self-conscious about her appearance usually, right now her body was a literal roadmap of all she'd endured. Bruises in every shade, cuts and deeper gashes, plus she'd lost a fair bit of weight over the last few weeks and her hip bones and ribs protruded in a very unattractive way.

If it wasn't for the greedy desire burning so brightly in Cooper's eyes, she would have covered it. Instead, all she could do was watch in wonder as he kissed his way down her chest, pausing to feather the lightest of kisses to her nipples, making them both pebble. When he got to the apex of her thighs, Willow pressed them together.

"You don't have to if you don't want to," she said shyly. While she'd had her share of sexual partners over the years, she hadn't been invested in any of those relationships and she'd never pushed any of those men to give her more than reasonably good sex. She certainly hadn't pushed for foreplay, and they hadn't offered.

"Oh, honey, I want to," Cooper assured her, nudging her legs apart.

When she stopped fighting against it, he hooked his hands under her knees and lifted them, bending them over his shoulders so she was completely spread open for him.

There was no room for embarrassment when he looked at her like he couldn't get enough of her, and when that first stroke of his tongue slid along her center, Willow forgot how to think altogether.

All she could do was feel.

Each swipe of his magic tongue, the vibration of his lips as he moaned when he took her already trembling bud into his mouth and suckled on it.

A finger slid inside her, then another, and a third, filling her almost as delightfully full as his erection would have. Those fingers stroked relentlessly, hitting that spot inside her with each thrust.

Sensations built.

Quicker than she was prepared for.

They swelled inside her, reaching out to claim every cell of her body.

Then when his teeth scraped across her bundle of nerves as he sucked hard and stroked deep with his fingers, she detonated.

White stars burst behind her closed lids, and she screamed Cooper's name at the top of her lungs.

There was no time to recover from the all-consuming orgasm because Cooper was moving up her body, and thrusting inside her. He set a fast, almost desperate pace, and all Willow could do was hold on and go along for the ride.

His mouth found hers, his fingers slipped between them to work her overstimulated bud, pushing her quickly toward a second orgasm.

This time when it hit, she wasn't riding that wave alone.

Cooper was right there with her.

They clung to one another as pleasure zinged along their every nerve ending, and Willow loved every single second of it.

For so long she'd been all alone. One person's desire to make a name for themselves had changed the entire course of her life. The last twenty years she'd thought all those changes had been for the worse. She'd lost her dad in the most horrific of ways, and then her mom to grief and guilt. While she enjoyed her career, it probably wasn't what she would have chosen had her dad not been killed the way he was.

But now she felt anything other than alone.

She was one of the lucky few who managed to find their other half.

Because that is exactly what she thought she and Cooper were, two halves of the same whole. Split apart by the universe but destined to find one another.

It didn't matter that they'd found each other in the darkness, because through that battle for their lives they had forged a bond that nothing could break.

The man holding her so tenderly as he stayed buried inside her, his body warm and strong above her, his lips soft and gentle against hers, was more than she could have hoped for even if she'd been given a million wishes.

CHAPTER
Twenty~Three

July 21ˢᵗ
10:50 P.M.

"That's it, honey, ride me," Cooper urged as he reached up to grab one of Willow's pert nipples, tweaking it and drawing another moan from her lips.

Damn he was addicted to the sound.

Couldn't get enough of it.

There was nothing he loved more than getting her naked and making her moan until she screamed as her release hit her.

Over the last few days, they'd made out a lot. Like *a lot*. In pretty much every room of his house—which was feeling more like *their* house by the day—and he'd even convinced her to make love to him in the hot tub in his backyard, and under the wisteria covered gazebo the previous owner had left behind. He'd always intended to remove it, put in a pool instead, but seeing the softness in Willow's gaze as she'd looked at the pretty vine covered space, listening to her talk about summer picnics under the shade, and what a great backdrop it would be for photo sessions with kids or pets, he was glad he'd never gotten around to taking it out.

Honestly, anything that made Willow smile after everything she'd been through pretty much became his new favorite thing.

But nothing topped this.

With her head thrown back, which arched her breasts closer to his eager mouth, long, blonde locks cascading down around her, shimmering like spun gold in the bedroom light, she looked like a goddess.

"Oh, Cooper," she moaned, dragging out his name as he lifted his head off the pillow enough to capture a nipple. Doing the tongue thing she liked made her moan again and she sank down to take him fully inside her.

Any position he loved, as long as he was bringing Willow pleasure he was good, but seeing her like this was magnificent. He knew what had almost happened to her, what her death would have been if he and his brothers hadn't arrived when they did. Willow knew it, too. The first time they'd had sex when they got home, he'd been worried that it would trigger some of the trauma she was attempting to stuff down.

Not that he'd let her stuff it down.

While of course he wouldn't do anything to trigger her, especially since she'd told him how Mahmoud had violated her, he was also going to make her talk about her ordeal. Burying stuff never worked. He knew. In fact, it was the suicide of one of his Delta Force teammates that had been the catalyst for him getting out and joining Prey.

So, talking things through was a no-brainer to him, and he'd led by example being sure to articulate with her all the mess of swirling emotions tangled inside him. It seemed to have helped them both, and they both also had appointments set with Prey's on-staff psychiatrist.

Bad days would come and go, in fact just the day before had been Willow's worst as anxiety had gotten the best of her and she'd had nightmares and a couple of panic attacks. Totally normal, but awful to both endure for her and watch her endure for him.

Tempered throughout the bad, were moments like this.

Moments where he swirled his tongue over her pebbled nipple while one of his hands palmed Willow's backside, gripping onto her as she rolled and lifted her hips, and his other played with her bud, knowing just the right amount of pressure to exert in just the right way to have her orgasm building steadily until she was a writhing, pleading mess.

Every time she lifted up until only his tip was left inside her then sank back down, a groan fell from his lips. She felt so good, so tight and hot, and it was such an honor to know that even with what she'd endured she was comfortable enough with him to be completely vulnerable and allow him to touch her, and bring her pleasure.

A gift he'd never forget.

When her internal muscles began to quiver, Willow upped the pace until she was riding him in a near frenetic haze, moaning and gasping. Pressing harder against her bud, he managed to hold himself back as he watched her fall apart, his name screamed into the air.

As soon as he felt her begin to float back to earth, Cooper grabbed both her hips and began to thrust into her in earnest. Angling his thumbs so he could brush them against her bundle of nerves, when her second orgasm rushed through her only then did Cooper allow himself to hit his own peak as she clamped around him.

Wave after wave of pleasure washed over him, and by the time it began to ebb, Willow had snuggled herself down against his chest. As much as he loved sex with her, these moments, when they were both basking in the afterglow, somehow seemed better. This was when he felt the closest to Willow and wished it was possible to freeze the clock and hold onto these precious seconds for as long as possible.

Stroking his hand up and down the length of her spine, Cooper inhaled Willow's soft jasmine scent. Over the last few days, he'd come to associate the fragrance with Willow. It was obviously her favorite because it was in her perfume, body wash, shampoo and conditioner. Curious, he'd asked if jasmine was also her favorite flower, and she'd told him it was. Which meant he would be planting as many as he could in the yard.

"Gotta get up and clean you," he murmured.

"Mmm, don't want to move," Willow whispered, snuggling closer.

"Don't want to move either, honey, but still gotta clean you up. I'll be right back," he promised as he lifted her and pulled out of her.

Moving as quickly as he could, Cooper hurried into the attached bathroom, disposed of the condom, ran a washcloth under warm water, and returned to the bedroom. Willow's legs fell open as he moved between them and it was damn tempting to find another condom and bury himself inside her all over again, but she needed sleep. Her body still had a long way to go to recover and sleep was the best thing for it.

Once she was clean, he returned to the bathroom, tossed the washcloth in the sink, flipped off the lights, and returned to bed. As soon as he lay down Willow was there, curled against his side. Cooper had no idea how he was going to be able to go to sleep ever again without feeling her weight pressed against him.

In such a short time, she'd made such a huge impact on him and his life.

There was no going back, nor did he wish to go back.

Right here, this was where he wanted to be.

Just as he was starting to drift off, lulled toward slumber by Willow's deep, even breaths, and the puffs of warm air against his chest, which she was using for a pillow, his phone began to ring.

Normally he might ignore it, but with the new information they'd learned from Willow about his mom and Tarek Mahmoud, his brothers had been working almost round the clock to see if they'd learned enough to figure things out. Cooper was grateful they were allowing him to focus on Willow while they worked on intel, and if they'd found something he wanted to hear it.

Reaching over as carefully as he could so he didn't disturb Willow, Cooper managed to snatch up his cell phone from the nightstand. It was his little brother Cole's name on the screen, and he accepted the call as he brought the phone to his ear.

"Yo, little bro, what's up? You find something about mom?" he asked.

"No." Cole's normally relaxed and calm tone was now tight with stress, and Cooper was immediately on edge.

Something had happened.

Something bad by the sounds of it.

"What's wrong?" he demanded.

"You know my neighbor?"

"The pretty one who lives next door to you that you're obsessed with?" he asked, that was the only one he could think of, although why his brother would be calling him late at night about her, he had no idea.

"I'm not obsessed, I just don't like her."

"Sure, bro. Whatever. What about her?" If Cole was bickering with his pretty neighbor again, that had nothing to do with him. If he hated the woman so badly, Cole might as well move and get away from her for good. Instead, Cole stayed right where he was and constantly complained about her.

"She just turned up at my door beaten to a pulp," Cole said, voice tight with barely controlled emotion. "I don't like her, yeah. Don't agree with her life choices, but, man ... damn ... Coop ... it's bad."

It was clear his brother was badly shaken up, and since they were family that meant only one thing. "Hold on, little bro, we're on our way."

What will Cole Charleston learn from his neighbor and will it help his family in their quest for answers? Find out in the second book in the action packed and emotionally charged Prey Security: Charlie Team series!

Shadowed Lies (Prey Security: Charlie Team #2)

Also by Jane Blythe

Detective Parker Bell Series

A SECRET TO THE GRAVE

WINTER WONDERLAND

DEAD OR ALIVE

LITTLE GIRL LOST

FORGOTTEN

Count to Ten Series

ONE

TWO

THREE

FOUR

FIVE

SIX

BURNING SECRETS

SEVEN

EIGHT

NINE

TEN

Broken Gems Series

CRACKED SAPPHIRE

CRUSHED RUBY

FRACTURED DIAMOND

SHATTERED AMETHYST

SPLINTERED EMERALD

SALVAGING MARIGOLD

River's End Rescues Series

COCKY SAVIOR

SOME REGRETS ARE FOREVER

SOME FEARS CAN CONTROL YOU

SOME LIES WILL HAUNT YOU

SOME QUESTIONS HAVE NO ANSWERS

SOME TRUTH CAN BE DISTORTED

SOME TRUST CAN BE REBUILT

SOME MISTAKES ARE UNFORGIVABLE

Candella Sisters' Heroes Series

LITTLE DOLLS

LITTLE HEARTS

LITTLE BALLERINA

Storybook Murders Series

NURSERY RHYME KILLER

FAIRYTALE KILLER

FABLE KILLER

Saving SEALs Series

SAVING RYDER

SAVING ERIC

SAVING OWEN

SAVING LOGAN

SAVING GRAYSON

SAVING CHARLIE

Prey Security Series

PROTECTING EAGLE

PROTECTING RAVEN

PROTECTING FALCON

PROTECTING SPARROW

PROTECTING HAWK

PROTECTING DOVE

Prey Security: Alpha Team Series

DEADLY RISK

LETHAL RISK

EXTREME RISK

FATAL RISK

COVERT RISK

SAVAGE RISK

Prey Security: Artemis Team Series

IVORY'S FIGHT

PEARL'S FIGHT

LACEY'S FIGHT

OPAL'S FIGHT

Prey Security: Bravo Team Series

VICIOUS SCARS

RUTHLESS SCARS

BRUTAL SCARS

CRUEL SCARS

BURIED SCARS

WICKED SCARS

Prey Security: Athena Team Series

FIGHTING FOR SCARLETT

FIGHTING FOR LUCY

FIGHTING FOR CASSIDY

FIGHTING FOR ELLA

Prey Security: Charlie Team Series

DECEPTIVE LIES

SHADOWED LIES

Christmas Romantic Suspense Series

THE DIAMOND STAR

CHRISTMAS HOSTAGE

CHRISTMAS CAPTIVE

CHRISTMAS VICTIM

YULETIDE PROTECTOR

YULETIDE GUARD

YULETIDE HERO

HOLIDAY GRIEF

HOLIDAY LOSS

HOLIDAY SORROW

Conquering Fear Series (Co-written with Amanda Siegrist)

DROWNING IN YOU

OUT OF THE DARKNESS

CLOSING IN

About the Author

USA Today bestselling author Jane Blythe writes action-packed romantic suspense and military romance featuring protective heroes and heroines who are survivors. One of Jane's most popular series includes Prey Security, part of Susan Stoker's OPERATION ALPHA world! Writing in that world alongside authors such as Janie Crouch and Riley Edwards has been a blast, and she looks forward to bringing more books to this genre, both within and outside of Stoker's world. When Jane isn't binge-reading she's counting down to Christmas and adding to her 200+ teddy bear collection!

To connect and keep up to date please visit any of the following

www.ingramcontent.com/pod-product-compliance
Lightning Source LLC
Chambersburg PA
CBHW050425260626
47156CB00003B/1163